MW00468694

# SLATER'S GOLD

## MATT BANNISTER WESTERN 13

## KEN PRATT

Published in the United States by Wolfpack Publishing, Las Vegas

CKN Christian Publishing
An Imprint of Wolfpack Publishing
5130 S. Fort Apache Road 215-380
Las Vegas, NV 89148

cknchristianpublishing.com

Paperback ISBN: 978-1-63977-918-5
eBook ISBN: 978-1-63977-917-8
LCCN 2022934312

# SLATER'S GOLD

# Dedication

This book is dedicated to all the pastors and Bible teachers out there who still teach the truth of the Bible without compromise. I don't believe there is a higher calling than teaching the Word of God. My highest respect to you all.

I was not raised in a Christian home, but I have been blessed to have known and been greatly influenced by men and women who like you, who are pastors or Bible teachers. Here are a few of the people who have touched my life: Pastor Dan and Nancy Wentworth, Dr. Dewey Bertolini, Pastor Gerry Clark, Pastor Bill Wertz, Pastor Phil Magnan, Pastor Tim Bunn, along with Bob and Diane Reynolds just to name a few.

# Chapter 1

Oliver Rohloff entered the marshal's office with a scowl on his face and a harshness in his eyes that revealed the annoyance on his chest. He stopped at the three-foot-tall partition and spoke before deputy Phillip Forrester could greet him, "Is the marshal in?" His tone was as sharp as a slap across the face.

"Mister Rohloff, hello. Yes, he is this time. Give me one minute," Phillip said, and went to Matt's office and knocked on the private office door. He opened it just enough to speak to Matt. "Mister Rohloff is here again. He sounds a little irritated."

Matt Bannister stuck his hand out to shake as he approached the older man with a long gray beard. "Mister Rohloff, it's nice to meet you finally. I heard you have come by a few times looking for me." Matt was a tall man with broad shoulders. He was in his mid-thirties, handsome, with brown eyes and a nicely trimmed beard and mustache while his long dark hair was pulled into a tight ponytail, He was dressed in black pants and a blue button up shirt with the sleeves rolled up.

"Yeah, I was expecting you to come out to the mine and talk to me. I asked these men to have you come out to see me."

"Generally speaking, I don't go searching for people just because they come by the office. What can I do for you?"

Oliver's jaw clenched tight, and his nostrils flared at Matt's response. "Maybe you could better serve the community by taking an interest in the people around here when they need you."

Matt grinned despite the old timer's coarseness. "Mister Rohloff, I apologize if I have offended you. I promise you I try to serve this community the best I can. Now, since we're talking face to face, maybe you can tell me how I can help you?"

"All right. My name's Oliver Rohloff and I own the Rohloff Mining Works. We're located on the Modoc River around the bend from the Slater's silver mine. They own the mountain and a lot of the land around there; I won't argue that. My claim borders theirs on the southeast side. It's my claim, and as you might know, claims don't stop at the surface. I own the ground and every valuable mineral found there clear to the center of the earth. I believe the Slaters are mining under my claim. I think the gold they found is mine. I need your help to verify it."

The grin left Matt's expression as the seriousness of the accusation warranted his attention. "What makes you think so?"

"I can feel the vibration of explosives. I filled a pot with water and rested it on the ground to verify that. I stayed put and watched that pot for hours until I felt that vibration and sure enough, it rippled the water. Black powder isn't that strong to shake the ground if it is far away. It has to be straight under my claim. I spoke to one of the employees there and he said the gold was in the southeast. I believe they are mining gold out from under me."

"Have you talked with Ron Dalton or anyone at the Slater Mine?"

"I have been approached several times over the past two years by them wanting to buy my claim. I won't sell. I wondered why they wanted to buy me out, now I know. I need you to investigate and find out if they are encroaching onto my claim and pirating my gold. I already know they will deny it, but I'm telling you, they are. I need more done than just asking them, Marshal."

"I'll need a copy of your legal claim and a map of its borders. Ron Dalton is a good and honest man. He married my cousin, so I'll talk to him and get back to you. If they have infr inged on your claim, that's a matter for the courts. But I can find out if they have or not."

Oliver's lips turned down as his eyes rolled with aggravation. His right hand clenched. "It figures you'd be related to the Slater's business somehow. I guess I can count on being robbed of a fortune and nothing will come from it. Except for maybe a percentage in your pocket, right?" He continued with a sharp tone, "Well, we're a smaller mine, but we'll start blasting down right over them, and when their men are killed, keep in mind it's my land! All is fair in the name of corruption. Right?" His beady blue eyes peered at Matt with a fiery disposition.

Matt remained serene and spoke softly, "You can do whatever you want on your claim, but how about you let me do my job and let me see what I can do for you. If they're in the wrong, you'll have your proof for the court of law."

"And if not?"

"If not, what? If they're not infringing on your claim, then you're wrong. If they are, you will have proof for a massive lawsuit. I don't know what else you're asking me. If you're insinuating that I'm going to hide the truth from you because I'm corrupt, then I need to prove myself to you, and I will. The courthouse should have a map of all the registered claims in the county, but I'll need to see your deed. I'll take those and compare them to the silver mine's maps. Ron isn't going to lie to me about it."

"I know they are pirating my gold, or they wouldn't be trying to buy my claim," Oliver stated as a fact. "I filed for a patent and the claim is mine. Bought and paid for from the center of the earth to the sky."

"That very well may be, Mister Rohloff. How about you let me do what I can to investigate that allegation for you."

"Don't do me wrong, Marshal. I'm a Christian man, and I hear you are too. I hope you can stand on the high ground if what I hear is true."

Matt answered, "I stand on solid ground. I'll come by your mine later today and let you know what I find."

\*\*\*

Matt carried a circular leather tube containing the county's claim maps into Ron Dalton's office at the Slater Silver Mine. Ron had graciously greeted him and listened with concern as Matt explained what Oliver Rohloff was accusing the mine of doing.

"No," Ron denied the accusation with a surprised chuckle. "I can show you our company maps which our engineers carefully update every month to keep our progress up to date. The maps need to be precise because people's lives could be in danger if not. Let's compare maps and you can let Mister Rohloff know we're staying within our boundaries. We have maps for everything and every purpose, but the overview will probably settle any dispute with our neighbor."

"Is it true your company has tried to purchase Rohloff's claim?" Matt asked as he followed Ron down a hallway.

"Yes. The Slaters have offered him fair amounts to buy him out. The Rohloffs bring their ore to our stamp mill to have it processed. Their mine is tiny, but the ore yields are promising, and our engineers speculate there are a lot higher yields deeper than the surface, where the Rohloffs are mining. The Rohloff Mining Works is a tiny family-owned pick and shovel operation with no idea what they are sitting on or how to extract it. Of course, we want to buy him out."

Ron led Matt into a room with a large and wide table with a stack of maps on it. "We have a wide variety of angles of our mine. It's probably more than we need to be honest, but Wally Gettman is probably the best investment William Slater ever made. His maps are carefully updated every month and precise. His maps cover everything from fifty feet of new track to areas of weakened rock. We can look through all kinds of maps, but to answer your question, the overview of the mine relative to the geological topography of the area and where our diggings have extended from the portal will probably settle any dispute with our neighbor."

Ron flipped through the most recent map and found the top overview of the mountainous terrain of the surrounding area and the Modoc River as it flowed, twisting and curving through the wilderness within a two-mile radius of the map. The Slater Silver Mine claim borders were platted with solid black lines. The map of the mine's workings and any information gained by the map was far too complicated for Matt to understand. The map was nothing more than thin lines that seemed to lay one on top of another with no identifying information other than a capital letter and a series of numbers. To Matt, the map revealed nothing except a confusing mess of lines.

Ron revealed his expertise as he traced his finger along a fine line on the map. "The drift you are primarily interested in is to the southeast and nearly seven hundred feet underground. As you can see, it extends quite a way, but we are clearly within our boundaries. You can see the border between the Rohloff claim and ours is here." He traced his finger along a solid black line. "Rohloffs might feel some light vibrations from our blasting, but truthfully, I wouldn't think so. I think it's far more likely that he is hoping to get a higher offer for his property which is about two thousand feet away from where we discovered gold. Two thousand feet isn't that far, but six charges of black powder nearly seven hundred feet underground shouldn't be too noticeable that far away."

Matt couldn't translate the map's information, but he could understand the mountainous terrain and river perfectly. He examined the map and followed the river around a bend where a finger of land called a spit narrowed the river into a short white water run. He put his finger on the spit. "This doesn't match, Ron."

"What doesn't?" Ron asked with interest.

"The county claims map shows this finger of land along the river belongs to Rohloff, but your map has his property line way over here. I'll show you." Matt pulled the county claims map out of the leather tube and spread it across the table. Matt explained, "This is the official state map of mine claims for this section of the county. I don't know where your tunnels are, but your map is wrong about this part anyway. Are your workings under his property?"

Ron frowned, took an interest in the county

map, and flipped through the company maps to compare them. "Wait a minute," he said and quickly went to a storage closet and dug around for a bit before coming back to the table with two maps. After a brief ten minutes of grabbing and comparing older maps, Ron was dumbfounded. "I don't believe it, Matt. Look at this. This map was from one year ago. It matches your county map perfectly as far as the Rohloff border goes. Now, look at this map from seven months ago when we started the southeastern winze. They moved Rohloff's borders approximately two thousand yards to the east while suggesting we dig an exploratory winze." Ron placed his hand over his thick mustache and mouth and rubbed his face thoughtfully. He shrugged before exhaling with a troubled expression. "Our winze and drift go directly under Rohloff land." He cursed loudly.

"Which means he's right? You're digging Rohloff's gold."

Ron nodded in agreement. He cursed loudly again. He shook his head and pointed at the map. "That could not have been done on purpose, but it can't be an accident either," he said thoughtfully. "Someone made a massive mistake, and it wasn't caught until now, almost a year later." He looked at Matt with sincere concern. "I read those maps every day and I didn't catch it either. I'll probably lose my job today, but I'm shutting that side down right now. Give me fifteen minutes or so. I'll go to town to talk with William Slater. I'd appreciate you coming with me and bringing that county map."

"Is it possible William knew gold was there and did this on purpose?" Matt asked.

Ron shook his head. "We didn't know gold was there until we got close to it. And it's a good load of gold. It makes no sense at all."

"You don't think William knows he's hijacking his neighbors claim?"

"No. I cannot imagine so."

# Chapter 2

With a heated sneer on his thin lips, William Slater peered through the spectacles set on his long and pointed nose at the three maps spread out along the tables in the conference room. "How can this happen?" he asked with a severe gaze at the company engineer Wally Gettman. The map-making fell under Wally's supervision.

Wally was perplexed. "I'm...speechless. It's an error of the most erroneous magnitude. How I did not catch that when it was brought to me for finalization? I do not know," Wally admitted. He rubbed his bottom lip nervously as the responsibility fell on him. He explained, "The emphasis of our maps is on the production and accurate measurements of the work underground. It would be easy to miss the things we ignore, such as the borders. They never change!" he shouted angrily.

William struggled to keep his fiery temper under control. His gut tightened as an invisible hand gripped it in a clenched fist. The honeypot of gold they had discovered and collected over the past two months wasn't legally his. The expense of hiring guards to guard it and protect his treasure was for nothing. The investments he had been making in funding other mining ventures were promised by the millions in gold he had discovered. William felt sick to his stomach as the total weight of the impact of what was at risk could not be realized yet.

William shouted, "How could it be changed? Don't you dare say you don't know! You're a damn engineer; figure it out. You're in charge of map-making, Wally; this falls on you! Who did this? I want a name and I want them fired right now."

Wally, red-faced with a glaze in his eyes, said, "I'm the one that signed off on it and take responsibility. The borders are stationary, meaning they never change. The focus of our maps is always the production, geology and progress to keep our mine up to date..."

William cursed with a loud shout, "I know that! Tell me something I don't know, like who did it!"

"I am, William!" Wally snapped with a harsh glare. "What I'm telling you is this is no accident or innocent mistake. The border was intentionally moved about two-thousand yards and the exploratory winze suggested by my assistant Uriah Davidson. Remember him?"

"The jackass that wanted to court my daughter?" William asked with a scowl.

Wally turned the map to face William and pointed at the small square scale with two initials, Uriah

Davidson's and Wally's. "He drew it. I signed off on it."

"He quit!" William yelled. It angered him even more, to know that he didn't have anyone responsible for the map to fire other than Wally.

Wally grimaced. "I hate to say it, but Uriah may have done this intentionally to hurt you. Remember, you humiliated him at Debra's birthday party when he asked for your permission to court her?"

"My daughter has nothing to do with this! The last thing I need around the office is a young jackass slobbering over my daughter when there is work to be done."

"Yeah, but Uriah's heart was set on courting Debra, and you humiliated him."

William interrupted him with a scowl, "Debra is too good for him. I'm not going to let some weak-willed little weasel court my daughter. Maybe he should not have asked me in front of my guests. Huh? Did he think I would give my permission because I had guests? The kid is a jackass. So, he's the one that did this? Intentionally?"

Wally answered thoughtfully, "Yes. Debra's birthday party was at the end of August and Uriah made this map in the first week of September. It looks like he made this map and quit once I approved it. Unfortunately, the change to the border Uriah made has been used since."

William stood up, cursed and threw his chair across the conference room, enraged. "Well, fix it! This should have been discovered long before now. You men are failing to be observant enough to do your job, and now we have to pay for it!" His red-dened face and angry eyes fell on Matt Bannister, who stood back quietly after bringing the error to their attention. "Marshal Bannister, is there any criminal wrongdoing here? Are we negligent of a criminal action?"

Matt shook his head. "No. If Mister Rohloff wants to precede with a lawsuit, he certainly can, but there are no criminal charges."

"Then please excuse us. I have a lot of yelling to do and maybe some firing as well. Before you go, can you do me a favor? As you can see, this is an outrage. I need a day or two to digest this. Can I ask you to wait a day or two before you tell Rohloff that he can buy my company?" he asked with a stern glare at the men that sat around the table. All were humbly glancing down at the table, wondering where William's fury would land when the marshal left.

He continued, "Matt, you don't owe me anything, but if you could give me a couple of days to come up with a fair offer or maybe even a partnership with Rohloff, I'd appreciate it. I'll even ride out to his place with you and admit our error. I just need some time."

Matt agreed. "I can do that."

"Wonderful. I'll have Debra walk you out. Debra, please," he asked with a wave of his hand towards the door.

She smiled as she closed the conference room door behind her. She exhaled as they walked along the corridor to go downstairs. "I haven't seen my father that angry in years. This is really bad. We have a wagon load of processed gold waiting to be escorted to San Francisco right now. The detective agency my father hired is on its way here to take it under guard. Now I don't know what's going to happen."

"I didn't know there was a Rohloff Mining Works until he came to my office. Ron told me it's a small outfit?" Matt asked.

"Family owned and run with a few employees. What little ore Mister Rohloff does find he brings to our stamp mill to process. We have a good relationship with him as far as neighbors go, but he is no competition. I just hope we can work something out with him." She stopped at the door to leave the W.R. Slater Mining Company office. She leaned her shoulder against the door jamb with her hand holding the knob closed. "So, Matt, I understand your wedding is coming up in a few weeks," Debra Slater said. She was a very attractive young lady with blonde hair and pretty, blue eyes on a heart-shaped face. She watched him with a cute coy smile as she lightly scratched at the collar of her dress around her neck.

"It is."

"I haven't gotten my invitation yet," she hinted.

"We have a pretty full guestlist with limited seating in the church. We couldn't invite everyone, I'm afraid."

She smiled flirtatiously. "I think you're just afraid I'd cause a scene when the reverend asked if anyone has a reason why you two shouldn't be married. You know I think you should marry me," she said with a pointed finger, lightly jabbing his chest.

He laughed lightly. "I don't think your father would like that too much. He'd be calling me a jackass before too long if he doesn't already."

"Well, certainly he does call you a jackass, but only when he hears you're marrying a dance hall girl. She has no future, Matt. I think of Lawrence Barton, who worked in the mine. He lost his leg and can't work anymore. Luckily for him, his wife has talent and can make beautiful pottery. I've bought some of it myself. But your bride-to-be can dance and sing, but when she gets older and loses that youthful beauty, she'll have no future. You should think about that because you have a high-risk career and if you're ever hurt, she can't support you." She paused to grimace while tilting her head slightly to the left. "I'll toss this out there. I could."

He grinned slowly, uneasily. "Debra, you're a very pretty lady and I suppose you could. But you know, I'm in love with Christine."

Her eyes went to the front desk where the receptionist Martha Puglisi stood at the counter, listening to their conversation. Debra pushed the door open and stepped outside while circling around the door to close it after Matt followed her out. She leaned against the closed door while keeping eye contact with Matt. "You never gave me a chance."

"What?" Matt was taken off guard by her statement.

"You never gave me a chance. You just assumed I

was like my brother, who I know you don't like, or my father. You never gave me the opportunity to prove to you that I'm not like them."

"I'm in love with Christine," he said slowly.

"I know and you're engaged too. I'm sorry. I'm..." she hesitated. "I just always wanted to know you. I wanted to get to know you and hoped we would start a courtship. When that Chinese criminal had you, I was scared I would never see you again. I thought this man is the only one I want to get to know. I want to spend time with him and if something happens to him, it will break my heart. Then when you were found, I saw you on the street with Christine and your hands were all wrapped up and the thought occurred to me, if you had lost your hands, she couldn't support you forever. And I knew right then that I could, and I would. I'm not a bad find, Matt."

Her sincerity touched his heart, and he had no desire to hurt her feelings or bluntly break her heart. He was flattered to have one of Branson's most desired young ladies interested in him. He would be enraptured to court such a beautiful lady if he was single. Unfortunately for her, he had no interest in her or anyone other than his fiancée. He spoke gently, "Debra, as much as I appreciate that, and I do, I hope you can understand that I'm committed to Christine. If I were single, you would be a dream come true. And for some man down the road, you definitely will be. But whether Christine can support me or not, she's the lady I'm in love with. I thank you, though. It never hurts to be friends." He held out his hand to shake.

A slight tug on her lips pulled the corners upwards as she took hold of his hand. "I'll take what I can get. But if she doesn't treat you right, I'm stepping in."

Matt chuckled.

"I'm serious. You deserve better."

The door pushed against her back, forcing her to take a step forward. The receptionist, Martha Puglisi, stuck her head out the door and glanced at the two of them. "I apologize, but I have to interrupt. Your father says to get your fanny back upstairs."

Debra shook her head with a small tight smile. "It's a bad day here and I'm needed. I hope we get a chance to talk before your wedding day, Matt. I know I'm a little bolder than most ladies," she shrugged, "but I can afford to be because I don't need a man to support me. You see, I'm looking for a man that I can support and who will love me for me. I always kind of hoped it was you. Anyway, I have to go before it gets too bad up there."

# Chapter 3

It was mid-afternoon when Matt collected his horse from the stable and rode to Bella's Dance Hall to surprise Christine with a horse ride. He wanted to rent the buggy from the livery stable for a more comfortable ride, but the buggy was unavailable. He knocked on the door and waited in the foyer by the stairs while Gaylon Dirks went to notify Christine he was there.

Christine came out of the reading room carrying a broom and a duster. She set them aside and approached him with a discouraged expression on her lovely face. Matt narrowed his brow curiously while he watched her draw near.

"Are you okay?" he asked as he raised his arms to invite her inside them.

She struck his chest with her palms while his arms wrapped around her. "Ugh! Your sister is driving me crazy!"

Matt grinned. "Welcome to the family. What's

she doing now?"

"I have been telling Annie for a month now that she needs to come to town and get measured for the bridesmaid dress while there is time for Missus Lesko to make it. I just received a wire delivered from her telling me to relax, she'll come when she's good and ready. Last week the wire Annie sent asked if I wanted her measured with or without bloating! Matt," she paused to stare at him with a flabbergasted expression. "Your sister is driving me nuts. She can't be serious. Is she?"

Matt held her close in his arms. "You never really know until you get hit."

"I'm serious. This is our wedding, and I don't want my bridesmaid wearing dirty ranch boots and jeans or, at best, one of Helen's old dance dresses. Helen has been measured and her dress is going to be beautiful. I can't afford to wait for Annie to come to town at the last minute. Should I have Angela be my bridesmaid instead? Do you think Annie would be mad?"

"No. I think she would be hurt," he answered honestly.

Christine's eyes widened with uncertainty and a touch of frustration. "She's not communicating! I wire her and have sent letters begging her to please come to get measured, and I get these short responses that I don't know if they're supposed to be funny or if she's really that stupid. It may not be important to her, but this is our wedding, and it's coming up fast. Three weeks is not very long. Please tell me that she's not going to ruin our wedding by waiting until our wedding day and expecting the dress to fit."

"It sounds to me like she's just trying to get your gander up. I'm sure she sent those wires for her own entertainment."

Christine shook her head with annoyance. "I love your sister, Matt. But I don't have time to wait for her to be good and ready and not bloated at the same time. That day may never come. Should I ask Angela to step in? I know Annie is busy on the ranch, so I'm asking for your opinion, honestly." Her large brown eyes locked onto his, waiting for his reply.

Matt squeezed his eyes tightly closed and wrinkled his nose with a groan. "I wasn't supposed to tell you, but she'll be here on Friday to get measured. Act surprised and mad when you see her."

Christine sighed with relief. Matt could feel her body relax in his arms as her palms fell from his chest to wrap around him. "I hate her." A grin appeared on her lips. "Do you think I could beat her in a fight if I hit her first?"

Matt chuckled. "No. But I can't either, so don't try it. You'll get us both beat up before our honeymoon."

"That does remind me, I have made some inquiries. We can take a stage to Walla Walla and then board a sternwheeler in Wallula down the Columbia River. We would have to change boats twice because of a waterfall and rapids and pay for three sternwheelers to reach Astoria, or we could take the Oregon Short Line train from Walla Walla, but we'd have to change trains in Portland. The train is the most practical and least expensive way, but wouldn't it be romantic to take a sternwheeler? We'd have our own room, and we could take strolls around the deck. I heard it's a very beautiful trip down the river despite the inconvenience of changing boats and wagon travel around the dangerous parts of the river."

"You know me, cheaper is always better, but you just talked me into it," Matt said with a wink and a smile. "I've heard about the portages around the falls and rapids of the upper, middle and lower Columbia. It would be a more interesting trip than sitting on a train."

"I was hoping you would say that."

Bella walked into the foyer with a no-nonsense expression. She spoke with her raspy voice, "Matt, your sister needs to get herself to Lesko's and get measured for that dress. You need to ride over to her place and bring her back or tell her she's out of the wedding. We have waited long enough."

"She'll be here on Friday," Matt answered. A few weeks before, Bella had expressed some concerns that nearly ended the engagement, but since apologizing, Bella had become the mother figure Christine had never had and made the wedding her priority.

"Good!" Bella exclaimed while waving her hands, indicating one more concern settled. "I spoke with the owner of Redlin Meats, Henry Redlin. He gave me quite a discount for the occasion on the price of chicken for the reception dinner. He also wanted me to tell you that he'd make plenty of his meat-balls as a wedding gift. I had to try one and they are fantastic. I think we have a grasp on the food for the reception. The only big concern I had was your sister doing her part." She sighed with relief as she crossed her arms over her chest. She smiled proudly. "It's going to be a beautiful wedding."

Rose Blanchard descended the staircase, in a casual blue dress, with her red hair in a ponytail. She was one of the most attractive ladies in the dance hall, even though she appeared to have just woken up from a nap and dressed to help cook dinner. She smiled at Matt as she spoke, "I have no doubt it will be a beautiful wedding," she agreed. "And I, for one, look forward to the reception and the party that's going to take place. It is going to be so much fun. I'll warn you now, I have my eyes on your deputy."

Bella laughed.

Matt grinned. "Which one?"

"Truet is my first pick, but I'll settle for the younger blond one. I don't know his name, but I saw him when he came here to take Christine to the hotel that night when the Chinese trouble was going on. He's a very stout and handsome man."

"Nate. He's a very good young man," Matt stated.

Christine spoke frankly, "You might have some competition because Nate's been asking about Angela since that night. He watched her walk me down the stairs and I think her beauty struck him. He's asked me about her twice now, I think. He's just too shy to come down here to meet her." She addressed Bella, "It's so funny. He's a deputy U.S. marshal, but he's afraid to meet Angela," she snickered.

Bella waved a hand with a chuckle. "Well, bring him here and make him dance. If he's too shy to do that, I can send Angela to the marshal's office with a letter for him with eight simple words, 'Nate, ask her to join you for dinner' and tell her to wait for his response."

Matt said with a growing grin, "You better not. He'd just turn bright red and start stuttering and she'd walk away thinking he's a fool. He's gotten his heart broken a few times now and is a little gun shy when it comes to pretty girls."

Rose stood at the bottom of the stairs listening. "I'll gladly go to the marshal's office and ask him out for dinner myself if I have to. But I hoped to meet him here. I thought it would be more romantic in the setting of a wedding. He might be asking about Angela, but I can change that."

Christine answered, "I don't mean this in a bad way at all, but I think Angela would be perfect for him. Nate is very innocent regarding women, and Angela has much more in common with him. In my opinion, they are almost a perfect pair for each other. Don't you think?" she asked Matt.

"I think Nate needs to take his time before he falls head over heels for another girl, period. He falls hard and as of yet, none of them have shared his affections."

"I will, even if it's just for a little while," Rose volunteered. "Angela is too young and naive to make a man out of an inexperienced boy. But if she is competition, I'm up for the game. Have a good day."

She walked towards the kitchen without waiting for any response.

Bella watched her walk away and shook her head. "The girls are always competing and bickering over something. Anyway, take Angela with you sometime and surprise him by taking them out to dinner. I don't know him, but I do trust both of your judgment."

"We will," Christine said. "Maybe tomorrow we can take them to dinner at the Monarch Restaurant. I don't think Angela has been there yet."

"We can," Matt agreed. "I'll make sure Nate is there. In the meantime," he spoke to Bella. "I have my horse outside and wanted to take Christine for a ride. Only for an hour or so. She'll be back in plenty of time for your supper."

"I don't care," Bella said with a compliant wave of her hand. "You two go have fun."

\*\*\*

Matt could feel Christine pressing against his back as she held onto him tightly. If he were driving the buggy, he would have stayed on the road up to the other side of the hill where it was a more moderate climb to the top, but he told Christine to hold on and rode up the steep incline where there was no road. He knew it would be a rough ride and soon regretted the decision knowing how uncomfortable it was for his beloved lady. She had not cursed him, but she wasn't appreciative of sitting behind the cantle of the saddle while gravity longed to pull her off the horse. Her hands were locked tightly around Matt's midriff and her face rested against his shoulder.

They crested the hill and Matt turned the horse to look out over the view of the city of Branson, the valley and towering mountain ranges that encircled them. Matt could feel Christine's locked hands loosen as she relaxed her grip and felt her warm sweet breath on his neck as she gazed over the view. He didn't need to turn his head to know there was the mesmerizing look in her eyes that always held her spellbound when gazing at the natural beauty of the valley. There was nothing more soothing to his heart than to see the joy in Christine's eyes when she was at her favorite place to picnic.

"I love being up here, but next time take the road," she said with a quiet hug from behind.

A warm smile spread across Matt's lips. "Do you want to get down?"

"In a minute. Sometimes I just want to hold you."

They sat quietly while the horse ate the green grass for a few moments. Matt held her hand while she slid off the horse and walked to the edge of the hill. He stepped out of the saddle of his recently acquired buckskin gelding from the deceased Jude Maddox. Jude was a cowboy and had trained the horse well. Matt could release the reins without concern of the buckskin wandering away. He had found out from those who had spoken to Jude that the gelding's name was Jek.

Christine turned her brown eyes to him. "You forgot to bring a picnic basket."

The warm smile had not left his face. Some men promised to rope the moon for their beloved ladies, but Matt couldn't promise the impossible. What he could do was try to make her dreams come true. The longing expression in her eyes when she was on the top of the hill revealed her dream to build a home where they stood. It was a far more realistic goal to strive for than roping that bright moon on the clearest night. He quenched the temptation to blurt out the reason he brought her there.

"I considered bringing a picnic basket, but I'm trying to save money. Those sternwheelers are going to be expensive."

She turned to look at him with an easy smile. "I think between us we can afford them."

"Maybe," he paused. "This hill doesn't have a name. If we built a house here, would you give the hill a name?"

Christine shrugged her shoulders questionably. "Home?"

"That's good enough." He grinned with a short chuckle. "I checked with Lee, and no one owns or has claimed this land. So, I claimed it."

"You bought this hill?" she asked with excitement.

"We're buying it."

Her mouth widened into a joyful grin. "We're buying it? This will be ours?"

"As long as we keep our end of the deal."

She leaped into his arms and wrapped hers around him tightly. "I love you, Matthew Bannister! I cannot believe this is where we will raise our children. I'm so excited. Thank you, Jesus!" she shouted. She skipped away from Matt like a fawn frolicking in an early morning meadow, dancing in circles while spreading her arms out wide with her beautiful face exposed to the sunlight, praising loudly, "Thank you, Jesus!" Her voice echoed across the valley.

Matt never wanted to forget the glow of the sun on her face or where she danced with her voice echoing through the valley. If time could stand still only for a moment, watching her celebrate was the moment he would forever treasure. If only he had a photographer to capture the moment.

# Chapter 4

The westbound stage from Boise City pulled into the Branson stage stop. A man named John Painter collected his grain bag of belongings and shook hands with a well-dressed gentleman he had met along the ride. "Dan, where are you staying while in town?"

"I believe it's called the Monarch Hotel. Do you happen to know where it is?" Don Franklyn was very tired. He had traveled a long way and hoped this would be the last stop before he could return home. The train wasn't a bad way to travel, but stagecoaches were a dying mode of long-distance transportation in the east. Unfortunately, they were still necessary in the west, to get to Branson anyway. He was anxious to lay his body down and get some sleep.

"Hell, I grew up in this town. Like I told you, my father's a reverend." He laughed. "Walk with me and we'll find it. It is probably on Main Street. As

I said, I haven't been home in twelve years. I sure hope my parents are still alive." He laughed with a friendly tap to Dan's bicep. "They're going to be surprised to see me if they are alive, and I'll be surprised if they're not. I don't know what I'd do then." He pulled a silver flask from his inside coat pocket and shook it. "But first, I have to refill my flask. I'm optimistic my parents are fine, but I can guarantee my parents won't have any liquor in their home."

Dan had endured long hours of discomfort with a group of friendly and decent people, but none spoke quite as much as John Painter. John was one of those men that thought he was humorous by ignoring common courtesies in a small, crowded area with ladies aboard and took offense when corrected. Dan was a professional, well-groomed, courteous to others and faithful to his wife as a Christian man. Along the way west, John Painter had made it known he valued none of the qualities that Dan respected from other men. "I'm sure I can find it, John."

"Grab your stuff. I'll walk you there." John watched a middle-aged lady who had been stretching her legs after a long and uncomfortable ride. She was traveling to Walla Walla to catch a train further west. "Hey, Jane, remember what I said. If you come back this way, look me up. We'll have supper or something."

She gave a fake smile and then turned away without interest. She was relieved to be away from the foul man.

John chuckled. He tapped Dan's arm again. "I

don't think she liked me too much—snooty woman. I feel sorry for her husband. He probably can't button his pants up right living with a woman as perfect as her." He was a bit offended by her relief to be rid of him. "Well, Dan, let's go. It can't be too far; Branson is not that big. So, who are you looking for anyway? Do you think I'll hear about a gunfight tomorrow if you find them?"

"I told you, it's confidential information. But to answer your question, no."

John laughed with another tap to Dan's arm. "Come on. Pinkertons don't come across the nation for nothing. Who are you arresting?"

"I'm not a Pinkerton. That's a different detective agency. John, it is no big deal, believe me. And I wish you wouldn't talk so loudly. Any criminal on the street might hear you and assume I'm looking for them. That's trouble I'm not here for or want."

"Fine. As I said, this is my hometown, but I haven't been here in about twelve years. I have never heard of the Monarch Hotel before, but it sounds nice. Can I come inside and check out your room when we get there?"

"No, I don't think so," Dan said as he carried his leather suitcase along the Main Street boardwalk. He had asked the stage stop attendant where the hotel was and knew where he was going. But John was persistent to follow.

"Oh, come on," John pleaded in a loud voice. "Let me take a peek. I might need to rent a room myself if my parents are dead," he laughed.

Dan shook his head uninterested. "I'm sorry,

John; I just want to check-in and get some rest."

"What about your urgent business? Do you need my help to guide you around town? I can take you around wherever you want to go for a price. You know, it's only fair to be paid a small fee for my expertise and knowledge of the area."

"John, I'm not going to need your help, but thank you for offering," Dan answered tiredly.

"Well, if you're going to be in town for a few days, my goodness, let's get together," John said. "This big stone building is it. It looks like a nice restaurant, doesn't it?" John asked as they passed by the windows of the Monarch Restaurant. "I sure am hungry, but I'll go see what Ma and Pa have on the stove."

Dan had paid for John's meals along the way west because he didn't like to see anyone go hungry. John had not made any friends on the stagecoach and was nearly left behind in a rural stage stop due to his rude comments and foul body odor. If it weren't for Dan paying a little extra and negotiating John's travel, he would have been stranded forty miles away in the middle of nowhere. Dan stopped at the door of the Monarch Hotel and put his hand out to shake. "Thank you for guiding me here, John." The hotel wasn't hard to find. It was a few blocks up the road from the stage stop.

John shook his hand. "My pleasure. Hey, what do you say about taking my flask in there and having it filled with wine or whatever they have?" He shrugged uneasily. "I'm a little low on money, you know. I'd appreciate it for showing you the way here and all."

Dan set his case down and pulled out his bill-fold. "As a Christian man, I'd rather not do that. But here," he handed John a dollar bill. "John, you seem like a broken man to me. When you go home to see your parents, I hope you pick your Bible up again. You know the Lord has a path planned for your life, and I don't think you're on it."

John chuckled as he took the dollar. "You don't believe we're just puppets on strings?"

Dan shook his head. "No. We are not puppets at all. If you don't want anything to do with God, that is your choice, but don't blame him for that on Judgment Day. You're a minister's son; you should know that."

"Yeah," John said bitterly. "But God didn't do me right, did he? What a path he has put me on, huh?"

"Did he? Or was it you?"

John grinned after a quick offended glare. "Thanks for the dollar."

"You're welcome. Take care, John." Dan said and walked into the hotel.

\*\*\*

John had walked to Rose Street and had his flask filled with a dollars' worth of whiskey before walking to his parents' house across town. He knocked on the door and waited with butterflies fluttering in his empty belly.

Reverend Eli Painter and his bride of forty-three years, Beatrice, were entertaining friends, the newly-married Henry and Sylvia Redlin and Sylvia's daughter. Barbra. They had them over for dinner and were seated in the family room, enjoying some friendly conversation.

Beatrice spoke of their mutual friends, Roger and Martha King, "I know Martha and Roger have had some troubles fairly recently, but they seem to be overcoming them. I think it was wonderful of you, Barbra, to help them when Martha's arm was broken, and Roger's knee injured. They needed the help."

Barbra was a seventeen-year-old girl with long brown hair and blue eyes on a thin oblong face with hollow cheeks. She was attractive but shy and quiet. She smiled at the bit of praise as the evening's conversation finally moved to her. "Thank you."

Sylvia Redlin volunteered, "Roger was so impressed with how hard Barbra worked that he gave her a job at the Monarch Hotel."

"Is that right?" Beatrice asked. "What are you doing there?"

"I clean rooms and keep the hotel clean. Roger says, eventually, I will work my way into a front desk job with Pamela. But I think I'd rather just clean. I'm not good at talking to people like Pamela is."

Henry Redlin laughed. "Until you get her home. When I start wanting to go to bed, she wants to talk. Barbra's like a coo-coo clock. At ten o'clock, she turns into a chatterbox."

"Is that right?" Beatrice asked her with a humored grin. She was a robust lady with long gray hair that was often in a ponytail. Her round face with warm brown eyes behind her spectacles were always welcoming and loving. She had a way of making people feel comfortable.

Barbra's face reddened. "Yeah. I don't have to be at work until eight."

"So, you're up late?" Reverend Eli Painter asked.

"Yes," Sylvia answered. "She's always kind of been that way, but it's getting worse."

"What do you do late at night?" the reverend asked.

"Read or write."

"Oh. What do you write? If I may ask," he questioned.

"Poetry. I like to read poetry too."

"Really? Before you leave, I'll show you my library, and you can borrow one of my books if you'd like. We have collected quite a few books of poems. There may be some you haven't read."

"I'd like that."

"Do you have a favorite?" There was a knock on the door. "Hold that thought," Reverend Painter said, getting to his feet. He opened the door and stood staring momentarily at a face he didn't quite recognize at first. "John?" he asked with a touch of repulsion in the tone.

"Hello, Pa. A bit surprised, huh?" John asked with a grin.

"Come in. How are you, son?" He hugged his son. He wrinkled his nose at the stench. "What are you doing here? Where is your family?"

"Long story."

Beatrice had gotten to her feet and gasped when she saw her son. Tears filled her eyes.

"Hello, Ma," John chuckled before hugging her.

"Ugh! You smell of the witches' brew." She fanned her hand in front of her nose as they separated.

John grinned. "I met a man on the stage that bought me a few drinks when we got to town. But I came back like the prodigal son, yeah?"

"Where is Sue and the children?"

"Ah…it's a long story, Ma. But in short, she took the kids and divorced me."

Beatrice gasped and covered her mouth emotionally. "What? Where are our grandchildren?"

"Last I heard, either Mississippi or Louisiana."

Henry tapped Sylvia's leg and whispered, "Let's go." He announced to his hosts, "We're going to go home and let you visit with your son."

Eli Painter spoke, "Thank you, Henry. Henry, you remember John, of course."

"Of course. How are you, John?" he asked, shaking the man's hand. He was surprised by John's appearance. Twelve years before, John was a clean-cut kid with a bit of fire in his eyes and acne on his skin, with big dreams and a knack for wanting adventure. He'd left Branson to attend Andover Theological Seminary in Andover, Massachusetts. Henry expected that John would accomplish his endeavors and become a well-known theologian. It took John twelve long years to come home, and he was dressed in rags and most unkempt and filthy. John had long brown hair that was greasy, tangled and fell lifelessly onto his shoulders. He had a shabby brown beard about six inches long that was too thin and spotty to be worn respectfully. He smelled of whiskey mixed with severe body odor and hadn't eaten in some time by the baggy rags used as clothes.

John shook Henry's hand. "Henry."

"This is my wife, Sylvia and our daughter, Barbra. This is John Painter."

John's eyes roamed over Sylvia with desire. He glanced at Henry Redlin and grimaced. "How in the hell did you talk such a good-looking woman into marrying someone as ugly and fat as you, Henry?"

Both Eli and Beatrice's cheeks reddened, whether from humiliation or angered at the comment, wasn't made clear, but their disapproval was made known either way.

Sylvia answered before anyone could respond, "His character and heart brought out the beauty in him. I find him most attractive and cuddly. If you'll excuse us, we'll leave you with your parents to visit. Barbra, come along."

John chuckled. "As they say, beauty is in the eye of the beholder, huh? Well, I can see where your daughter gets her good looks. I'm John; I'm single and always looking for a good time." He extended his hand out to shake Barbra's hand.

Reluctantly Barbra extended her hand. John gently bent over kissed the top of it. "My pleasure to meet you, Barbra. I'll be calling on you before the week is through."

"John, why don't you sit down while we say goodnight to our guests," Reverend Eli Painter

36

suggested with underlying displeasure in his voice.

"What?" John said with a roll of his eyes, quickly picking up on his father's disapproving tone. "I'm being friendly."

Reverend Painter stepped outside and closed the door behind him to speak to Henry as they were leaving. "I apologize for my son. His manners are terrible."

Henry frowned. "No reason to apologize. It smells like he's been drinking."

Eli was flustered. "I don't know what to say except I am embarrassed. We'll have you all over for dinner again, and Barbra, we'll talk poetry then. I'm sorry my son came home, smelling of whiskey, and obnoxious." He shrugged.

Eli entered the house and glared at his thirty-year-old son. "Don't you ever embarrass me like that again. Henry is a long-time friend of ours and you know that."

John chuckled. "Pa, he's still ugly. Henry is the ugliest man I've ever known. I'm sorry, but how in the hell did he ever find such a cute woman to marry? So, do you think I have a chance of stealing her away from him, or shall I focus on the daughter?"

"I think you need to close your mouth and refrain from using that kind of language in our home. John, I am going to sit down and listen while you tell me what has happened to you?"

John laughed. "What happened to me?"

"Yes. We have not seen you in twelve years. So far, the homecoming has not been pleasant, so, please. Let's start over. Tell us about you."

"Pa, I am much more interested in learning about Henry's wife and daughter. Do you think I have a chance?"

Beatrice spoke pointedly, "If you want to stay in my house, you will never speak like that to our friends again, period." Her stern eyes glared at him warningly. "You embarrassed us. Don't you ever be rude to our guests again!"

"What? Does the way I look embarrass you?" John asked and raised his palm questionably. "It's the only clothes I have, the ones in my bag are worse."

"No. The way you treated our guests is the problem. Now, where have you been?" Eli asked pointedly.

# Chapter 5

Don Franklyn had a relaxing hot bath before getting a good night's sleep in a comfortable bed. He ate a hearty breakfast at the Monarch Hotel and even bought a coffee cup with the Monarch Hotel's front emblazed on it to keep as a souvenir from such a grand facility. He got directions and walked to Rose Street and banged on the front door of Bella's Dance Hall. There was a sign on the door stating they were closed until later that evening on the door. He continued to knock loudly. After several minutes, he looked at his watch. It was after ten in the morning. He banged on the door again. He had been forewarned to wait until around ten before knocking.

A man in his thirties with a well-groomed mustache and short brown hair peeked out a covered window before opening the door. A heavy chain allowed the door to open five inches or so to allow him to answer the door safely. By the gauge of the thickness of the chain, Dan guessed the anchors connected to the chain were solid as well. The gentleman asked in a friendly voice, "Can I help you?"

"Yes. I can see that you are closed for business, but my name is Dan Franklyn. I am a detective with the Mission Detective Agency in Indianapolis, Indiana. I was hired to contact a young lady named Christine Knapp. May I inquire if she is employed here?"

The gentleman behind the door appeared unsure of what to say. "Hold on a minute." He closed the door and locked it. Dan waited patiently before the sound of the door being unlocked and opened fully to reveal an older woman in her late fifties, heavy set with brown hair and a rough exterior. She asked in a raspy voice, "I'm Bella and this is my place. I understand you're looking for someone?" Two men stood behind her, watching curiously.

"Yes. As I explained to the gentleman, I have been hired by a certain individual to locate and relay a message to one Christine Knapp. I have traced her westward travels to Denver and the most unfortunate circumstances that happened to her there. I know she worked for you in Denver and came here with you, but I do not know if she is still employed with you or not. I am merely here to ascertain that."

Bella asked curiously, "Is she in trouble?"

Dan smiled. "Not at all."

"Can I ask what your business with her is?"

"That is confidential. But I assure you it is nothing criminal. I assume Miss Knapp is still employed here?"

"She is."

"May I have a few moments of her time? I assure you my business will take no more than twenty minutes."

Bella lowered her brow. "You came all the way from Indiana to see her for twenty minutes?" Bella asked skeptically.

Dan nodded. "Believe it or not, someone is paying a large fee for that, yes."

"Come inside. Have a seat at one of the tables in the ballroom. You can talk to my husband Dave and Gaylon while I let Christine know you are here to see her."

Dan made small talk with the two gentlemen until Bella came downstairs with an uneasy smile. "She is getting dressed. I told her you came from Indiana and now she's very concerned that maybe you're here to tell her that her grandmother passed away. Is that why you are here? Because if it is, it would be better if I told her in the privacy of her room."

Dan appreciated the sincerity of Bella's concern. "I can offer no information about why I am here except to Miss Knapp, herself. However, the answer is no. That is not the message I was given."

"Good," Bella said with relief. "Christine is getting married shortly and the last thing she needs is bad news." She noticed the fading of Dan's upturned lips to downturned corners at the news of a wedding. "What? Is it bad news?"

His lips squeezed together. "Not particularly."

Before too long, Christine came nervously

downstairs dressed in a simple brown dress. Her hair was thrown into a quick bun on the back of her head. "Hello, I am Christine."

Dan, still talking to the others, turned to face her. "Miss Knapp. It's a pleasure to meet you finally. Please, let's have a seat and a bit of privacy." He continued when they were seated at a table, "My name is Dan Franklyn and Miriam MacArthur hired me to locate you. Do you know who Miriam is by chance?"

Christine shook her head. "No."

"She is your mother's cousin, your second cousin. Your grandmother moved to Indianapolis to live with her older sister Ruth. Your grandmother had written Ruth's address down on a piece of paper that she intended to put in the envelope that she gave you that contained the money from the sale of her farm. After she left you, she found that piece of paper in her coat pocket while on the stagecoach bound for her sister's. It broke her heart knowing she would never hear from you again."

"Mine too," Christine said with a quivering voice. Her eyes filled with thick tears.

Dan frowned understandably. "Your Great Auntie Ruth has a daughter named Miriam. Miriam was close to your mother in age, and they were close friends in their youth. Miriam and her husband own a few businesses in Indianapolis and are well off. Two years ago, Miriam moved her mother and your grandmother into her home, as both ladies were too elderly to take care of themselves during those freezing winters. Last fall, Ruth, unfortunately, passed away."

"Does she want my grandmother to come live with me?" Christine asked with concern.

"No. Miriam hired our company to find you. Your grandmother is welcome to live with Miriam and her family. Christine," Dan said softly, "your grandmother is not well. Her time upon earth is getting shorter and she has one wish. She would like you to come stay with her. If you agree, I am hired to escort you safely back to Indianapolis, where Miriam is offering you the opportunity to spend the last months of your grandmother's life with her. That is your grandmother's wish. There would be no financial cost to you, and you are welcomed into their home. Miriam said she has always wanted to meet you."

Christine buried her face into her arms on the table and burst into harsh sobbing. It wasn't a gradual gathering of tears slowly falling, but an emotional reservoir four years in the making that burst through the hardened soil of time. She had not known if her grandmother was still alive, but she did know she would never see her again. To learn she was alive and wished to see her was more than her heart could restrain.

Dan was touched by the obvious love Christine had for her grandmother. When Christine had gained control of her emotions and raised her head to look at Dan, he continued, "I know your mother committed suicide right after you were born, and your grandmother raised you as her daughter. I can imagine this comes as quite a surprise, although a good surprise, I hope."

Christine repeatedly nodded as she wiped her cheeks and eyes of tears. "Yes," she said with a grin.

"I was told you are getting married soon."

Red-eyed and with a tear-stricken face, Christine answered, "In three weeks." She sniffled.

"I don't know if you're willing to postpone your wedding or not, but Miriam has offered to pay for your travels and everything you would need to come to stay at her home for as long as you want to spend the remaining time with your grandmother. It is a once in a lifetime opportunity because, as you know too well, once someone is gone, they don't come back."

Her lips puckered emotionally as her eyes filled with tears again. "I could see my grandmother?"

Dan smiled softly. "For as long as you want."

"She's the only family I have."

"Miss Knapp, I went to talk with your grandmother, and that's exactly what she said about you. I am merely the messenger, but I took a liking to your grandmother and if you can, I highly suggest taking the opportunity to see her."

Christine covered her face with her hands and wept.

"You have a lot to think about and I don't mean to put added pressure on you, but I am leaving tomorrow morning at nine on the stage. So, if you would like to come back with me, I'll need to know soon to purchase your ticket. I'm not pressuring you, but I wish I would have had a chance like this to spend time with my parents before they went to

44

heaven. I know she is the only mother you ever had. If your fiancé understands, postpone the wedding for a month or two and see your grandmother. You'll never regret an opportunity like that. I'm staying at the Monarch Hotel. Please let me know before too long."

When Dan left, Christine wrapped her arms around Bella and sobbed.

"I don't know what to do," Christine wept.

"Christine, sweetheart," Bella released the hug and put her palms on Christine's cheeks to look into her eyes. "If you don't go, you will always wish you had. Take the night off to pack and spend some time with Matt. He'll understand, sweetheart. And when you come back, your room will be here waiting. I want you to go."

\*\*\*

Matt's excitement to see Christine enter his office faded as she told him she wanted to postpone the wedding to travel to Indiana with a stranger to see her grandmother. She had explained what had been proposed to her and at the conclusion, she asked, "Are you mad at me for wanting to go?"

Matt's eyes blinked a few times to force away any sign of moisture before answering. He was dumbfounded. "Ah…no. I'm not mad. Who told this again?"

"His name is Dan Franklyn. He's staying at the Monarch Hotel until tomorrow. I need to tell him I want to go because the stage leaves in the morning.

Will you come with me?"

"The stage leaves in the morning? How long do you think you'll be gone?" A hole was beginning to form in his heart.

"I don't know," she said softly. "Matt, don't be mad at me, please. You know how important my grandmother is to me. She is the only mother I know."

"I'm not mad. I'm surprised, but not mad. I'm a bit overwhelmed. Yesterday we were talking about sternwheelers and making plans for our honeymoon, and today, it's canceled."

She shook her head slowly. "Not canceled, just postponed."

"Until further notice." A thin coat of moisture glazed his brown eyes.

"I didn't plan this. I want to see my grandmother before she passes away. Can you understand that?" she asked emotionally.

"Of course, I can. It's just very sudden." He took a deep breath as she blurred through the lens of his moistening eyes. "I want you to see her, but that's so far away."

"You can come with me. We can go there for our honeymoon."

Matt rubbed his beard anxiously. "By the time we got there, you'd only have a couple of days with her before we had to come back. That wouldn't be fair to you." He took a deep breath. "We've waited this long; I suppose we could wait longer."

Her sad attempt at a smile revealed her own heartbreak. "I hate that I am doing this to you."

"It's not the worst thing you could do. It's fine."
An uncomfortable silence grew between them.
There was probably a lot more that needed to be
said, but Matt couldn't think of anything. He was
filled with a sadness that he wasn't used to feeling.
It wasn't the ending of their engagement, but it kind
of felt similar. "Shall we go talk to this detective
and make sure he's who he says he is?"

"Please. And thank you. I was hoping you would,"
Christine admitted.

Matt's brow lifted warningly and raised one finger to make a point. "If I don't like this Dan fellow
or get a bad feeling from him, you're not going with
him. Agreed?"

Tears filled Christine's eyes like an ocean tide. "I
hope he's being honest because I'd give anything to
be with my grandmother again. Matt, if he's lying,
I'm going to be hurt."

He stood and put on his gun belt. "Let's go find
out. If he is lying, I'll hurt him."

\*\*\*

After spending an hour talking over lunch with
Dan Franklyn and checking his credentials, Matt
was satisfied that he was telling the truth and an
upright Christian man who agreed to provide safe
passage to and from Indianapolis when Christine
returned.

Matt held Christine's hand as they slowly strolled
along Main Street back towards the marshal's office. He was in no hurry and certainly didn't want

to see the day come to an end. Fortunately, she was given the night off work to pack and prepare for her travels and spend time with him. It would be a long night but didn't seem long enough.

"You're awfully quiet," she said softly.

"I'm sad," he replied with a hint of a comforting smile. "I understand, though. Christine, I'm excited that you get the chance to see your grandmother. I know how much that means to you. I'm going to miss you, but I will wait for you, no matter how long you're gone. I want you to treasure the time with your grandmother."

Her bottom lip twitched. "You don't know how much that means to me. I was scared you would get angry and tell me to stay there."

He laughed. "Never. You won't have any regrets when you come back, and we will have the rest of our lives to be together. Until then, just rest on knowing you're loved."

"I know I am. You prove it more to me every day. Don't doubt I love you, Matthew Bannister. I want to marry you."

"So how do we start to postpone a wedding when invitations have been sent out? I suppose we had better start with Redlin meats before Henry kills twenty chickens."

"I don't have time, but I can have Bella send out cancelation notices. I imagine the gossip will take off in a variety of ways of why it's canceled."

"Undoubtedly," Matt agreed. He was going to respond as they strolled along the boardwalk hand in hand when his eyes went to a group of eight men riding their horses up Main Street with two pack horses. As they rode closer, Christine could see they all wore silver badges and appeared to be a mean and hardened bunch of men. One of the men pointed towards Matt.

Matt's eyes hardened with recognition.

Christine narrowed her brow curiously when she noticed Matt grow tense. "What?" she asked. He silently released her hand and stepped to the edge of the boardwalk to lean against a support post of the awning above him. His thumb casually removed the thong from the revolver's hammer. Frightened, she stepped away a few steps.

Matt stared at the approaching riders. The group leader tipped his hat towards Matt and passed with a scowl on his rough face without saying a word. One man rode by and said, "Matt."

"Ed," Matt replied with a scowl.

One young man riding towards the back of the column glared at Matt and threatened, "You better change that glare, half breed, or I'll lay you out in front of your woman!"

"Toby!" the group leader shouted as he turned his horse. He was angry. "Shut your damn mouth! You all get to the hotel and get checked in." The leader rode back and stopped his horse in front of Matt. He was an older man in his late fifties with short gray hair, a prominent nose on his weathered face, and gray whiskers from not shaving for a week or so. His cold hazel eyes watched Matt sternly. His voice was deep and strong, "I didn't know you were in town until I just saw your office. I apologize for my man. He's young and stupid. You won't hear a squeak from him again. I'll see to that."

Matt spoke coldly, "I warned William Slater not to invite you here. We don't need the trouble that comes along with you all. I won't tolerate any trouble, Jeff. You better tell that stupid kid I don't put up with much," Matt warned.

Jeff Blackburn twisted his lips before stating, "There won't be any trouble. We're here to escort a gold shipment to San Francisco, that's all. We're here for one night and there will be no trouble at all. You have my word."

"I didn't see Duggan. Is he with you?" Matt asked. There was no friendliness in his voice.

Jeff ran his tongue on the inside of his cheek. "He's dead. You'd think he'd get shot, but no. He got gut kicked by a horse."

"I can't say I'm sorry to hear that. Keep your men on a tight collar."

"Will do." Jeff turned his horse and continued up the street.

"Matt, who was that?" Christine asked.

"That is Jeff Blackburn. The leader of the Blackburn Marshals. They're nothing but trouble," he replied as he watched Jeff ride away.

"You know them?" she asked skeptically.

"Some of them."

"Are they a gang? They all wore badges," she inquired.

Matt sighed. "You remember when the two Pinkerton Detectives came here searching for Sarah Pierce? Allan Pinkerton started a whole new profession when he started the Pinkerton Detective Agency. There are many detective agencies around the country now, such as the one in Indianapolis hired to find you. Along the same lines, there are private police forces hired by ranchers, the railroads, mines or any company or person that needs protection primarily. The detective companies may do more investigating as Dan searched for you. The private police forces mostly regulate and protect. Jeff Blackburn prefers to call his men marshals rather than a militia or a police force to separate them from the others. The Blackburn Marshals wear a badge like mine; it looks like a federal marshal badge, but it's not. My badge carries the authority of the United States government. Theirs are nothing more than a metal star with the word marshal on it. They have no authority anywhere in the United States. They are paid thugs and Blackburn doesn't care what the job is as long it pays, he'll do it. And that's who they are."

"Are they dangerous?" she asked with concern.

"Every man hired by a private detective company or private police force is dangerous. You have to be dangerous to be in that line of work, but that doesn't make them a danger to the public. What makes the Blackburn Marshals dangerous is they are mostly outlaws and killers already. I'm surprised to see Ed with them, but I hope they just do what they are paid to do and leave."

"Matt, are you going to be okay when I leave? I don't want anything to happen to you when I'm gone." Her sincere expression once again warmed his soul.

"I'll be fine. It sounds like they'll be leaving here soon. I don't want to spend my last evening with you talking about them, though."

"You make it sound so final."

He laughed lightly and put his arm around her shoulders and pulled her close to him as they walked along the boardwalk. "Until you come back to me."

# Chapter 6

William Slater sat with his elbows on his desk, with his long fingers intertwined in front of his chin. He stared at Jeff Blackburn and Jeff's close friend, Ira Kelly, from overtop of his silver-rimmed spectacles. "Trust me, gentlemen, Matt Bannister is not going to be a problem."

Jeff spoke in his deep voice, "I was surprised to see him here is all. You contacted us, and we agreed to escort your gold shipment to the railhead and then to San Francisco. You did not mention anything about guarding your house or your mine from your employees."

William's fingers extended and relaxed with a slow shrug. "There's been some changes since I requested your help. Recently my employees threatened to strike if I didn't meet their demands about halfway. I had to give in some to keep my mine flowing. Strikes don't make me money, and we hit a nice vein of gold—good quality gold at that.

However, we slightly miscalculated and followed the vein right into another company's claim. In essence, we're processing their gold."

Ira Kelly laughed. "I'd make the same miscalculation." Ira was a medium-height man with medium-length light-brown hair, and a well-groomed mustache that had a touch of gray on his oval-shaped face. He wasn't a broad man but a muscular, blue-eyed fellow. He was in his early forties and appeared to be the more vocal of the two men.

William continued, "It was an honest mistake. A former employee who was angry with me decided to change our boundaries on our company map, which is updated every month, and no one caught it. In his act of sabotage, he found us a fortune. I should send him an apology note and offer his job back with a large raise and permission to court my daughter, and when he shows up, tell him to get lost! I should and perhaps I will. And I hope he spends every last damn dime he has to move back here."

"You sound a little angry about that," Ira said with a grin.

William stared at Ira irritably. "Our neighbor mining company is small and of no concern, except they discovered our mistake and want to be compensated. You can imagine the cost he wants. It is everything we have processed."

"Imagine that?" Ira asked while tapping Jeff on the arm. "The rightful owner wants a big part of his gold." He laughed.

"It's my gold," William said slowly. "The Rohloff Mining Works is a small family-owned business that would never be able to dig as deep as we have to find it. They bring what ore they find to our stamp mill to process because they can't afford a single stamper or the means to process it. We are the only ones that can get to the gold, and we have."

Jeff Blackburn spoke, "That doesn't concern us. You made a good offer to do a job that we are prepared to do. Half paid now and half when we return with your men and the treasury note. We are ready to leave in the morning. You are not the only one that wants to retain our services, and waiting in town without being paid is not something I am willing to do. I don't know what you're getting at, but unless it pertains to us and getting paid, I don't care about your problems."

Josh Slater sat in a chair not far from his father, listening. He spoke, "Well, it does involve you. We need time to work out a deal with our neighbor, and to create the time needed, we need a distraction. We are going to force our employees to strike. They'll hate us for a while, but we can't haggle with our neighbor if we're too occupied haggling with our employees. Do you see how that works? We just need some time to run our neighbors out of business and buy them out. And that's where we need your help. You'll be paid handsomely, but we need some heavy hands and some ideas, perhaps."

"What about your people?" Jeff asked.

"We have armed guards at the mine, but they are not professionals. They're just simple people with a job to do."

"I'm talking about your miners. Don't they have

families?"

Josh answered, "Of course, some do. Hey, they threatened to strike first; we're just helping them decide to do so while it's beneficial for us. It's only for a couple of weeks at most and then we'll make things right. In the meantime, all production will stop, and we'll maneuver to run the Rohloffs out of business and buy their claim."

"How are you going to do that?" Jeff asked.

William Slater smiled like a snake eyeing a crippled mouse. "That is where you and your expertise come in. We'll write up an offer for a fair amount and you'll get him to sign it by whatever means is necessary."

Ira grimaced with a growing grin. "If you want him strongarmed, why don't you just say so. You don't need a strike to do that."

Josh explained, "We think Oliver Rohloff will be much more likely to sign over his company at a much lower price if we are down and appear to be struggling to reach an agreement with a bunch of angry strikers. In the meantime, he will have some problems of his own that he may not be able to afford for long, but that's to be discussed later. Right now, we need to discuss the price to keep half your men here while the other half escorts the shipment."

"It's a ruse?" Jeff asked catching on.

Josh grinned. "Completely. But we will have a furious bunch of employees and we've never had a strike before and don't know what to expect. Hence your protection and expertise would be greatly appreciated."

Jeff raised his brow and exhaled. "We've never encountered this before. Most mines try to avoid strikes, not plan one."

Ira answered, "Yeah, but most mines know their legal boundaries." He chuckled.

Jeff spoke frankly, "William and Josh, we're not known for being big-hearted for anything, and we will do a lot more than most private companies will that is illegal. In fact, we are pretty good at that. But let me tell you something; I fought with the Confederate army and after the war, I saw many hurting families. Most men in my hometown were killed during the war and I came home to famine and poverty as I've never seen before." He raised a finger before continuing slowly and thoughtfully, "I have one soft spot and that is hungry children and women that have nothing to eat. If you want this owner to sign over his mine, we can get that done today. There is no need for you to put these men out of work and force their wives and children to suffer. How are they going to eat?"

Josh narrowed his eyes, perplexed by the question. "How would they eat if they went on strike at their own accord? That's not our problem. Our problem is teaching our employees how good they have it without asking for more. We're going to take everything they have away and when they are hungry enough and get what they have back, they'll be content and happy as a fed cow. There are two parts to our plan, and both are winners for us."

Jeff's hardened eyes glanced at Josh curiously.

"Have you ever gone a day without eating Josh? I don't mean fasting for your church. I mean not being able to eat because you have nothing, not even a mildewing potato and no way to barter for a slice of bread. Have you ever had to feed your kids a slice of bread and a cup of water for supper?"

Josh chuckled. "No."

"I didn't think so. We'll do what we're paid to do as long as the price is right, but I'm also going to warn you that I am a pretty straightforward man. If we're hired to keep the peace or something more violent, we'll do it if the money's right. But it's a straight punch; I don't play games with people's lives. We'll protect your shipment with our lives, and we'll get that man to sign your offer in one hour. We'll even protect you and your property from your employees, but do not ask me to harass or lay a hand on your employees, because I think it's a rotten thing you're doing. Rotten to the core. And if you try to cheat me like you are your neighbor and your employees, it will be the most unfortunate error of your lives, if not the end of them. Now being warned, let's talk money."

William's eyes peered over his spectacles at Jeff. "Let's be clear, I don't want any of my employees hurt. I don't want a single hair on their heads touched. I'm not kicking them out of their homes or harassing them. I just need them to strike for a little while as a distraction for plan A and learn to be content with what we offer on plan B. Your job will be to protect me, my family and my interests. Now about money, let's discuss it."

# Chapter 7

"I plan on getting a job, Pa. What do you think I plan on doing?" John Painter asked his father irritably. They were sitting at the supper table trying to enjoy a meal, but the prodigal son's homecoming wasn't going quite as well as John had hoped.

"I wasn't sure," Eli answered. "You haven't made it clear if you were visiting or planning to stay. That is what I was asking."

"I'm not sure. I'm testing the waters."

"A bath would be a good idea, Son."

John laid his fork down with a roll of his head in frustration. "And I should cut my hair, shave my beard and put on a suit, right? I don't have a suit. Hell, I don't even own a razor. I pick pocketed and begged for money to just buy a stage ticket here and begged for food on the way. I don't own a damn thing and I haven't bathed in I don't know how long. I stink and the folks on the stage let me know it. I was almost left behind in some little place far from here, but one man on the stage came to my rescue. Okay? Now you know, your son is a criminal and a beggar. I didn't reach the pinnacle of the Christian life as you wanted."

"Excuse me," Beatrice said emotionally and left the dinner table to hide her tears. His words broke her heart.

Eli watched her go towards their bedroom.

"Sorry, Pa, I didn't mean to upset her."

Eli stared at his plate of food with a heavy heart. He spoke softly, "She had much more hope for you. You are such a smart man, John. How do you balance that sort of life with your Christian upbringing?"

John answered plainly, "I don't. I don't call myself a Christian. It's great for you and Ma, but I don't need it."

"We all need the Lord."

"No, I don't."

"No?" Eli asked.

"No. I'll give you credit, you're a Christian, but not even you're perfect. How many hypocrites come to your church? You can't go to a church or a seminary without finding a bunch of hypocrites, phonies and charlatans. That's all that goes to church. I'm sorry to tell you that because I know you and Ma are not, but even you two are far from perfect. I don't want to be around that."

Eli took a bite of food and chewed it slowly. "Maybe you should come to church and show all the rest of us how not to be a hypocrite, phony or a charlatan. Maybe that is your calling to be an example of the perfect Christian."

John laughed. "No, I know I'm not."

"Do you think you'd fail at being the perfect Christian? Perhaps someone will call you a hypocrite and use you as an excuse of why they don't go to church."

"Okay. I know not everyone is perfect. I get that. But there are some terrible people in churches, and you know that. How many so-called Christians would look at me right now and give me the time of day? If I went to church looking and smelling as I do right now, how many people do you think would want to talk to me?"

"I would hope many."

John scoffed bitterly. "If I was wealthy, they would, no doubt. How many people in your congregation would look at me and then look away and avoid me without a second glance, except to wonder what a beggar is doing in their church. I guarantee most of them would think I was there looking for a handout. You see, my spiritual life would not be their greatest concern. My appearance and my financial standing would override it. I know that from experience, Pa. Do you think I haven't tried to come back to the Lord? I'm not wanted. I think John Calvin had it right. Some of us are just not chosen by God and it's pointless to even try."

Eli's eyes hardened a touch. "Horse crap! John Calvin was dead wrong. God does not pick and choose who goes to heaven and hell. We are not predestined before birth. We are given free choice to choose to serve the Lord or not. Our eternal destination depends on that choice, but everyone has to make that choice. What does the word, *whosoever* mean?"

"Whoever."

"What does whoever mean? Who does that word include?"

John shrugged. "Anyone. Everyone. Whoever."

"*For God so loved the world that he gave his one and only Son, that whosoever believes in him shall not perish but have eternal life. For God did not send his Son into the world to condemn the world, but to save the world through him.* John 3:16 and 17. It does not say Jesus came to save those chosen or predestined. It says *whosoever believes in him shall not perish.* It is very inclusive to anyone and everyone. Jesus did not come to *condemn the world but to save the world through him.* The world means the world, right? Not fifty-one percent to have a majority. The idea of predestination and having no choice of your eternal destination is ludicrous. Worse, those that believe in Calvinism waste no time trying to reach the lost souls and tell them the good news of Jesus Christ. I'll tell you right now when I stand before the Lord, I want to be able to say, 'Jesus, I spent my life trying to tell people about you and gave my all to increasing the number of people coming to heaven.' I do not want to have to say, 'Um, well, they were predestined to hell, weren't they?' I'm afraid Jesus's answer might be a thunderous and angry shout of, 'NO!'" Eli shook his head and spoke softly, "Why would Jesus tell the disciples to go spread the Gospel to the ends of the earth if we are all predestined? We have a mission, Son, to share the good news of Jesus with the world around us. If you know the Lord, then it's your mission too. Maybe not the same way I do, but in your circle of life and in your own unique way using your God-given gifts and talents."

"Not me, Pa. I left that behind when Sue divorced me. I prayed and prayed, and it did no good. She took my kids and I'll never see them again. That's what the Lord did for me. Anyway, can I borrow a few dollars for a bath, shave and haircut? I thought I'd go downtown and get cleaned up. I might have better luck getting a job if I looked about half respectable around here."

"We have a bathtub and scissors here. You can use my straight edge razor as well."

"Pa," John said with a grin. "I would like to come back cleaned up and maybe even in some new clothes if you'd loan me enough, and surprise Mother. I know she's disappointed in me right now, and I'd like to, you know, surprise her."

Eli took a deep breath. "We don't have a lot of money to spare. But if you promise to use it for what you stated and not drink or gamble, it might be a nice surprise for your mother. I'll agree to it if you promise to use the money to clean yourself up and buy new clothes."

"Of course. I look at this homecoming as a new start to get back on my feet. To start over," John said sincerely. "Who knows, maybe I'll be revived in church."

Eli smiled. The words were pleasing to his ears.

"We can always afford to help with a turned-around life. I'm glad you're home, Son. We'll do what we can to help you reach your God-given potential. Do you think twenty dollars would be enough for a new suit and some everyday work wear?"

# Chapter 8

Matt sat with Christine on a quilt she had brought to the top of the high hill where they could watch the sunset over the western mountains one last time. His arm held her shoulders close to him as they cuddled as lovers do. He could not shake the sadness that filled his heart even though she was right beside him. It was the last moments they'd be together until she left him for an undetermined time. They were in no hurry to see the sun go down or for the evening to come to an end. If time could stand still…if only he could make it last.

He had bought an apple pie to share and now that it was half-eaten the pie sat near their feet on the quilt. The sunset's orange, red and yellow glow filled the sky as beautiful as it always did, but this one was special somehow. Only the glory of the father in heaven could paint such a magnificent display of colors, images and beauty. The only thing that compared to the beauty of the sunset was seen when Matt turned his head and gazed at Christine as a slight breeze touched her hair. A mist coated his eyes.

She knew he was staring at her, and her lips raised just a touch as she turned to face him. Her soft voice reflected her own tormented emotions, "I'll be back."

Matt spoke slowly through a deep frown. "I want you to know since I've met you, I've had the best time of my life. You've become the best part of me and without seeing you every day, it's going to take some getting used to. I'm good at a lot of things, but I don't know how good I am at missing you."

She sniffled as his lips tightened. "I'll miss you too. I wish you could come with me. It's the last chance you'll ever have to meet my grandmother. It's the last time I'll get to see her." Her brow furrowed as her eyes went downward. "I don't know how long I'll be gone, Matt. It might be only a week or two or maybe months. I don't think I can leave her until she goes to heaven. Will you still wait for me even if it takes longer?" Her sincere concern was revealed in her eyes.

"I'll wait until the end of time if need be."

"Thank you." She moved her lips forward slowly and kissed him gently. "How did I ever meet someone as wonderful as you?" she whispered.

"By being you."

She leaned her forehead against his. "I hate to leave you. I'm excited to see my grandmother, but I don't want to leave you."

He rolled his head upwards against hers to touch

the tip of her nose with his. "It will be a good visit for you. You'll come back grateful for the time with her and ready to move on to the next stage in life, marrying me." He tried to pucker his lips to reach hers without moving the tip of his nose from hers, but his lips wouldn't touch hers. He tried again without moving his nose.

"You're making me think my nose is big," she stated while she waited for him to kiss her.

"Maybe mine, but not yours." He pulled his face back to gaze into her brown eyes. "I thank God above for you. I am thankful that I never married Elizabeth when I was young because I would have missed out on the greatest blessing in my life – you. It'll be hard to see you leave in the morning, but I'll keep reminding myself that it is just temporary until the day you come home."

She snuggled close to him as his protective arm welcomed her. Christine closed her eyes, comforted by his touch. "I think it will be harder for me because you won't be there to hold me when I am scared or sad or need to be held by you. I love you, Matt." A tear fell from both of her eyes. "I don't want to leave you. I want to stay here and marry you."

Matt lifted her chin gently to look into her eyes. "The Lord is blessing you with an amazing opportunity to be with your grandmother when she needs you the most. There is no way I would ever ask you to miss that for me. We can get married when you come home. We'll still have the rest of our lives to live together. Your grandmother has limited time.

You enjoy her and ask questions about her life so you can share them with our children. Have your picture taken with her and honor the time with her. When you come home, I promise, I'll hold you close to me for the rest of your life or for as long as the Lord will allow me to. And I will honor every minute we have together."

Her eyes closed as another tear slipped out and ran down her cheek. She pressed her head against his chest and wrapped her arms around him. Her gaze went to the setting sun. She didn't need to hear anymore. She just wanted to hold and be held by him for as long as she could.

# Chapter 9

John Painter stood in front of the Branson Baptist Church, focusing on a stained-glass window beside the door. The window portrayed a sunrise over a flock of sheep on a hillside eating the green grass peacefully while a large cross on the hilltop overlooked the flock. Two structural masterpieces made the church different from any other church in town; one was the tall belltower, and the other was the stained-glass window that invited anyone to come inside and find some peace in their lives.

John swayed on his feet as he lifted the jug of cheap red wine to his lips and drank. The gallon jug was nearly empty. John lowered the jug from his lips and stumbled as he tried to see clearly through his double vision and heavy eyelids. He had not bought new clothes or got a shave or haircut. He had bought the jug and gambled the rest of the money away at the card table in the Green Toad Saloon.

A lit lantern in the coat room of the church gave the window a soft glow through the night. The longer John glared at the peaceful work of art, the angrier he became.

John groaned with disgust. "You never did nothing for me, did you? The sun comes up and goes down and I'm one day closer to dying. You have done nothing for me. Where's that good path you have for me?" He chuckled eerily. "I'm not chosen by you. I guess that makes me a wolf! Is that my role in life to be a wolf instead of one of the sheep? Is that the role you wrote for me?" he asked loudly in the silent night. He snarled as he stared at the church. "I might be condemned, but at least I'm not a wolf in lamb's clothing! I'm just a plain wolf. You have enough wolves in your church gossiping to separate the congregation. You don't need me for that."

John raised the jug, finished what little wine was left, and stumbled backward. His double vision was taking over as a familiar feeling churned in his stomach. He tried to belch to relieve some of the pressure building in his stomach but to no avail. He shook his head as a wave of sorrow came over him.

He spoke loudly, "Why don't you want me, God? I wanted to serve you, but you sure closed that door, didn't you? You made sure that I felt every hurt and heartache along the way. You want me to be a wolf, fine. I'll be a wolf!" He raised the empty gallon jug to realize it was empty. Angry, with a yell of fury, he threw the jug across the short yard through the large stained-glass window—the sound of shattering glass echoed through the silent street.

He chuckled eerily. "Shh! Don't tell Pa I did that." His grin suddenly fell into a scowl as he shouted, "You chose everyone else! Why not me?" He questioned miserably. "I'm a wolf, that's why." He howled like a wolf into the night and then screamed, "I'm a wolf!" He cupped his hands to his mouth and howled again.

A man two houses down the street flung open his bedroom window and shouted, "Shut up! People are trying to sleep!"

John cursed him and then stumbled through the grass to his parents' house next door. He tripped on the single step and fell into the door with a loud bang. He grumbled as the door opened.

Reverend Painter stood in his night clothes and robe, staring at his son. "Good heavens, John, what have you done?"

John chuckled. "About a gallon. It's a...it's a... What did you say?" he asked, squinting his eyes at his father.

"I said, let's get you to bed and we'll talk in the morning. Let me help you up."

John howled like a wolf again as he lay on the doorstep.

"Stop it! People are trying to sleep around here."

"I'm a wolf." He howled as his father helped him on his feet and guided his son to the davenport. John was too intoxicated to walk up the stairs to the extra bedrooms.

Beatrice stepped out of her bedroom in her robe and gasped, bringing a hand to her chest. Her heart was broken to see her adult son being helped to the davenport drunk. His eyes closed as soon as his head hit the cushion. "Oh, Father," she called to the God above with the silent pleading of her aching heart.

John howled and opened his eyes wide to stare at his father. "I hate spinning rooms," He slurred. "I don't want to be a wolf. Wolves hurt..." His eyes closed for a moment and then opened. "The room is spinning faster than..." His breathing quickened and with a sudden eruption, a solid flow of reddish-black liquid spewed out of his mouth onto the davenport cushion and ran down the edge to pool on the wood floor. A second heave brought more of the rancid liquid with the sickening abdominal choking sounds and the horrific scent of wine mixed with stomach bile. Furious, John's stomach rejected the quantity and perhaps quality of the wine and forced what remained in his stomach out onto the cushions and floor. His head fell into a pool of vomit on the cushion and his eyes closed to sleep.

Beatrice turned away and went into her room to weep. Eli's body shivered with disgust. He could see the weight of John's head pushing the cushion downward, inviting the vomit remaining on the davenport cushion towards John's nose and mouth. Eli shivered again. He was repulsed, but someone had to clean up the mess and keep John from drowning in his own pool of vomit.

Eli went to work with rags to wipe up the warm and vile mixture of regurgitated wine and bile off the cushions and his son's face, hair and beard. The pungent smell was one he could not stomach for long as it caused his stomach to churn. Eli carried an armload of dirty towels and rags he had wiped the mess up with to the back porch and tossed them outside. He cleaned himself up with a bucket of water and covered his son with a blanket.

Eli got on his knees beside his son and prayed, "Father, I have tried to be a good father and Beatrice is a wonderful mother. I don't know what we did wrong for John to be like this. I ask your forgiveness for our failures if we are to blame. I do not know. He left with a Godly foundation and now here he is passed out drunk on our davenport. I raise my hands to you and say, Lord, I don't know what to do. I ask that you make yourself known to him and bring him back to you. He is your child that has wandered away and is lost. Jesus, please come find your lost lamb and bring him home to us renewed and on fire for you. You're the only one that knows what is in his heart and why. I ask you not to let Beatrice or I interfere with your plans for him. I surrender him and his life to you. I just know our hearts are broken to see him like this. I ask for your help, Jesus. Amen."

"Amen," Beatrice said with a sniffle from their bedroom door. She walked forward in the faint light. "I was woken up by someone howling and yelling outside and I prayed it wasn't him. It was. I don't mean to sound haughty, but I am embarrassed by him tonight. All our neighbors probably heard him and looked out their windows. I can only imagine what they are going to say?"

Eli put his comforting arms around her. "I don't know what they'll say, but if they are our friends, they will understand. There's nothing more we can do. Let's go to bed and we'll talk about it in the morning."

\*\*\*

The smell of stale wine filled the house in the morning when Beatrice made breakfast for Eli and herself. John snored loudly on the davenport, while Eli sat at the table reading his Bible and drinking a cup of coffee to start the day. .

A knock on the door came quite a bit earlier than usual. Eli answered the door and forced a smile while trying to block the view of John sleeping on the davenport; the snoring and foul odor couldn't be hidden. "Robert, good morning. How are you, neighbor?"

Robert Fasana was leaving for work when he noticed the window broken out of the church. "Good morning," he said with a step back as the smell reached his nostrils. "Reverend Painter, someone broke the stained-glass window on the church. It's shattered."

"What?" Eli asked with concern. "Show me." Having retrieved the church door keys from the nail by the door, Reverend Painter entered the church with Robert beside him. It only took a moment to discover a gallon jug of wine had been thrown through the window.

Robert picked up a stained-glass piece and shook his head with disgust. "This is going to be expensive to replace."

Reverend Painter sat down on a bench and buried his face in his hands.

"I'll stop by the hardware store on the way to work and ask them to send one of their boys over to board up the window for now, just until we get a glass pane delivered. We can order a stained-glass replacement," Robert said, taking the initiative to get the church window handled.

Reverend Painter glanced at Robert with a mist in his eyes. He had no doubt who threw the wine jug through the window. "I'd appreciate that."

Robert hesitated. "Well, I have to get going. Don't worry about the window. Boards will cover it for now, but we'll have a window again in a week or two. It might take a few months for the stained glass, though. I would stay and help clean up, but I have to get to work."

"No. No, thank you for letting me know. I'll clean it up."

"Are you alright, Reverend?" Robert asked, taking notice of the broken sound of his tone.

Eli nodded. "Yeah. Thank you." He entered the sanctuary and took a seat on a pew facing the cross on the wall behind the pulpit. . His heart was broken by the knowledge that it was his son who had broken the window. "Well, Lord," he shrugged his shoulders wordlessly. "It was my son."

Beatrice Painter entered the church with a gasp and found Eli on a pew. She sat beside him with a sniffle while a tear rolled down her cheek. Eli silently put his arm around her as she leaned on his shoulder.

"He did it, didn't he?" she asked solemnly.

Eli was hesitant to speak, "Yes. Twenty dollars of our income was thrown through our two-hundred-dollar window and wiped up off our family room floor."

Beatrice closed her eyes and shook her head. "Where'd we go wrong, Eli?"

He stared at the cross for a moment in thought. "I don't know if we did. But John needs our prayer and our help now. I will have a serious talk with him today. For now, let's pray for our son."

# Chapter 10

A tightness gripped Matt's chest and there was a strange lump in his throat as he held Christine tightly in his arms. He could hear her sniffling on his shoulder and her body jerking as she wept. His eyes were warm and moist as he looked at the stagecoach in front of him with a sinking sensation in his heart. Her small chest of clothes was loaded, and the driver checked the luggage for the final time. Don Franklyn waited by the door for her.

The wagon driver hopped down from the luggage rack to the street and said curtly, "Time to go, young lady."

Don spoke, "Christine, it's time."

She pulled her head back and stared Matt in the eyes. "I don't want to leave you."

Matt's lips tightened. "Just come back to me."

She hugged him tightly again and wept.

" Let's pray." He cupped her head with his hands and placed his forehead against hers as they lowered their heads. He sniffled. "Jesus, my heart is breaking but I ask you give Christine a safe journey to Indiana and Lord, may your blessing be upon her as she visits with her grandmother. Thank you for this awesome opportunity for her. Again, I just ask for your protection over her. Amen."

"I have to go." She kissed him. "I love you, Matt."

"I love you, Christine." He watched her slowly walk to the stagecoach and climb in hesitantly. She was weeping.

Don said, "I'll take good care of her, Matt."

Matt stood next to Bella and Dave, and together they watched the stagecoach drive away. Matt felt like a fifty-pound grain bag had taken residence in his chest. His jaw clenched tightly as his bottom lip twitched. He took a deep breath as the stage drove around the corner and out of sight.

Bella's arm went around his shoulder comfortingly. "She'll be back. This is just temporary."

Matt blinked the moisture away from his eyes silently.

\*\*\*

Matt went into his private office and closed the door. He wanted to be alone for a while. She would be back, but it felt like a final goodbye and an eternity until she would be in his arms again. He stared at his hands; they held Christine moments before, but now the space between them was empty. The external visual was a mirror of the growing sadness within him. Knowing she left town left him feeling alone.

It didn't take very long before there was a knock on his door. It opened and Phillip peeked inside to see Matt slumped over his desk staring at his hands. "Matt, Mister Rohloff is here to see you."

Matt didn't feel the usual energy he had to go out and greet someone. He stayed seated at his desk and said with no enthusiasm, "Send him in."

Momentarily, Oliver Rohloff entered the office and spoke immediately, "I haven't heard anything since I came to see you. Have you spoken with the Slaters?" His aged eyes burned into Matt. He was dressed in filthy canvas pants and a wool shirt patched and sown where it had been torn over the years. His floppy wool hat drooped downward.

"Have a seat," Matt replied softly.

"I don't need to sit to get an answer. Did you talk with them or not? Did you find out anything at all?" Oliver Rohloff's patience had run out and he was in no mood for anything but a yes or no answer.

"I did…"

"And?" Oliver asked in an impatient, loud tone. "They're stealing my gold. I can guarantee it. What did they say? Do they deny it?"

"No."

"They're not?" He was surprised. "Did you arrest them?"

"No."

"Then what are you doing? How come you didn't come out to the mine like you said you would? A man should keep his word! I'm the one losing a fortune here, not you. Did they cut you in on the deal or something, Marshal?"

"Are you going to shut up and listen?" Matt asked sharply. He continued now that he had Oliver's attention, "The Slaters admit they made a mistake. I believe it is their business to explain to you how it happened. I believe it was purely accidental and without criminal intent which means, it is between you and the Slaters. If he makes you an offer that is not agreeable, take him to court. I've done all I can do to confirm that yes, Mister Rohloff, they are mining under your property. From this point forward, it does not concern me because it was not intentional."

"So what am I supposed to do?" he asked.

"Wait. William said he wanted to make you a fair offer. His office is just down the road, stop in and talk to him. It is between you, him and the court of law if you two can't agree on something."

"But he is mining under my claim?"

"He is. But again, it was not intentional, and I'll let him explain that to you. Now, if you don't mind, I have work to do."

Oliver exhaled with a satisfied smile. "Thank you. I guess I'll go home and tell my boy and employees to stop working. We're going to celebrate today." He grinned for the first time.

Matt smiled slightly. "You have reason to, Mister Rohloff. Apparently, it's quite a motherlode."

When Oliver left, Matt closed his private office door and rested his head upon his hand. He already missed Christine.

# Chapter 11

The Slater wagon with boxes of processed gold had left that morning under the guidance of four of the Blackburn Marshals and four of William Slater's hired guards. They would escort the wagon to Walla Walla, load the gold boxes into a rail car, and escort it by rail to San Francisco. The earnings would be transferred into Slater's account. It was a simple job without much to do unless bandits tried to rob them.

William Slater scheduled a mandatory meeting with his mine employees at the end of the day shift when the swing shift would take over for the day. It wasn't that long ago when his employees gave him a list of demands to be met or they would strike. Under normal circumstances, he would have let them strike and come back to work when they were starving, but since uncovering a pocket of gold, he made certain compromises to keep the men working. Once again, circumstances had changed. The southeast winze was shut down for reasons that were never told to the employees, and he didn't want the cause known.

A wagon was placed in a wide-open area near the river where the men could congregate and listen. Four Blackburn Marshals stood in front of the wagon with their badges shining in the sun and rifles in hand. Jeff Blackburn placed six other guards hired by the mine in specific places to surround the large group of men. Jeff stood on the wagon with William and Josh Slater, Ron Dalton and Wally Gettman. Jeff watched the expressions growing hostile on men's faces while William spoke.

William shouted over the grumbling of the miners, "Furthermore, it has come to my attention that a fire sparked in one of the tunnels was from a cigarette. Therefore, no more smoking will be allowed inside the mine, period! If you are caught doing so, you will be terminated on sight and lose your housing immediately."

"Where? Where was a fire?" one man yelled.

"Rocks don't burn, you dumbass!" another yelled.

William continued, "I don't want to hear your comments. I know only what my supervisors tell me, and there will be no more smoking." It was a lie, but the goal was to infuriate the men to strike. "Furthermore, there will be no more talking during working hours. You are paid to work, not gab like a bunch of cackling women! I understand you ladies are wasting two hours a day on average because of talking. That ends today! Anyone found talking about anything not work-related will be terminated and lose your housing immediately."

"That's bullcrap!" one man yelled.

"What? Who the hell told you that? Two hours a day, my ass!"

William continued above the growling and cursing of the men, "One more thing, you men wanted some sort of financial funding for the families of the injured and fatal accident victims. Fine, I don't think it's fair that I should have to pay for your fellow miner's stupidity. Therefore, one dollar will be deducted from your pay every day to create a fund to support you and your co-workers. That starts today."

The roar of curses and hostile screaming overwhelmed William's voice.

William rubbed his forehead and waited for the men to quiet down just enough to talk. "These rules start right now! That's all I have to say, get back to work!"

Joe Thorn, furious, picked up a good-sized rock and threw it at William. It barely missed his head. Jeff Blackburn stepped in front of William and pointed a finger warningly at Joe while his other hand gripped his revolver. "The next person who throws a rock will be carried out of here in a box!" Jeff yelled.

"Kiss my arse!" an Irishman yelled and threw a rock that hit William's side. More stones were thrown from deeper in the crowd of angry men. The angry words and curses rose from the men like a chorus taking up a song.

A rock thrown by Joe hit Jeff Blackburn on the

eyebrow, creating a gash that bled swiftly. Furious, Jeff pulled his revolver, pulling the hammer back while taking a quick aim at Joe Thorn. His hand was jerked down by Ron Dalton as Jeff pulled the trigger.

Ron yelled angrily, "Don't you dare shoot my men!" His fury dropped like a ton of rock as he heard the familiar voice of Newton Collins cry out, "Joseph! Lord, no!" He began wailing, momentarily joined by his other two sons, James and Johnny.

With a sickening wave of dread filling his stomach, Ron stared with a horrified expression down from the wagon and saw the youngest son of Newton's, Joseph Collins, laying on the ground with his father and brothers kneeling over him, wailing. Joseph had been shot in the head and fell dead where he lay. Newton had lost his son, Jason, in the mine explosion a few months before. Ron's throat tightened as his eyes teared, knowing it was partly his fault.

"Let's go," Josh Slater said to his father.

Jeff glared coldly at Ron. "I wasn't aiming at him. That's on you!" He spoke to his gunmen. "Be ready!" His four marshals raised their rifles to the crowd of men to keep them at bay as the news of Joseph Collins being killed made its way through the large group.

Mark Sperry stepped out in front of the crowd and gazed down at young twenty-year-old Joseph's body.

With blood running down his face, Jeff Blackburn yelled over the miners, "My name is Jeff

Blackburn, and these are my marshals. The new rules apply whether you like it or not. Be at work tomorrow, or we will fire you and remove you from your company homes, rain or shine. Sorry about the young lad, that was accidental. I meant to kill that man right there!" he pointed his finger at Joe Thorn.

Mark Sperry turned to Jeff with a cold rage in his green eyes. "I don't give a damn who you are. You're going to pay for taking Joseph's life. We'll meet again!"

Jeff smirked, entertained by the threat. "I'll be here to enforce the rules. If you feel lucky, make your move."

Joe Thorn stepped forward to stand next to Mark. "Take your rules to hell with you! I say we strike right now!" he yelled, turning to face his fellow miners. "Joseph Collins is dead! Shot by that man for no reason. Right now, I say we strike! Who's with me?"

The entire crowd of men roared in angry agreement.

William Slater climbed into the safety of his coach with his son, Josh, and corporate engineer, Wally Gettman. William smiled uneasily. "Well, that happened sooner than I thought it would."

The coach door opened suddenly, and Ron Dalton glared fiercely at William. "Not a damn word you said was true and now a young man is dead! You don't know that kid, but I do. I heard Matt warn you about these gunmen months ago, and they haven't been here half an hour and Joseph's dead! What are you doing, William? This makes no sense."

Josh spoke before his father could, "The kid's death is your fault! My father has nothing to do with it. The rules stand and if they strike, so be it."

Ron glanced from Josh to William thoughtfully. "Why do I get the feeling you want them to strike?" He was dumbfounded.

The corners of William's lip curved upwards. "Ron, I employ you. If you want to remain employed, I suggest you go home and keep your mouth shut about our Rohloff error completely. You never saw the map. It doesn't exist. Understand?"

"No. What are you doing?" Ron gasped.

"You heard me, Ron," William said. "You have a nice job that pays for your nice home. And a bonus is coming if you go home and stay out of sight for your own safety. This will blow over soon enough." A rock hit the side of the carriage with a loud bang. The miners were angry enough to pull the Slaters out of the carriage and beat them to death and probably would if it wasn't for the five gunmen aiming their weapons at the crowd. Several men were looking for rocks on the ground while others hopped forwards to chuck the stones they had found along the river bed.

"Joseph's death won't blow over! If these men strike, how many more are going to be murdered by your hired killers?" Ron asked, appalled. He had no idea that William planned to show up and demand a meeting, nor had any knowledge of the fabricated complaints that William claimed he had heard.

William shook his head. "The boy wouldn't be dead if it wasn't for you, Ron. Keep your mouth shut and wait until the strike is over. We're leaving," He pulled a string that rang a bell by the driver. The carriage jerked forward quickly as Josh closed the door in Ron's face. Several rocks hit the carriage as it drove quickly across the bridge to leave the mine. One good throw broke through the glass on the door.

A rock hit Ron's back and he arched in pain, making eye contact with Jeff Blackburn momentarily as Jeff rode past him on horseback. Jeff said, "Better run! We're leaving."

Ron was shoved to the ground from behind unexpectedly. He was quickly surrounded by more boots than he could count and felt the first hard kick penetrate deep into his leg muscles. The pain was immediate but forgotten just as quickly as a boot connected with his side, just before someone stomped on his back. A kick to the side of his head left him barely conscious enough to understand that his employees were attacking him. He was helpless to protect himself from the rugged boots that kicked and stomped all over his body.

"Stop!" Joe Thorn yelled as he ran to Ron's side. Joe pushed one man back and hit another in the face to get the four men to stop kicking Ron. "Stop! Ron's not one of them! Stop it!"

Mark Sperry quickly joined Joe's side, as did Tony and Wade Rosso to create a barrier between Ron and the growing crowd of angry men.

The man punched by Joe accused, "He is one of them! Who do you think told William we talk too much? It's his fault!"

"Kick his teeth out!" one the crowd encouraged.

James Collins was the twenty-five-year-old brother of Joseph. He pointed at Ron and shouted with tearful eyes filled with hatred, "He killed my brother! Get out of the way, Joe! We can drown him in the river."

"Get a rope! We can hang him from the rafters of the stamp mill!"

"Let's hang all of the supervisors!"

"None of this would have happened if it wasn't for him!"

The chaos of so many angry men yelling and fights breaking out between each other and at-tacking supervisors was far more chaotic than Joe Thorn could stand. He climbed on the back of the buckboard William had spoken from, to be heard loud and clearly. "Stop!" he yelled. From his vantage point a few feet higher, he could see further back in the crowd where a group of men had knocked su-pervisor Jim Longo to the ground and were beating him as they had started to Ron. He cursed loudly, "Stop them!" he pointed. "Listen to me! Stop that fight! Stop them! For crying out loud! Jim Longo had nothing to do with this! Didn't you guys watch Ron's expression when William was speaking? He had no idea this was coming. Did you, Ron?" he asked as Ron was helped to his feet by Mark Sper-ry and Wade Rosso. Ron held the side of his head where a boot had kicked him. He shook his head painfully in answer.

Joe continued as more men quieted to hear their respected leader who had led the Slater's negotiations a month before for some needed changes. "It's not Ron's fault Joseph was shot! The fault lies with the man who shot him. I don't know who that man is, but they are the enemy, not any of us here."

"Ron got my brother killed!" James Collins yelled again in his sorrow.

Joe waved the thought off. "No! Ron was trying to save my life and what happened to Joseph was a terrible accident. The fault lies with the man who pulled the trigger. He shouldn't have pulled the gun to begin with, James. Didn't you hear what Ron said? We're his men. Ron didn't screw us over. Ron Dalton is the best friend we have against William and Josh Slater. Hell, we should know that from when the Chinese sabotaged the mine." He paused as he watched Jim Longo stumble through the crowd with a large gash in his forehead and a deformed nose as he approached the safety of the front of the group where Ron was. "Help Jim. Put him up here with me. We need to get Jim to the doctor. Ron, get up here." He hollered over his fellow miners, "We're fighting the wrong men. I say we strike, but we fight the right men. And I'll talk to Matt Bannister and find out who these men are."

A roar of agreement followed.

Joe pointed at the mine portal where the six or so hired armed guards by the mine had assembled when the fighting began for their protection. "Those men aren't our fight either. Our fight's in town. If we destroy this mine or the equipment, we only hurt ourselves. We want to work, but we expect it to be fair."

"They killed my son," Newton Collins yelled, still holding the body of his youngest boy. He mourned bitterly along with his two sons.

James Collins shouted at Joe, "I don't give a damn about the job! I want that man's blood on my hands!"

Alan Rosso climbed on the wagon after helping Jim Longo onto the buckboard. He raised his right hand smeared with Jim's blood on his palm. "You'll have it, Jimmy. I agree; our fight isn't with Jim Longo or Ron or anyone else still here. Our fight is with the Slaters and the men they brought to town. Who are they, Ron?" he asked.

Ron sat weakly on the short side rail of the buckboard, holding a knot on his head. He spoke loudly, "I don't know who they are or how bad they are. All I know is William threatened to bring them here once and Matt Bannister warned him not to. They're called the Blackburn Marshals. Matt said they are bad men. Dangerous men." He paused. "I didn't know this was going to happen. None of us said that stuff to William Slater."

Joe was angry. "Did you hear that? Ron never said any of the crap William said. The Slaters brought in bad men to force us to labor like slaves. I say we take his plans and shove them right down his throat. I say we strike!"

A loud cheer went rose as the men agreed in unison.

Joe Thorn waved his arms. "Men! Listen, we all saw how fast that man reacted and would have killed me if not for Ron. Unfortunately, young Joseph was standing in the wrong place, but it could have been any of us. Newt, you and your family will be avenged. I swear it, but we have to be wise enough not to get ourselves killed. Let's hit them where it hurts. Load Joseph up here and let's take him to town. It's time the newspaper prints some bad things about the Slaters and their new guests."

"Should we grab our guns?"

"I am!" Mark Sperry exclaimed. "If they want a war, I'll call in my brothers and their friends. I'll give them a damn war. Newton, James, Johnny, I promise you that man's blood will be spilled by my hand for what he did to Joseph."

Alan Rosso ordered, "Bring down the mules and the other buckboard and fill it with rocks from the tailing pile. Let's show the town what we think of the Slaters."

# Chapter 12

Jeff Blackburn had the carriage stop shortly after leaving the angry mob. He handed the reins of his horse to one of his men and got into the carriage with William, Josh and Wally Gettman. "Those animals took to beating your manager when we left," he said as he entered and took an uninvited seat next to Josh to face William and Wally.

"Why didn't you go back and help him?" Josh asked with concern.

"I'm not paid to protect him. I told him to run."

William's eyes penetrated Jeff incensed. "You are hired to protect my interests and people. Especially Ron since he manages the entire mining operation. Get back there and make sure he's okay!"

"He received a few kicks and stomps, but another group of men stepped in to save him. I think he's fine. I didn't hoist him behind my saddle because I didn't think you'd mind since he is a liability to your whole plan and all. The way you cast the blame on him, I figured he was disposable. Besides, it was his fault that boy was killed. That was unfortunate."

"Yes," William agreed as he peered out the broken window. He rang the bell for the driver to continue. "But maybe it was a blessing in disguise because I have no doubt that they will strike now. A man doesn't make money during a strike and that will be their strength, so to say, but my striking employees don't know that they are saving me millions that I don't have to share with Oliver Rohloff. That man has been mining for years and barely earns enough to cover his costs and survive. I call that a failed enterprise and I won't share my success with a failure. He hasn't earned it."

"It's just his gold," Jeff quipped with a slight chuckle. His face was covered with a thin layer of drying blood, though it was still moist and thickening on the gash above his eye.

"Rohloff would never know it was right under his feet because he'll never be able to explore that deep underground. His small pick and shovel four-man crew barely move two feet of rock a day, I'll bet. The man was no more concern than a garter snake in the garden, but now he is a liability to my gold. Despite a young man's death and a beaten manager or two, I'd call today a successful venture. I'm confident we accomplished what we planned to do," William offered with a nod to Jeff.

"Except for that kid," Wally added. He was troubled by the accidental shooting. He had never witnessed a young man alive and well one minute and then a second later laying dead. He couldn't get the memory out of his mind and his hands still shook from the horror of it. "Does anyone know that kid's name?"

Josh answered, "Number four-sixty-five, Wally. No, we don't know his name. You don't know him, so what difference does it make? He's just a number on a piece of paper and no, I don't know his name or real number."

"Accidents happen, Wally," William said without any concern. "It wasn't intentional." His mind was already on the next step of convincing Oliver Rohloff that he was too busy negotiating with his striking miners to concentrate on negotiating a deal with him. William was terrified of losing the fortune he had discovered, and he was getting desperate to take over the Rohloff claim. "Are your men experienced with explosives?" he asked Jeff.

"For the most part. A stick of dynamite isn't hard to light. Why?"

William continued thoughtfully, "I'm considering sabotaging my mine just enough to blame my employees. I want Oliver to think my hands are too busy battling my employees to negotiate with him. Maybe we could even sabotage the Rohloff mine by closing their portal and blame our employees. That would make Rohloff more inclined to sell. We have been trying to buy their claim for about two years now because we believe there's good silver ore there. He doesn't know that, but we do. Those men better strike or all this is for nothing."

Wally had worked with William for years and knew William wasn't the most ethical man, but sometimes his ideas were not well thought out. He asked, "Why would our employees be interested in destroying the Rohloff mine? There would be no reasonable explanation for them to consider doing that."

William gave him a coarse glare. "Because I want it done!"

"It wouldn't be reasonable. It makes as much sense as a man with a grudge against the bank teller burning down a bread store. Why don't you invite Oliver Rohloff to the office and tell him the truth? He will never be able to reach the gold in his lifetime with his little outfit. So make him a fair offer for his claim with a small percentage of the gold. Set him up for life and we're all happy," Wally explained with a questionable shrug.

Jeff Blackburn chuckled lightly. "William, you said you wanted Mister Rohloff to sign an offer to sell all his property and rights over to you. I'm not here to tell you how to do your business, but Wally is right, this strike and all the antics are unnecessary. Make the man an offer and if he refuses, I told you we could force him to sign that offer whether he wants to or not. I can guarantee it will be done. But since you wanted a strike, I can tell you right now that you're not taking the greatest threat seriously."

"Oh? What's that?" William asked.

"Your employees. You infuriated them and that young man's death, though accidental, just raised the stakes. Right now, I can promise you some of those men are stirring up others for violence. I drew blood, and blood begets blood. They'll want my blood, and they'll want yours. I can protect my-self, you and your family, but I have four men with me, and you have about eight or so inexperienced gunmen at the mine. I need experienced killers, to be blunt. We don't play around and if the family and friends of that boy get the idea of striking back, it's best to crush them early."

"That's why we have a marshal's office. Matt can help you."

Jeff grinned, half-humored by the statement. "You must not know him too well. Matt won't help me."

"He will if I tell him to. If it weren't for a few of my pals and me, he wouldn't be a marshal, pe-riod. He'd still be a deputy marshal in Wyoming somewhere. I paid a handsome sum to help build his office and manipulate the rules a bit to give him the legal authority over Jessup County. My friends and I did that just for situations like this. We don't need Matt here if he isn't of any use when we need him. He'll help keep the peace; trust me on that," William said with an authoritative tone.

"Keeping the peace isn't what I'm talking about, William. I think it's probably better if Matt and his deputies have nothing to do with us and stay far away. That's why I want to hire a few more experi-enced shooters that are not afraid to pull the trig-ger and aim well under pressure. I don't have time for your inexperienced guards. Did you see your guards run to the opening of your mine when the crowd got hostile?" He chuckled. "Cowards, every one of them."

"I don't want any of my employees hurt," William stated.

Jeff grinned with a short chuckle. "I'm not talking about hurting them, but you'll need protection if they come for you. This might be a ruse to you, but to them it's now deadly serious. There's a dead miner back there. They'll be coming to get even."

"We can place an ad in the paper," William suggested.

"What would your ad say? Experienced gunmen wanted to end a strike when the time is right? That might not go over well. How about you leave that to me. Do you gentlemen know any low-down and dirty gunmen? I hate to phrase it like that, but I find it works best if my men have a lower sense of morality."

Wally spoke with disgust, "I don't partake in an environment that would introduce me to such people."

William's brow lowered in thought. "I've got an entire mine full of them, I'm sure. I don't know about gunmen, but wretches, every one."

Josh Slater narrowed his eyes. "I do. Father, you'll remember the man that was tortured by that dirty Indian? I know his name was Wes and he was a soldier in the Indian Wars. He massacred them at Bear River, the story goes. He might be worth talking to."

"Sounds promising. Is he married? I don't hire married men," Jeff explained.

"I don't know him myself. I've seen him around

town, but I don't think he is."

"I want to talk to him. It's a start anyway. Anyone else?"

Josh shook his head. "As Wally said, we don't mix with that crowd. William Fasana, but he's Matt's cousin. He's not around anyway. He went to Portland for a little while."

William spoke, "Josh, set up a meeting with Wes. If he is morally low enough, he'll have friends just as low as he is. We all flock with our own kind."

"I'll set the meeting up."

William pulled the string to the bell that communicated with his driver. The carriage came to a stop. "Josh, tell him to take us to the house. I have no reason to go to the office. I want you to set up a meeting with Wes at the house this evening. We'll have a few drinks with him. Also, Josh, I think Wally's right. I need you to set up a meeting with Oliver Rohloff at the office tomorrow. Let's see if we can be reasonable, to use Wally's word, with Oliver before unleashing the beasts," he said, waving a hand towards Jeff Blackburn.

# Chapter 13

John Painter sat in the family room of his parent's home with his head lowered. He had slept a good portion of the day and now endured the disappointment of his mother and father. "I'm sorry, Pa. I didn't mean to make such a mess in here. It was bad wine, I guess."

"Bad wine, John? Is that your excuse for breaking the stained-glass window of our church?" Reverend Painter asked patiently.

"Yeah. The bad wine made me mad, I guess."

"Mad about what?"

"I don't know. I feel awful, though." His head lifted to look his father in the eyes. "But I am bound and determined to get a job and pay you back for the money you loaned me and the window too. It might take me a little while, but I'm determined to do that."

"I appreciate that. Robert Fasana lives across the street and is the granite quarry manager. I'm sure we can talk with him and see if he is hiring. If not, Jim Longo is a supervisor at the mine and might get you hired on there. We'll do our best to get you working and you can make payments to us. We want you to do well, John."

John seemed hesitant. "I'm not one for hard work, Pa. I tend to be my best in an office-type environment. Cleaner work, if you know what I mean."

Beatrice Painter narrowed her eyes skeptically. She had held her tongue to allow her husband to do the talking, but she also knew her husband always saw the best in people and overlooked the bad often enough. Her eyes saw people for what they were and sometimes the bad was far easier to see than the good in someone. Her son once had a great heart, but he had fallen far, and she wasn't going to be fooled by his attempt to be sincere. She squeezed her lips together and lowered her head as her husband continued.

"John, I don't know if they have those kinds of positions open. It seems to me like you need to take what you can get and work yourself up the ladder."

"I'm too smart for that, Pa. You know I am. What about the church? Do you need an accountant to handle the funds?"

"No, we certainly don't," Beatrice blurted out. "What company is going to hire you to sit behind a desk looking as you do, John? You look like a beggar, and you haven't bathed yet. You stink! My home stinks. Maybe I could believe your words a little bit if you bathed, shaved your face and cut that hair off. I hate to say this, Johnny, but you haven't cleaned your teeth in how long? You look horrible." Her eyes filled with deep pools of water. "I didn't raise you to be like this! Get cleaned up and make something of yourself or get out!" she shouted while standing from her chair. She quickly left the room, beginning to sob.

John's eyes flickered angrily for a moment. "Wow," John said slowly. "Maybe I'm not wanted here, after all. Huh, Pa? Do you want me to leave too?"

The Reverend Eli Painter took a deep breath. He had not heard his beloved wife raise her voice in a long time. He yearned to hold his weeping lady. "No, son. I want you to clean yourself up and find some work. You are thirty years old, almost thirty-one..."

"You're not going to compare me to every other person in your church that's my age, are you? Trust me, all the successful people my age have never walked in my shoes. If they had, they wouldn't be so successful either. Just saying," John said with lifted open palms and a tilted head shrug.

"Is that an excuse? Life's hard, so I quit trying?" Reverend Painter asked.

"I never quit trying."

"Then please explain, John? Because I have to admit I am shocked by your appearance, your lack of knowledge about your children and your actions since you have shown up here. When has it ever been acceptable to drink a jug of wine, stain our davenport with vomit, and vandalize the church? This is supposed to be home, where you feel most welcome, but it's like we don't know who you are anymore."

John bit his bottom lip and looked away from his father. "I lost my wife and my children, okay? They're not coming back. Hell, I don't even know where they are!"

"Why did Sue leave you?"

John snickered. "Pa, you don't want to know that. Listen, I'm going to see if I can find some of my old friends. It's been a good talk, but some things I don't want to talk about."

"What about your faith? You left here for seminary but never came back. Wrote letters to say you were married, the births of our two grandchildren and we were so excited to meet them someday. And then nothing, not a single letter for years until you knocked on our door. What am I missing, son? Talk to me," Reverend Painter pleaded with his son with great care.

"About ten to twelve years of my life, Pa."

"And whose fault is that?" Reverend Painter asked.

"It's no one's fault. I just found better things to do. I'm going to look for a job. I'll see you later."

Beatrice came out of the bedroom when John left, shaking her head. "He's not coming home tonight. I don't know how you can keep a calm demeanor when you talk to him. He is not the boy we sent away. I don't know my son anymore." She sat in her chair heavily.

"He is traveling through the muck and mire of the world right now, but we have to love him anyway. He came home, Beatrice. He may, deep down, be asking for our help to get him on the right path again. We know no one is too far gone for Jesus not to reach them and bring them back to the cross. As he said when he arrived, the prodigal son has returned."

Tears filled her eyes. "The prodigal son in the Bible came home ready to submit to his father's will. He was broken. John isn't broken, Eli. He doesn't want to change; he just wants an easy life at our expense. And we can't afford to support a thirty-one-year-old grown man that acts like a child."

"Sweetheart, it's only been two days. I won't give up on him."

"Don't give him any more money."

"I don't plan to. He'll have to work for it from here on out."

\*\*\*

John Painter wore his tattered clothes to Main Street and collected a few bits from strangers he passed on the boardwalk. He stopped outside the marshal's office and read Matt's name on the window. Having been told Matt went to his father's church, John entered to be greeted by a clean-cut young man with short light brown hair and a clean-shaven face. "Hey," John began, "this is Matt Bannister's office, huh?"

"Yes, it is. I am U.S. Deputy Marshal Phillip Forrester; can I help you?"

"Is Matt here?"

"He's in his office, yes."

"Can I speak to him?"

A moment later, Matt came out of his office with a friendly smile and handshake. "I'm Matt Bannister. How can I help you?" he asked.

"I'm John Painter. I understand you go to my father's church."

Matt's smile faded despite himself as he gazed at the man who appeared homeless for some time. "You're Reverend Painter's son?"

"Yeah. I just got back in town. I've been traveling around back east for a while. I thought I'd come home and see the folks. I heard you were a church member and wanted to meet you. I have never met too many famous people here in the west anyway."

"Nice to meet you, John. I suppose if you just stopped by to meet me, then we'll meet again in church on Sunday."

"Yeah. Hey, I hate to ask, but my father said you might help me out. My pa was going to loan me about five to ten dollars to get cleaned up, you know for a bath, shave and haircut, perhaps some new clothes. I think they might be a little embarrassed by the way I look," he said with a wrinkled nose. "But they just bought a new davenport yesterday and are a little shy on money until payday. He said he'd pay you back then if you could lend me the money?"

"Oh…" Matt said, taken back. It was evident by the body odor  and filthy tattered clothes that John did need to clean himself up. It was odd for Reverend Painter to refer someone to him for money as the church kept a small fund to help people who needed some assistance. However, it would be like the reverend not to use the church funds for his own son. Matt smiled slowly. "Your father doesn't want to use the church fund, huh?"

"I guess not," John said thoughtfully. "You know, I'm just his son." He laughed. His plaque-coated teeth were yellow and quite noticeable.

"All right. Phillip, give Reverend Painter's son ten dollars out of the safe. Tell your father he can pay it back when he can. Nice to meet you, John. I have to get back to work."

"I'll let him know. Thank you. I'll see you Sunday, but you may not recognize me," John said with a cheerful laugh.

"I'll look for the new fellow sitting beside your mother. Nice to meet you, John," Matt said and went back to his office.

John watched Phillip open a small safe bolted to the floor in the corner and take ten dollars out of an envelope. John thanked Phillip for the money and walked towards Rose Street.

# Chapter 14

One wagon carried the injured Jim Longo to the doctor's office and the body of Joseph Collins to the Branson Gazette newspaper's office to be propped up for all the citizens to see and be photographed.

The other wagon, filled with waste rock from the mine's tailing pile, stopped in front of the W.R. Slater Mining Company office with the big silver-painted false front with the company name painted across it. A large crowd of seventy-some miners followed on foot and grabbed rocks from the wagon's bed. With all the fury that a man can hold, and without a word of warning, they began throwing the fist-sized jagged rocks at the building. The yells of rage and cursing of so many angry men were drowned out by the loud and consistent storm of rocks pelting the boards and shattering the office windows. One stone was thrown, and another was grabbed as the men frantically tried to destroy the front of the office building. Behind the rock throwers were a limited number of men with rifles and sidearms to protect their friends from the gunmen William had hired.

Inside, the receptionist, Martha Puglisi, hid under the counter as the windows around her shattered. Broken glass showered the floor as heavy stones hit the interior wall with a loud bang and ricocheted to the floor close to her. The constant banging on the exterior wall was as loud as thunder and was terrifying with the background roar of a large crowd of angry men's curses. Martha covered her head protectively and dashed into the hallway further inside the offices to escape the danger of being hit by one of the rough stones weighing between one to five pounds.

"What's going on?" the company accountant, Grant Rogers, asked coming out of his office with his assistant, an older lady named Pauline.

"They're attacking us!" Martha cried.

"Who?" Grant asked.

"I don't know!" Martha yelled.

Debra Slater came out of her office and glanced out a distant window. "Oh, no." She was the only person in the office that knew what her father had planned to do to cause a strike, but they weren't expecting the strikers to do something like this. She swallowed nervously. The miners were furious and the only way out of the building was the front door. She feared when the rock-throwing stopped, the men would force their way into the building. If so, she and her three other office employees would be trapped and at the mercy of the men. The consequences of being the victims of a rioting mob could be life-threatening for her in particular, as she was William's daughter.

"Debra," Grant yelled as Debra joined them through the thunderous roar of the rocks pelting the building, "Why are they doing this?"

"I don't know," she answered quickly. "But we need to get out of here before they come inside."

Grant held a protective arm over Martha. "The sheriff will be here soon, I'm sure. Maybe we should wait for him," he suggested.

Debra shook her head nervously. "There are too many of them out there. I'm not waiting for them to come in here. We have to get out!" Debra exclaimed in a shaking voice.

Grant understood that outside the building meant anything done was in public view, but no one would witness anything if caught inside. "Okay. As soon as the rocks stop, I'll go out first to be a shield while you ladies run as fast as you can away from here. Do you think they'll burn the building down?" he asked Debra quickly as a second thought. The files, payroll, expenses and all those essential documents couldn't be replaced.

Debra was more concerned about their safety. "I don't know."

"Where's your father?" Grant asked with a scowl. "Why are we the only ones here?"

"I don't know!" Debra yelled over the commotion.

"Those are our employees out there. What did your father do?" Grant asked anxiously.

"I don't know!" Debra repeated, growing desperate to escape the building. It wasn't her job to notify the office employees of her father's plans.

"Listen, the boardwalk is going to be covered with rocks, so be careful and don't fall." Grant glanced at his gray-haired assistant, Pauline. "Pauline, I will escort you across the boardwalk. They might hurt me, but they won't hurt you."

Debra put her hand on Grant's forearm appreciatively. "If we can just get outside, we'll be okay."

The rocks pelting the boards of the office came fast and furious, but as the wagon emptied, the rock-throwing began to ease intensity. Some men picked rocks off the ground and threw them again, trying to crack and break the boards of the building.

"Let's go," Grant said and carefully opened the door with his hands raised. "We're coming out." A rock hit him in the shoulder, and he spun around to be hit in the back by another. He went to his knees in pain.

Fearing she would suffer the most if trapped inside by the furious men, Debra shouted to Martha and Pauline, "Run!"

Martha Puglisi ran out the door and nearly slipped as her foot landed on a jagged rock. She kept her balance but was quickly grabbed by one of the men. "Hostage! I got a hostage," the man yelled as he led her towards the crowd of men on the street.

Debra tried to urge Pauline to run, but the gray-haired lady sat against the wall, too afraid to move. Hearing the men cheer after capturing Martha,

Debra's heart quickened. She hated to leave Pauline behind, but she had to escape before they came inside. She darted out the door, turning sharply to run, but her foot landed on an unevenly shaped rock, and she felt the popping and searing pain of her ankle twisting and fell onto the stones that were lying on the boardwalk. A jolt and painful jab of landing on a stone placed just below her shoulder blade would have made Debra cry but getting away from the men was the greater concern. She had barely turned to her hands and knees and attempted to stand when a man's arms wrapped around her and yanked Debra to her feet. Helpless to get away from him, the man carried her around the two mules that pulled the wagon to take her to the other side.

"I got Debra!" he yelled victoriously. "I got William's daughter!"

The cheer that followed and the scowling faces of the men left no doubt that their resentment towards her father would be taken out on her. Any strength she may have had inside the office disappeared and she began to sob petrified by fear. "Let me go!" she sobbed. "Get your hands off me!" The pain of her ankle could not compare to the panic to get away from the mob.

"Take the women back to Slater's Mile and keep them for ransom," one of the men suggested with a scowl.

"Yeah! A thousand dollars to start!"

"I'll keep her in my cabin!" another man volunteered with a laugh.

"Throw the women in the wagon and let's move!"

"Fellas, this isn't right. Leave the women be," one of the miners suggested.

"Shut up! You aren't in charge."

"Hurry up and toss them in the wagon!"

Debra struggled but breaking free from the man's iron grip was impossible as he had her arms trapped at her sides. The unnamed miner carried her towards the wagon, but as he lowered his arms to heave her upwards over the short side wall, he stepped on the hem of her long dress and nearly tripped. Debra, watched as in an unbelievable dreamlike state three other men with coarse expressions lifting Martha Puglisi uncaringly into the wagon's bed. Martha was screaming in terror. Another man hollered as he yanked the terrified Pauline out of the office roughly by the arm. Grant laid on the boardwalk in a fetal position while two unnamed miners kicked him with their hardened boots.

Glancing around desperately in hopes of seeing some help, Debra caught a glimpse of the Branson Sheriff, Tim Wright, standing back watching with a lost expression on his face. He dared not to interfere with the angry mob. Realizing the law wasn't going to interfere on her behalf, the hope of rescue faded and the terror of being held captive by the savage men consumed her. She had been confident the noise and mayhem would attract the attention of the town's lawmen, but if the sheriff and his deputies weren't going to do anything, the only hope she had left was Matt. But if Matt wasn't in town, she would become a mining camp whore and the idea of being abused by countless men was a nightmare that was more terrifying than she could conceive. Disease, pregnancy, shame, she would not be able to endure it. Terrified or not, if the sheriff was not going to help her, then she had to fight for her life on her own.

Debra screamed as loud as she possibly could, "Let me go! My father will have you killed if you don't leave me alone! Help. Someone, help me! Help!" She fought the best she could and tried to kick repeatedly at the man trying to grab her legs to help throw her in the back of the wagon.

Two town citizens came forward to end the mayhem and free the women, but they were quickly besieged by a group of miners and on the ground helpless and beaten themselves.

Lawrence Barton had left the pottery shop and used his crutches to approach the crowd of his old co-workers quickly. He shouted at Joe Thorn, "Hey, Joe! No. Stop this before it goes too far. Leave the women alone!"

"Go home, Lawrence!" Joe yelled. His eyes were filled with fire.

"Help me!" Debra screamed desperately at Lawrence.

Lawrence was helpless to do anything himself with a missing leg. He glanced around the street to see many townspeople watching, but not one dared to intervene after witnessing what had happened to the two gentlemen that tried. The mob contained too many violent men filled with rage and it seemed to be growing in madness as they stormed into the Slater office and dragged out an old woman, who was now screaming too, towards the wagon.

"Joe!" Lawrence yelled. He stood in front of the mules to stop them from leaving. "Joe, take control of this before it gets bad! You're better than this. Let the women go!"

"Shut up!" Paul Buff, a middle-aged miner with long yellow hair and beard, sneered. He was tired of listening to Lawrence and shoved him to the ground. "Stay out of the way, you little piss ant, or I'll crush you like a fly!" Paul was well known for his short temper and plain meanness. He turned back to the others, "Load 'em up! Let's take them home!" he yelled.

Debra, desperate to save herself, forced her boot between the wagon wheel spokes and twisted her foot to wedge it between the spokes. The man holding her jerked on her to break her foot free, but Debra refused to straighten her foot despite the agonizing pain his pulling on her caused. She knew if her boot was freed, she'd be thrown in the wagon and held down until she was a prisoner in one of the cabins at Slater's Mile. She screamed in agony, and through her terrified sobs, "Help me!" she cried, but was losing the strength to keep screaming.

Richie Thorn had enough messing around, he slapped her face so hard it stopped her screaming. Her foot went limp, and Richie pulled it from the wagon spokes. He squeezed her cheeks together to open her mouth and pulled his face close to hers so she could hear him. He sneered with a hateful scowl, "Your father doesn't know one of our names, but we all know you. And you're going to get to know me!" He moved forward to kiss her opened mouth and then released her cheeks and grabbed her feet to lift her and help throw her in the wagon.

Matt Bannister didn't say a word as he quickly approached. He pulled his revolver and pushed three men out of his way to reach the man who had his arms wrapped around Debra. Matt slammed the butt of his pistol against the man's head viciously. The man dropped to the ground unconscious taking Debra with him. The fall had pulled her feet free from Richie's clutch. Matt knelt to help Debra to her feet with his left arm while holding his revolver on Richie. Debra turned her face into Matt's shoulder while she held onto him tightly sobbing.

Matt turned his revolver to the men holding the terrified Martha Puglisi down in the wagon. There was no bluffing in his stern voice, "Let her go, or I'll kill all three of you right now!" His rage-filled eyes held no doubt as he pulled the hammer back until it clicked. The gun did not shake a bit. His eyes shifted to the two men holding the old woman. "You, too! Let them go, now!" The authority of his voice quieted the crowd of men.

The men released Martha and she quickly ran towards Matt sobbing so hard she could barely catch a breath. Debra continued to sob into his shoulder. Matt spoke to her, "Debra, take the ladies to my office. Go," he said as the mob began to curse Matt.

"We should have known you were with the Slaters!" Joe Thorn accused.

"I can't walk," Debra whimpered. "My ankle."

"I'll help you," Lucille Barton volunteered anxiously from beside her husband. She put her arm around Debra to help her escape  the mob of angry men.

"What is going on?" Matt demanded to know from Joe Thorn.

"You're playing with fire, Marshal!" Mark Sperry shouted as he stepped through the crowd. He wore his gun belt and carried a Smith and Wesson repeating rifle in his hand.

Matt's eyes scanned Mark up and down as he answered, "I always am, Mark. What is going on here?"

The urgent voice of Lawrence Barton caught his attention, "Behind you!"

Matt turned around quickly enough to see Paul Buff's yellow hair and beard coming at him with a hunting knife in his hand. Paul stopped as Matt turned, but Matt continued his momentum and slammed the revolver against the side of Paul's head. Paul Buff fell to the ground, losing his grasp on the knife. Still conscious but holding his bleeding head, Paul reached up and clasped a front wagon wheel spoke to pull himself up to his feet. Matt drove his boot through Paul's elbow, dislocating it. Paul screamed in pain and turned to sit against the wheel while holding his elbow. "You broke my arm! You son of a..."

Matt shot a dangerous glance behind him at the men who watched without venturing to interfere.

Matt ignored Paul's words, holstered his revolver and retrieved the knife, and returned to Paul. He grabbed Paul's hair, jerked his head back and shoved the knife blade against the hairy exposed throat. Matt snarled, "You're damn lucky I broke your arm instead of killing you!" The knife blade was pressed firmly against the skin and drew a bit of blood.

Paul's rough and gritty demeanor lost its strength quickly. "You broke my arm. I can't work with a broken arm."

"You're lucky you're not dead, be glad of that! Next time, I won't hesitate to kill you. Stay here because you're going to jail." He faced the mob of men. He yelled with a grimace on his face, "Get these rocks picked up and get out of here! I don't want to see one rock left inside the office or out. Get to it!" He grabbed Joe Thorn's arm and questioned, "What's this all about?"

Joe Thorn waved his hand across the street where four Blackburn Marshals stood watching. They all held their rifles and watched the mob of men and Matt with interest. "Ask them."

"I'm asking you!" Matt demanded to know.

"They killed my brother!" James Collins exclaimed overhearing Matt.

"Who did?"

"Them!" Jimmy shouted with an extended arm towards the Blackburn Marshals.

Joe spoke, "That was an accident, James. Matt, let me explain."

The Branson Sheriff, Tim Wright and his deputies approached. "You beat us here, Matt." He pointed at the men picking up rocks. "Yeah, get all these rocks picked up and no more of this! You're lucky we're not arresting every one of you!"

Joe had taken several moments to explain what had happened earlier that day at the mine. Matt helped Paul Buff to his feet and guided him towards his jail when he finished talking to Joe.

One of the Blackburn Marshals shouted out as Matt walked past, "Matt, I think all this easy living around here may have softened you. Five years ago, you would have killed that yellow-haired man without blinking an eye."

Matt stopped and then walked over to them. "I was wondering if you were going to speak to me, Ed. So, this is what you're doing now, huh?" His eyes scanned the other three marshals carefully.

Ed Bostwick shrugged his shoulders. "It pays better than the federal government does. Not many of us get promoted to a federal marshal position. As I said, I think living the good life has made you soft."

Matt's lips edged upwards. "If you are hired by Slater, how come you didn't protect his property or his daughter, in particular?"

Ed's eyebrows rose innocently. "I didn't know he had a daughter. But to answer your question, we were in the hotel having a late lunch and just got here ourselves about the time you did. We thought we'd watch your show. Your town sheriff didn't just show up; he was hiding over yonder. We could see that from the hotel. He's sure sticking around now, though, isn't he?" Ed asked with a chuckle. "He might be trying to take some of your thunder when the big man comes back, huh?"

"He was watching?" Matt asked.

"Oh yeah. He was hiding over there," Ed pointed at a corner of a building. "Well, you haven't gotten too soft, I suppose, those men are picking up the rocks like you told them to."

"I can be as hard as I need to be."

Ed studied Matt carefully. "I'm finding it hard to believe that you are giving that man a second chance to kill you someday. He had a knife with the intent to stab you. The Matt I knew would have killed him quicker than snot in hay fever season. And not thought twice about it."

Matt spoke to Paul Buff, who was waiting on the street for him, "Go turn yourself into Phillip at my office. Get going." He waited until Paul walked away. "That man's nephew was killed today out at the mine. I just found that out. Paul thought I was teaming up with Slater and you guys and that's why he tried to stab me. I don't know what's going on, but I'm going to pay William and Josh a visit to find out. As you have seen, these men aren't carrying signs and handing out cookies like little old ladies striking at a mitten company. You saw their guns; I don't want this situation to get bloody. There's a lot of good men out there at that mine with families to take care of."

Ed laughed. "So, you broke a man's arm." Ed Bostwick was forty years old, almost six-foot, lean, muscular and as tough as a man can be. His straight

118

light-brown hair fell to the top of his shoulders, and he wore a well-groomed goatee that had traces of gray on his oblong face. His brown eyes revealed discontent but no malice towards Matt.

"Could've been worse."

Ed spoke sincerely, "Listen, as an old friend, do me a favor and stay out of any trouble between those men and us. I don't want to go against you, Matt. I didn't even know you were here."

"This is my community. My home." Matt's slight smile faded. "We won't have any trouble as long as you don't mess with it or my people."

The young man that called Matt a half breed the day before, spoke, "Is that a threat, half breed? You better watch who you threaten, or you might end up six feet under."

Ed backhanded the young man's chest with a noticeably hard whack. "Shut up, Toby! He'd have you six feet under before you could free the barrel." Ed shook his head, frustrated. "Sorry, Matt."

"I doubt that," Toby mumbled under his breath.

Matt looked at the young Blackburn Marshal and recognized the type. A young and angry criminal-minded man set on making a name for himself with his gun. Matt would be the prime target for the young man to make his name known. Avoiding a man like that was like trying to ignore being followed by a pack of wolves. It usually didn't end well. "What's your name? Toby?" Matt asked.

"Toby Stearns. Have you heard of me?" Toby had a slight build, medium height and was skinny as a skeleton. He had a touch of red in his short brown hair under his Stetson hat. A lighter color goatee was trimmed neatly on his chin. His bony face was clear of acne, and he had bold blue eyes that appeared as hollow of life as the hub of a wagon wheel.

"No, I've never heard of you. But you might get your chance before too long to put me in the ground; just remember, no one respects a coward. So, if you get that chance, make sure it's man against man and not an assassination like the coward Bob Ford. No one respects him for the coward he is."

Toby was offended. "Do you think I need to assassinate you to put you in the ground? Let's step out on the street right now!" He was held back by Ed Bostwick and another man.

Ed spoke coarsely, "Settle down! You won't be fighting Matt today, but if you ever do, listen to me!" he snapped to take Toby's eyes off Matt. "If you ever do, it had better be man against man and fair, or I'll kill you myself. Matt's an old friend of mine and I won't have it any other way."

Matt's lips rose. He didn't like Toby. Once in a blue moon, there were just certain people that Matt didn't like, and the young man was one. "You know, Ed, it's not too late to put a real marshal's badge back on."

Ed chuckled. "You've never been much of a comedian, Matt. But this calling a town home and that promotion seems to be bringing it out in you."

Matt grinned. "It's nice having a place to call home. Friends become like family around here. It's a good place to settle down. Until we meet again."

"Think that yellow-haired man turned himself in?" Ed asked skeptically.

Matt nodded. "Of course. He's not a bad man. He is hot headed, but he has a reason to be today. I'll send him to the doctor and let him go home in the morning. You're welcome to come along to see if he turned himself in or not."

"I can't. I have to stay with these fellas until our boss comes back."

"Babysitting?" Matt asked with a growing smile.

Toby cursed him.

Ed sighed with a hint of frustration. "Pretty much."

# Chapter 15

Truet Davis and Nate Robertson had returned from outside of town and looked forward to calling it a day when Matt asked them to go to the Slater mining office, lock it, clean the broken glass and board up the windows for the night. Phillip had rented a buggy from the livery stable and gave Pauline, Martha and Grant a ride to their homes before returning to the office. Matt wanted to talk to William Slater anyhow, so he carried Debra to the buggy and drove her home to the Slater mansion on top of King's Point, a high hill overlooking Branson. Below King's Point were the other mansions and large homes of the more well-off folks of Branson.

Matt had never been to the Slater's mansion. He had been invited to various parties, but he had never attended. Wealthy people had a certain arrogance that often kept their noses above the stench of their guests of lesser stature. Matt wasn't one to put himself above or below anyone else and found his greatest comfort was among the regular working people of the community that didn't think so highly of themselves. Knowing in advance that he wouldn't enjoy the company, he had always declined the invitations to join the King's Point parties.

Matt drove the buggy up King's Point past the other well-to-do homes and reached the top where a decorative wrought iron fence four feet high separated the property, with an arch over the driveway. Matt drove under the wrought-iron arch with stone corner posts and past a large, manicured yard with well-shaped bushes, roses and a variety of flowers. Matt stopped the buggy in front of a vast Queen Ann mansion three stories high with prominent gables extending from the roof line above symmetrical windows on every floor. On one corner of the large home, a four-story tower added to the King's Point name by giving the mansion a castle-like appeal with the tower reaching above the roof. The front of the home faced west and there was no doubt that the view of the setting sun must be spectacular, perhaps even better than the view from the hill where Christine wanted to build a home. A short four-step concrete stairway led to the massive front porch enclosed by a three-foot-high river rock pony wall separating the stone support columns for the porch roof. At the base of the stairs were concrete statues of proud male lions on either side.

"Nice lions," Matt stated as he stepped around the buggy to carry her inside.

She giggled slightly. "They weren't part of the architect's original plan. My father asked for them."

Matt lifted her with one arm supporting her back while she clung tightly onto his neck. His other hand went under her knees. She leaned her head on him as he carried her up the flight of stairs to the oversized porch. She pulled a decorative silver handle connected to a small chain that rang a bell inside the large double entrance doors. Momentarily, a middle-aged maid opened the door. "Miss Debra, are you injured?" the maid asked, taking notice of the boot in her hand and wrapped ankle that dangled in Matt's arms.

"I sprained my ankle, Betty. Where is my father?"

"I believe he is in the drawing-room with Mister Blackburn."

Debra guided Matt through a long rectangular room lined with beautiful wood paneling. It was a gorgeous room with the finest of decorations that went the length of the house with multiple doorways to other rooms on either side. A grand stairway in the middle led upstairs to the second floor.

"Wow. This is where you live? How many rooms is there here?" Matt asked, amazed by how large the home was. He had never experienced, in essence, a hallway larger than his house. He thought Lee's home was too big, but the Slater mansion seemed too clean, too perfect, silent and vast to be considered a home. It felt cold and lonely.

Debra rolled her eyes upwards as she counted the rooms. "A lot. The ballroom is on the third floor where we have our annual parties. You'll have to come to the next one. Our bedrooms are on the second floor and down here is where we spend most of our time. The cellar has several rooms, too; it's where the help lives. We have five live-in employees. And my parents' wine cellar is down there. If you like wine, I could show you that?"

Matt shook his head. "No, thank you."

"You don't like wine? I could open a bottle."

"I don't."

"That's because you haven't tried better quality wines."

"Perhaps. So, where do you think we'd find your father?"

She giggled lightly. "Go to the door over there and I'll open it," she instructed. She opened the heavy oak door. Cigar smoke seeped out. Inside, William, Josh, Wally Gettman and Jeff Blackburn were seated in comfortable stuffed chairs or one of the two davenports. Cigars and a drink were either in their hands or set on one of the tables.

"What happened to you?" Josh asked before anyone else could.

"Set me on the davenport and sit beside me," she instructed Matt.

"What did you do?" William asked with concern.

Matt set her down and faced her father. "Your employees came to town and attacked your office with rocks. They caused quite an uproar and traumatized your office people severely. Debra sprained her ankle trying to get away. I took her to the doctor. She'll be down for a week or so."

"Matt, sit," she invited.

William's eyes narrowed. "They attacked my office?"

"I have Truet and Nate boarding up the broken windows."

"Thank you for that and for bringing Debra home," William said, quite sincerely.

Debra spoke to her father with intention in her voice, "Aren't you going to invite Matt to sit down and have a drink?"

Matt waved his hand. "No, thank you. However, I do want to say I heard one man was killed today and I almost had to kill another. You should know you could have lost your daughter today."

"What do you mean?" Josh snapped.

Matt continued, "Those men had your receptionist loaded in a wagon when I showed up. They were taking Debra out to Slater's Mile to hold her hostage."

"What?" Josh yelled.

"They touched my daughter?" William asked with a rage filling his beady eyes.

Debra answered, "Father, they were carrying me to the wagon to take Martha, Paula and I to their homes. I was terrified. Thank goodness Matt came when he did. He saved all three of us. Those animals beat up Grant, and I saw Tim Wright hiding! Lawrence Barton, who lost his leg when the mine exploded, came to help us, but the sheriff was hiding!"

"How many men were there?" Josh asked, hoping to spare his good friend's reputation.

"A lot. It was horrible."

William peered at Jeff Blackburn with anger burning in his eyes. "I want those involved ran out of their homes and out of town."

Matt spoke, "You wouldn't have a single employee left. This business with your employees does not involve me, but I will tell you those men came to town ready to fight with guns. I don't understand what caused them to strike, but there is a young man dead and many pissed-off men who will not be content holding signs. It hasn't been a day and there has already been a lot of bloodshed, including the beating of two innocent men who tried to help your daughter. Blood has been drawn and I don't want to see that continue."

Jeff spoke for the first time, "The killing at the mine was accidental. I did not intend to shoot him or anyone else. Ron grabbed my arm and yanked it down, and the gun accidentally went off."

Matt had no respect for Jeff, and it showed in his expression. "That is what Joe Thorn told me. But I have to ask why was your gun out to begin with?"

William answered quickly, "A rock about the size of my fist flew past my head. Jeff pulled his gun to protect me. It was not without cause. Now, what about the damage to my building? Are you going to arrest Joe Thorn and his trouble-making friends for vandalism? I'm sure he had something to do with it as the leader."

"The only arrest I made was Paul Buff for trying to stab me."

"Who is that?" William asked.

"One of your employees, and the uncle of the

young man killed," Matt answered.

"Hmm," William grunted. He asked Debra, "No one hurt you?"

"No. One of them slapped me really hard and then squeezed my cheeks and forced a kiss on the lips, but I don't know his name. It was disgusting." She shivered at the memory. "I'm just thankful Matt showed up, or worse things would have happened. I think it's best we don't go back to the office until the windows are fixed and we have guards to protect us."

"Do you know who slapped my daughter?" William asked Matt pointedly.

"I do."

"Who? He's fired and I want him thrown in jail!" he demanded.

"Maybe it would be better to end this strike," Matt suggested. "The more fuel you throw on the fire, the hotter it's going to get, and I don't like what I've seen already."

William's patience had run out. He spoke sharply, "I don't care what you like, Matt! It's my company and I won't give my employees everything they want at my expense. A strike is their idea, not mine. They can end it anytime they want. But I won't allow my administrative employees to be harassed, threatened or beat up by them. I expect you to hold them accountable to the law, starting with the man that slapped my daughter. Got it?"

"I do."

"Good. I hate to be rude, but we are expecting company. Josh will show you the way out."

"Father," Debra whined her disappointment.

"Sorry, doll, but I have a guest coming. Thank you for your help, Matt."

"Thank you, Matt," Debra said with great sincerity.

Josh closed the door behind him as he left the room. Debra quickly said, "Father, I like Matt and you are terribly rude to him. He saved my life and all you can do is give commands like he's your maid."

William took a puff of his cigar as he watched his daughter. "He's not good enough for you. Get your mind off him. Doves don't mingle with rodents. Aim higher, Princess."

# Chapter 16

Wes Wasson came home from work at the sawmill to discover a sealed note from a family friend and District Attorney, Jackson Weathers, addressed to him. The message was an invitation to attend a private meeting at the Slater mansion about a career opportunity. It advised dressing well, leaving his firearms at home and being at the mansion at seven-thirty in the evening.

Wes had been politely received by a maid and escorted to a room where three men greeted him with an offer of a drink and a cigar. Seated in a comfortable chair in the mansion's drawing-room, Wes was under the scrutiny of William Slater, his son Josh and a man named Jeff. There had been no talk of a job opportunity or why he had been invited to such an elegant home, but the idle chat of a greeting had become an uncomfortable silence. In most job opportunities, interview questions were asked, but there had not been many, and the awkward silence was becoming strange.

Wes finished his drink and leaned forward in his chair to perhaps leave. "Well, fellas, we have looked each other over and said our howdy-do's. Is there more you wanted from me or am I here for no reason?"

Jeff Blackburn stated with his deep voice, "I hear you were an Indian fighter."

"I was. My whole youth was spent fighting the red man here in the west and then Kansas, Nebraska and Montana, among other places. I was in the cavalry a good many years. So yeah, I did more than my share to settle this country."

"Is it true you hunted scalps?" Jeff asked.

Wes nodded. "I did. California was paying good money for them."

"I heard you partook in the Bear River Massacre twenty years ago and you harassed a local man who survived that? I heard he scalped you, but I see you still have a good head of hair?"

Wes was quickly irritated. "Harassed is the wrong word. He came at me and caught me off guard. Yeah, I was scalped, but the marshal got me to the doctor quick enough to sew it back on, and it took." He showed the scar at the base of his hairline.

Jeff questioned with interest, "What do you do for a living now?"

"Sawmill."

"Do you miss the excitement of the cavalry?"

Wes laughed. "Maybe you were never in the cavalry. First of all, the cavalry wasn't exciting. The battles were, but beyond that, it was plain boring, sometimes miserably so."

"But you kept reenlisting?"

"I did. I liked the danger. Those moments in battle made up for the stretches of misery. You don't get that kind of horror, danger and adrenaline and excitement anywhere else. It was worth it. May I refill my glass?" Wes walked to a bar and poured a drink.

"Have you ever heard of the Blackburn Marshals?" Jeff asked.

Wes shook his head. "No."

Jeff smiled for the first time. "I am Jeff Blackburn. My men and I are a private police force, if you will. We are hired to do a lot of things. Let me cut to the chase, Mister Slater has a strike starting at the mine and he asked us to oversee his property and family. You may have heard that the miners attacked his office today and tried to kidnap his women employees, including his beautiful daughter. Matt Bannister saved her this time, but my men and I will save her if there is a next time. I have four men here, and I am looking for a few more men to join me to work with the guards' Mister Slater already has to keep his interests safe. I'm looking for men like you who are experienced with your weapons and not afraid to use them if we must. And sometimes we do. Do you think you might be interested in quitting the sawmill in joining us?"

Wes returned to his seat. "How long do you expect the strike to last? I don't want to quit my job for a week or two and be out of work. My brother-in-law got me hired at a higher rate of pay and I'd be a fool to give it up for a temporary job, which I don't even know what the job pays."

"I pay well. If you join us, you have the option of coming with us when we leave. Is there a woman or anything holding you back from leaving when we do?" Jeff asked.

"There was. I don't know if she's ever coming back, so no." Billy Jo's father had kept his promise to take Billy Jo to live with her aunt somewhere along the coast and there was no way to find her. He had no other reason to stay in town. His short romance with Viola Goddard was nothing more than an attempt to make Billy Jo jealous and get information about Joe Thorn raping her. It had caused the breakup of Joe and Billy Jo as he had hoped, but he never foresaw her father taking her away.

Jeff continued, "I'll be honest with you, we spend a lot of time traveling by train mostly. Mines, railroads, politicians, ranchers, companies of various kinds and people hire us all over the west to do whatever they want to be done. There are times when I'll send two of my men to do a job. I need men without a weak conscience because we are paid to do whatever we are asked if the money is right. I have one rule, we do not kill women or children. Beyond that, it's a wide-open range. That's who I am and that's what we do. If you are interested, let me know. If not, we part ways now."

Wes took a deep breath. "I'm interested."

Jeff reached into his suit pocket and pulled out a badge. He tossed it to Wes. "Pin that to your shirt if you choose to join us. If not, toss it back. We wear those badges all the time, day and night. They never come off."

Wes held the badge in his hand looking it over. Slowly he pinned it to his shirt and asked, "How does it look?"

Jeff smirked. "The better question is, how does it feel?"

"Good."

Jeff took a deep breath. "Welcome to the Blackburn Marshals. Now that you are part of our family, the rules are simple. Everything we do is secret, and secrets are kept that way. What happens between Blackburn Marshals stays between Blackburn Marshals and there is no grace for exceptions. Understood?" His meaning was made clear with the cold glare of his eyes.

"Understood."

"Good. William?"

William Slater asked, "Do you know Richie Thorn?"

"I do."

"He is one of the men that tried to kidnap my daughter. Matt Bannister knew that but didn't tell me. I found that out by confronting the sheriff Tim Wright before you arrived. My daughter has a sprained ankle and is afraid to go back to work. Richie hit her and roughly kissed her. I want Richie Thorn hurt and then brought to me."

Jeff spoke, "Wes, this is your first job. I'll send some of your new brothers with you, but can you lead such a mission?"

"Brothers?" Wes questioned.

134

Jeff nodded with a serious expression. "We're all the family we have."

Wes answered, "Yes, I can set him up easily enough. Mind if I hurt his brother, Joe, in the process? That's a personal request."

"Not Joe," William said frankly. "I need him right where he is. I only want Richie hurt. He'll tell us the name of the other man that grabbed Debra. The office can be repaired, my other employees will get over it, but my daughter being threatened, I will not tolerate that! I want Richie in pain and brought to the carriage house." William stood up, "Thank you for coming. Congratulations on your new job."

Jeff added, "One more thing; if you know anyone else who might have your skillset and are interested in a part-time or potential full-time job, let them know I'm looking to hire maybe three more fellas."

"I know a few. Have you ever heard of the Sperry-Helms Gang? I'll wire them in the morning."

# Chapter 17

Patsy Jane Ohlund had been repulsed when John Painter entered Madame Collet's Brothel and wanted to purchase her services. He could not afford any of the other ladies except her, as the oldest and cheapest of the prostitutes. There were other brothels in town, but they were more costly and to find a cheaper prostitute than Patsy Jane was to risk a streetwalker. The business owners on Rose Street and the city ordinances as well outlawed independent prostitution outside of a brothel within city limits. Whatever happened to the women that were forced into streetwalking and run out of town, no one asked or seemed to care. Prostitution on Rose Street was strictly by employment with a brothel. Streetwalkers didn't pay the city taxes or fees and went unchecked for disease, and were therefore, the most undesirable of all people.

At Madame Collet's, at least Patsy Jane had a place to live, food to eat, a bath and a regular check-up by Collet, the Madam, to verify that she had not contracted a disease and, if pregnant, a skilled abortion. A prostitute's livelihood was dependent upon performing her duties, even if all it required was laying down. Unfortunately, time is the enemy of all the women unlucky enough to enter the business. The youngest and prettiest earn the most money and have the highest chance of winning a husband and leaving the business. They were the lucky ones. Most girls found themselves trapped in a life of enduring what no one wishes to endure, a life of degradation, abuse, and hopelessness. Suicide was a consistent way out that many women took when their empty lives couldn't bear another day of living. Suicide was the number one cause of death in the profession of prostitution, followed by alcoholism, consumption, disease and, of course, abuse.

Prostitution was an ugly world and the gentlemen a girl met in the upper society parlors usually treated the young and pretty girls like a lady. More youthful and prettier girls always replaced the belle of the ball, and as a lady's beauty fades with time, smoke, alcohol and abuse, so does her worth. Sooner or later, even the prettiest belle of the ball who was once the pride of the nicest parlor can no longer find a madam willing to house and feed her because few men would pay the asking price for her. Madams can lower the cost as Collet did for Patsy Jane, but at a certain point, even the lower costs become a burden when they no longer earn their keep. Prostitution was a cold business with no lack of competition as younger and prettier women bringing higher rates were continually entering the trade for one unfortunate reason or another.

Women like Patsy Jane were cut loose to survive in a world that cared nothing about them. Seeking a lower-class brothel was the usual next step, but Madame Collet's was Branson's lowest-priced establishment and she was the lowest priced whore. Patsy Jane being turned loose and replaced by another woman in the brothel was only a matter of time. It was going to happen as soon as a younger and prettier woman knocked on the door. Her future was bleak as her choices were few: try to rent a small shack and become a streetwalker, or travel to the railroad construction camp and join the lowest class of whores in a row of tents for the Chinese men to use.

The best Patsy Jane could hope for was finding a man that would accept her as a wife to cook and clean, endure abuse or whatever she had married into to avoid an even less appealing side of life. Or she could always look forward to committing suicide. The life of a whore was hard and offered no hope the older a lady became.

In hindsight, it was a life of fake smiles, artificial alcohol-induced laughter, and hidden repulsion, danger and roughness. Scars on her lip and thigh, among other places, were reminders of violent customers that had hit, kicked, tossed and cut her over the years. It wasn't always the customers that hurt her; madams could be brutal, not to mention other prostitutes for various reasons. It was a life of hardness through and through and it showed on her face more the older she became. Time was the enemy of all the women in her business. Like an hourglass emptying its last grains of sand, time was short, and Patsy Jane didn't have any idea what she was going to do when Collet's door closed.

John Painter was a filthy man, but he had been gentle. He was an alcoholic as he even now took a swig of his gallon jug of cheap wine as he put his filthy clothes back on. It was a strange world, but one truth was that people generally married within their own social class. Patsy would never marry into the families that live on King's Point or step into their beautiful homes, but perhaps she could have a home if she found a man willing to marry her. John wasn't much, but he seemed nice enough and after he was cleaned up, he was relatively handsome despite his unkempt appearance. He didn't seem to have a wife and didn't appear to be successful at whatever trade he was in. It didn't matter, she was desperate to find a man because she knew Collet would soon ask her to leave the brothel.

"John, do you have a wife?" she asked.

He sat on the edge of the bed to pull on a boot. "I used to. She took my children and left me. I don't know where they are. I suppose I don't care much either." The tone of his voice spoke differently than his words. He took a long drink of his jug of wine.

"I bet you do," Patsy Jane said as she cleaned herself. She had never been the prettiest girl in any of the brothels she worked in, but she had gained weight over the years and had a round belly with thin legs. She had a round face with narrow eyes and a broad nose. Her lips were thick and two of her front teeth were missing on the left side of her smile. Patsy Jane did have beautiful light brown curly hair that she kept in a braided ponytail to keep it from tangling, that reached below her shoulders. "You don't see your children?" she asked.

He glanced back at her casually. "They're somewhere in Mississippi or Louisiana. I don't know where."

"I don't know where my son is either. He'd be twelve years old now. My madam sold him to a couple for fifty dollars in Albuquerque. I got five dollars from the sale."

"You sold your kid?" he asked, appalled.

She shook her head sadly. "Not willingly. I didn't get a choice. He was taken as soon as he was born. I didn't get to hold or feed him. I don't know his name, but I love him, just like I'm sure you love your children."

He ignored her and put on his other boot.

Her heart quickened at the knowledge that he was leaving her room and she may never have the chance to speak with him again. She continued, "May I ask what you do for a living, John?"

"Nothing. I'm looking for a job." He stood to leave. "Well, until we meet again."

"John, I'm just going to come out and say it. I could make you a good wife." The anxiety of being rejected showed on her face.

"What?" he asked with a growing grin.

"I can clean, cook, sew and keep your house

clean. I can be a good wife. I can make your house into a home and do a lot of things to make your life easier."

He chuckled. "I don't have a home. I don't have anything to offer you. Maybe your next customer will take you up on your offer."

"I can help you get a job. I can read and write and have an education."

"I went to seminary. I'm not stupid, Miss."

Patsy Jane asked bluntly, "Then what are you? Because you don't seem to be doing too well. Your bath water was filthy, and your clothes are rags. I don't believe you'd be here and pulling on that jug like a baby sucking the nipple if you were teaching the Gospel. So, what are you?"

John's head tilted with a flame of aggravation filling his chest. He was speechless.

"I can help you," Patsy said nervously.

"Help me do what? Feel better about being a beggar and a bum?"

"No," she said softly. "I'll help you start over. We can start over together. I have enough money to rent a small place and if you worked, we could build a home. Maybe even start a family. I know I'm not much to look at, but I cook well, and I'm still young enough to produce babies. I'm thirty-three. I'll be faithful. And look…" She opened her bedside drawer and pulled out a black leather-bound Bible. "I'm a believer too. I'm just not living it because my whole life is nothing but sin. I want to change that. You can help me do that while I help you."

"You're a whore," John answered simply.

The hope that had shown on her face faded as she replied pointedly, "If you were a woman, you would be too."

He chuckled. "You think so?"

"I know so. What other choice would you have? If you're not working, how did you get the money for the wine, the bath and me?"

He chuckled. "I borrowed it."

"How are you going to pay it back?"

"I'm not. My Pa is." He chuckled.

"How old are you?"

"Thirty. Thirty-one next month."

"Yeah, if you were a woman, you'd be in my shoes. I don't know that you can judge my life without being the one living it, nor I you. But certainly, we both can do better than we are. Maybe we can help each other do better. I don't have any diseases; thank the Lord for that. This is a lonely life; you need a woman and I need a man. We're evenly matched and coming into this with nothing except ourselves and what we can build from there." She shrugged while squeezing her lips together tightly. "I doubt you'll get a better offer."

"Am I being charged extra for this time? Is this a ploy to swindle another two bits from me?" John asked skeptically.

She shook her head sincerely. "No. If you agree to marry me, I can get us a shack to live in tomorrow. In one month, we could walk down Main Street in clean new clothes, and no one would look down on us like they do now. You can have a new beginning as a man and not a beggar with a woman who will dedicate her life to making you better." She sniffled as she shrugged and tilted her head emotionally. "And I could have someone in my life to call my family."

"You're serious?" he asked. "Well, let me go get good and drunk and I'll let you know."

"John, your answer must be final. Because once I say I'm leaving here, I can't come back, and you'll be stuck with me. Consider it carefully, but I know I can make you happy."

"Hell, wine does that."

"No, it does not. Being content in a home of your own would, though. I can make that happen if you'll let me. All I ask is for you to work and don't hit me."

# Chapter 18

Beatrice Painter had been woken up during the night by some banging against the staircase wall. She was discouraged from thinking John was coming home drunk and stumbling on the stairs before going back to sleep. She woke up at her usual time just after sunrise, made breakfast and, as an afterthought, went upstairs curious if her drunken son had vomited again. She was far more shocked to see a strange, naked woman sleeping beside her son.

She went downstairs, where Eli sat at the dining room table with his toast and coffee. "Did he puke his guts up again?" he asked as she entered the dining room.

Beatrice sat down heavily with her mouth agape.

"What?" he asked.

Her eyes widened and she took a deep breath to collect her words. "There's a woman in his bed."

"What?" Eli asked, nearly choking on his coffee.

"There's a nude woman sleeping beside him and a jug of wine on the bedside table."

Eli groaned with frustration. "Well, we can't have that." He stood up and went upstairs to John's room and shook John's bare shoulder. "John, wake up! Wake up right now."

"Go away," John said tiredly and rolled over, ignoring his father.

"John! I said get up." Eli shouted.

Patsy Jane shuffled in her sleep and raised her head to squint at Eli. "Morning," she said.

Eli spoke politely but with a firm tone, "Miss, would you mind getting dressed and getting my son up to come downstairs, please. This is not acceptable."

"Sure," she agreed. "Johnny, it's time to get up," she said, caressing his cheek with a growing smile. It was the first morning she had woken up in a house in many years and her first morning not being a prostitute. "I'll make sure he gets up," she said to Eli.

Downstairs, Eli waited impatiently at the dining room table, drumming his fingers against the wood surface. It was the only sound as he and his bride waited for their son to come downstairs with his guest.

Before too long, a strange woman came down the stairs, wearing a pink robe with thick imitation fur along the front seam, with her boots on. Her awkward discomfort to come downstairs alone was evident on her red cheeks. "Good morning. I couldn't find a chamber pot; do you mind if I use your privy?"

Eli pointed at the rear door. "Out back." He watched her leave quickly out the door. He looked at his bride and shrugged unknowingly.

John lumbered into the dining room, rubbing his eyes. He didn't feel too well after drinking more than his share of the wine. "Morning," he said with a raspy voice. "Ma, that coffee smells good." The large purple and brown blotch from a midnight kiss on his lower neck was plain to see under his opened shirt. When Beatrice didn't respond, he glanced at his parents and noticed his mother refusing to look at him. His father stared at him sternly. "What? All I said was the coffee smells good."

Eli made the extra effort to keep his voice at a normal volume, "You know darn well what the issue is! We told you yesterday not to bring alcohol into our home, but today you not only brought a jug of wine into our home, but you also brought a woman to your room."

John grinned. "Did you get a good glimpse of her, Pa? It got too hot, so we kicked the covers off the bed." He gave a short chuckle. "It might've been a few years since you saw something that young, huh?" He grinned.

"Shut your mouth!" Eli shouted, angered. "This is a Christian home, and I will not allow you to stay here and treat it like it's not. We have rules, and those rules apply to anyone, including you. If you do not like them, you are free to leave. But you are not free to treat our home like your own. It is not yours! Am I understood?"

"Yeah, Pa, I understand that, but you'll understand that I'm not a child anymore, right?"

"I don't care how old you are. Our rules are our rules. You can take your friend home and then we are having a serious conversation about your future here."

John hesitated. "Um, Pa…Ma, I asked Patsy Jane to marry me. I guess she's going to be living here now too."

"You what?" Beatrice shouted with her fierce eyes glaring into John.

"Yeah. I decided I needed a wife. We're not married yet, but we're going to be as soon as Pa says so. We don't need the whole church thing; you could just say the words as soon as she comes in and marry us right now. She doesn't need a dress or anything. It might be beneficial to marry us now; that way, we're not having sex outside of marriage and breaking your rules." He yawned.

Eli's mouth dropped open. He was speechless as he stared at his son, wondering where he and Beatrice had gone wrong. "Where is my son that I sent to seminary?"

John widened his eyes. "Right here, back at home."

"I don't know you anymore, John."

"I'm not the same kid I was. I grew up. Anyway, Patsy Jane and I are making a go of it, and we'll see what happens. Will you marry us?"

Beatrice spoke, "You came home a few days ago! How in the world would you know you wanted to marry that woman?"

Eli added, "You can't possibly be in love. When did you meet her?"

"Last night."

"Oh, good heavens!" Beatrice snapped and turned her head in disgust. " Take her back to where you found her and grow up!"

"Last night?" Eli asked, stunned. "And you want to marry her today?"

John poured a cup of coffee. "We're not in love. It's a marriage of convenience. I mean, look at me. I couldn't win a heart if I tried. And she's no Bathsheba herself, if you know what I mean. I know she's not that pretty, but we have a plan. I need a woman to care for me and she needs a man. It'll work. And I'll never have to tell her I love her or hear her say it to me. It sounds great."

"You have to be kidding," Eli said with no humor in his expression.

"Here she comes, ask her."

Patsy stepped inside. "I feel so much better, thank you. Do you think I could have some coffee? It smells wonderful."

"Patsy, my folks don't believe we're getting married. I forgot to tell you my Pa is the reverend in the church next door. They're a little irritated about us sleeping together under their roof. I told him he could marry us right now and it would be fine. It would also settle that whole sin thing."

Her cheeks reddened. "I apologize. This must come as a shock. But John and I would like to be married. The sooner, the better."

"Who are you?" Eli asked her with a perplexed expression.

"My name is Patsy Jane Ohlund. I'm originally from Texas, but now I'm here. I know it's surprising, but I'd like to be your daughter-in-law."

Beatrice had absorbed the shock enough to ask, "Where did you meet my son?"

Patsy was hesitant to answer. John waved a hand. "Go ahead and tell them."

"Madame Collet's."

Eli lowered his brow questionably. He didn't recognize the name. "Is that a clothing store?"

"Brothel, Pa," John answered.

Beatrice covered her mouth. "You're a... Oh, good heavens!"

"Whore?" Patsy Jane asked. "I was. I'm not anymore. Now I'm going to be Missus John...what is your last name?"

"Painter. You're going to be Missus John Painter."

Eli gasped and rested his forehead on his palm. "Please tell me this is a bad joke."

John put an arm around Patsy Jane's waist. "Pa, we'll go to the courthouse and ask the judge to marry us or another church if you won't. But I'd like for you to."

Eli held up his other palm. "Don't talk to me right now, John. Just take the lady home, and we will talk."

Patsy Jane raised one shoulder and tilted her head skeptically. "I can't go back. I have nowhere to go if I can't stay here. John said I could stay. Please don't make me leave."

Beatrice abruptly stood and left the dining room towards her bedroom, upset.

John rolled his eyes and shook his head. "I hate how she does that. I think it's supposed to make me feel bad and all, but it doesn't."

"John," Eli said softly, "you're quite old enough to marry her if you choose to, but I cannot marry you two. I believe you both are making a big mistake and I won't do that. Even if you two do get married, you cannot live here. You're not working, she's not working, and we will not support two adults."

John asked sarcastically, "Would you be happy if my fiancée went back to whoring? We could pay your tithe then."

Eli Painter was a patient and Godly man, but he was a human being. He had tried to be reasonable, but he didn't understand his son anymore. He lost his temper and slammed his hand down on the table. He shouted, "John, pack what little you have and get out! I won't tolerate your disrespect for me, your mother and our home and church. Good luck with your marriage but get out!"

John seemed unfazed. "Can I borrow some money to get a place of our own?"

"No! I'm not loaning you a penny."

John chuckled. "Fine. You ought to know you owe Matt Bannister ten dollars. He loaned me ten yesterday, thinking you'd pay him back."

"Goodbye, John! I'm going in to talk to your mother. You have half an hour to leave our home. And you know, I'm at the point where I don't care if you don't come back." He glanced quickly at Patsy Jane. "Miss, good luck."

John sipped his coffee. "Maybe you could cook us up some breakfast before we go. Don't worry about cleaning up afterward. Ma will do it."

# Chapter 19

Phillip Forrester lifted his head from his work when the door opening rang the cowbell in the marshal's office. A black man around six feet tall with broad shoulders and a muscular build limped into the office, holding tightly onto a tree limb with a forked end to use as a crutch. He limped noticeably, favoring his right foot. He wore a tan, weathered hat with a wide brim over his short hair and had a six-inch-long black beard that was heavy with gray on his square-shaped face. He was dressed poorly.

The man's eyes scanned the office before he spoke in a gentle deep voice, "Good morning. I'm here to meet with a man that goes by the name Matt Bannister. I think he's expecting me. Are you Matt?"

Phillip stood from his desk. "I'm not. Can I get your name?"

"I'm Jeremiah Jackson. I just arrived in town."

"Is Matt expecting you?" Phillip asked curiously.

The man shrugged with an awkward smile. "I think so. I'm not sure."

Phillip went to Matt's private office and knocked softly. A moment later, Matt came out of his office with a friendly grin. "You must be Jeremiah? I'm Matt. Darius sent me a wire about a month ago saying you were coming to town. I expected you a couple of weeks ago." He extended his hand to shake. Darius Jackson sent a message to Matt stating he had invited his younger brother to move onto the Big Z Ranch with him and Rory. He asked Matt to take care of Jeremiah for the night when he arrived in Branson.

Jeremiah's hands were heavily calloused and firm as he shook Matt's hand. "My brother told me to come to see you when I got to town, and you'd get me taken care of for the night? It's early enough I could reach the ranch today, I think. But I'll be honest; I'm exhausted. I'll be leaving first thing in the morning for the Big Z Ranch. I guess you'll give me the directions?"

"No problem at all. Darius asked me to take care of you and I will do that. Darius is part of the family, like an uncle, if not a father figure sometimes." He spoke to Phillip, "Phillip, write up a letter to Roger King at the Monarch Hotel telling them to treat Jeremiah like our family. Access to anything he wants at no charge."

Phillip immediately reached for a piece of paper and pen.

Matt put his attention back on his guest. "The hotel is owned by my brother Lee. He doesn't charge family when they come to town. Being Darius' brother, that makes you part of the family too. It's the finest hotel in town with a bathhouse, restaurant, laundry services, and more, but they'll tell you about all that. You just make yourself at home and enjoy your stay."

Jeremiah smiled with relief. "I have to tell you. I've been sleeping on the ground from East Texas and frying up whatever I can find along the way, snakes, squirrels, pheasants, ravens and any fruit trees that crossed my path. A warm meal and a soft bed sound like paradise to me right about now."

"That sounds like a very long trip. I have to ask, did you cowboy in Texas?"

Jeremiah chuckled. "Started that way, but I married my missus and took up sharecropping. I farmed forty acres of ground for many years. Darius asked me years ago to come this way, but my missus had family there, so we stayed put and worked the ground. I can't read, but I had a friend write to Darius and tell him my missus passed away back before Christmas. He wrote back and invited me to live with him and Rory. I figured, I'm fifty-nine and he's quite a bit older, our time's shorter than ever to be brothers. We're both widowers now, you know." The lively eyes moments before dulled and revealed a deep sadness at mentioning his lost bride.

"My sincere condolences about your wife." Matt took the note Phillip had written and signed it. He blew on the ink to dry it before handing it to Jeremiah. "Take this to the Monarch Hotel, and hand it to the lady behind the counter. Roger King is the manager, and he will treat you right. I would walk you down there myself, but I am right in the middle of writing a report."

"I appreciate it. I don't have two bits to spare, so thank you so much. Can I ask a favor, though?"

"Certainly."

"I dismounted on a hill the other day and must've landed on my big toe wrong. My toe popped, it didn't hurt too bad at the time, but that dang gout took hold. I don't know if you have ever had gout or not, but I swear there isn't a worse pain when you're climbing in or out of the saddle, except for maybe just walking. The truth is, I can't walk too well. I noticed the livery stable is quite a walk from here. Do you think I can trouble you to take my horse to the stable for me? I'd sure appreciate it."

"I've never had gout, but I hear it is terrible. I will have Phillip come to the hotel in about half an hour and board your horse. What time do you plan on leaving in the morning?"

"Oh, around seven, I imagine."

"I'll have Phillip bring it to you at seven. We have a couple of excellent doctors in town if you want to have your gout looked at."

"No. It'll heal on its own. I'll rest it when I get to Darius's place. The good Lord never saw fit to give my missus and me children, so sitting in that little house alone at night just didn't seem right anymore. I came here to be with family and work on the ranch." He said with a grin, "Your uncle Charlie is not going to be impressed by me sitting at Darius's house for a week or so doing nothing, but it's about the best I can do with gout. I fashioned this walking stick from a tree branch to help me walk. It ain't pretty, but it works."

Matt listened empathetically. "Jeremiah, how about I meet you in the restaurant at about six this evening for supper? I'll see if I can't get you a crutch to use."

The man grinned. "Am I allowed inside? Being colored and all?"

Matt frowned. "Of course, you are. I'll meet you there at six."

Matt watched Jeremiah limp back to his horse with the help of his homemade crutch and gingerly stepped into the saddle. He spoke to Phillip, "I knew Darius had family, but I never expected to meet any of them. He seems like a nice man, doesn't he?"

Phillip agreed. "Are we paying the livery bill?"

Matt gave a slight smile. "Yeah, do that."

"I figured."

Matt went into his office and sat down behind his desk. An arrest report could be fun to write, but the monthly expense account for the federal government was no fun at all. He hated working with numbers and if better judgment were his strong suit, he'd have Phillip doing the monthly reports, but it was Matt's job and his responsibility to know where every cent went. The government didn't know that he was still paying the widow of Jed Clark his monthly wage after he was killed on the job. Lying to the government was not a good thing but watching Jed's wife and children starve and freeze over the winter would have been a far worse crime. That wage had to be accounted for in monthly increments here and there to add up in the final yearly budget. Every dollar had to be accounted for and benevolence wasn't what the federal government wanted the U.S. Marshal's Office to be known for. He started at the beginning and read back through each number to verify he wasn't overlooking something since he was interrupted.

A few minutes later, a gunshot echoed from the street, followed by a few screams and a touch of laughter. Matt stood up and put on his gun belt before leaving his office. Phillip left the office with him.

A growing crowd gathered in front of the Monarch Hotel near a weary-looking bay horse tethered to a hitching rail. Matt approached and pushed his way through the crowd to find Jeremiah Jackson lying on the ground with a bullet hole perfectly placed in his heart. Powder burns on his shirt proved the barrel was set against him. Matt knelt and felt for a pulse, but there was only his own heartbeat to feel. Doctor Ambrose pushed his way through the crowd and knelt quickly to check for a pulse as well.

"He's dead," Matt said coldly and stood. He peered through the crowd with a fury burning inside of him. "Who shot him?" he shouted with eyes as cold and hard as the knife blade that was set beside Jeremiah's hand. The letter Phillip had written was lying on the ground near him.

Phillip answered, "According to the folks over there," he pointed toward a young family that was shielding their young children from seeing the body. "Some of the Blackburn Marshals saw Jeremiah limping and told him to hop on his hurt foot. When he refused, one of them shot him."

"Where are they now?" Matt asked.

"They rode off as soon after it happened."

"Matt," Big John Pederson called. He carried a wooden box of food goods in his hands. "Wes Wasson shot him. I saw it happen as I came out of the grocery a block up. I watched him shoot that poor man, search his pockets, put that knife on the ground and ride off with three others wearing badges on their shirts. I overheard them say something about going to Richie Thorn's before too many folks woke up as they rode by. That man's no good. I should have killed Wes when I had the chance."

"You're sure it was Wes?" Matt asked skeptically.

"Do you think I'm blind? Yeah, it was Wes!"

"Phillip, get the two deputies' and my horses ready. We're going after Wes." He approached Jeremiah and knelt. He made eye contact with Doctor Ambrose, who had stood up. "Will you do me a favor and have him taken to the funeral parlor? I'll be there later to make arrangements."

"Did you know him?" Doctor Ambrose asked.

"Not much, but his brother is part of our family. Tell my Uncle Solomon, I'll take him to Willow Falls in the morning. This man's name is Jeremiah Jackson. Darius's brother."

# Chapter 20

Wes Wasson wanted to make a good first impression with his new fellow marshals somehow and spotting an old crippled black man hobbling outside of the Monarch Hotel was an opportunity to do just that. He knew perfectly well that no one would care about his killing a black man. If he was arrested, Wes knew the charges would be dropped by the family friend, District Attorney Jackson Weathers, just like they were for his brother-in-law, Frank Ellison, when Frank killed Chusi Yellowbear. Of course, Wes didn't mention any of that advanced knowledge to his new fellow marshals and his reputation was now well-founded within the group of men.

Wearing the Blackburn badge gave him the power as an opposing force of the strikers to finally get a chance to rid the world of Joe Thorn for good under the pretense of doing his job once he was allowed to do so. For whatever the reason,

William Slater made Joe untouchable at the moment, but eventually, if it were the last thing he did as a Blackburn Marshal, Joe would be dead. And then, when Billy Jo did come back home, Wes could earn her affections and win her heart without her choosing Joe Thorn.

It was still fairly early, and Wes hoped a good portion of the miners were sleeping when he, Henry Dodds, Jimmy Abbot and Toby Stearns rode into Slater's Mile to Richie Thorn's cabin. The idea was to get Richie on a spare horse and get out of there before a thrown-together militia of miners could assemble and trap them in the cabin. All the cabins were identical with a single window facing the road. A few were covered by curtains, but of the eighteen or so cabins they had to pass by to get to Richie's most curtains were pulled open to let the sunlight in. So far, there was no hint of trouble outside, but they were ready for a fight if it came to one.

Wes knocked on the door as a friend and was invited inside, the other three barged in behind Wes and in no time at all, the four of them had Richie on his knees, beaten, bloody and with no fight left within him. His roommate, Bobby Alper, stood in a corner under the rifle of Henry Dodds while Wes, Toby Stearns and Jimmy Abbot beat on Richie.

Richie dropped one hand to the floor to hold himself up while looking up at Wes. "I thought we were friends," he mumbled as a string of blood poured from a severely split bottom lip.

Wes knelt in front of him and pointed at the

badge on his chest. "We were until you laid your hands and lips on Debra Slater. I'm a marshal now. I can't let you get away with that." He quickly drove a fist into Richie's face that laid him out flat. "We're not killing you today, Richie. However, I do believe you might wish you were dead by tonight. We're taking you to town to meet with Debra's father, and what he says goes." He looked at Toby. "Hand me the twine and I'll tie his hands."

"What about his roommate?" Henry asked while holding a rifle on Bobby. They were told to let Wes make the decisions and report how he did. "What do you say, Wes? You know him."

"Bobby? Oh, heck, Bobby won't say anything, will you, Bob?" Wes asked.

"No," Bobby answered nervously. He didn't like having a rifle pointed at him.

Henry placed the rifle's barrel under Bobby's chin and lifted his head with the barrel. He pressed the barrel against Bobby's throat. "Better not, or I'll place a bullet right here to make sure you never speak again."

Wes tied Richie's hands behind his back and then grabbed his hair and an arm and pulled Richie to his feet. "Come on, old friend, let's get you to town."

Bobby spoke, "Wes, if you do this, Joe and the rest of them are going to get even."

"Are you?" Henry asked, pressing the barrel into Bobby's throat a bit harder.

"No."

Henry Dodds continued, "Then I guess we will be expecting you to be the voice of reason around here. I'll hold you personally responsible if your pals cause any more trouble." He pushed the barrel of the rifle harder into Bobby's skin. "Understand?"

"Yes," Bobby replied through gritted teeth.

"Good." Henry pulled the rifle back and began to turn away from Bobby but then rammed the stock into Bobby's abdomen as a parting gift.

Toby Stearns, expecting Henry to do just that, waited for his chance to take a small step and kick Bobby in the face as he bent over. Bobby flailed back against the wall and slid to the floor, dazed. "Keep the peace, or it will be worse," Toby finished.

Wes pushed Richie out the front door towards a spare horse on a lead rope. They put him in the saddle and tied the rear leather saddle straps around the twine confining his wrists. Wes slapped Richie's thigh. "Who else was holding Debra Slater?"

Richie shook his head. He had been severely beaten already and had no idea what would happen to him once he was taken away, but there was no way he was going to tell Wes who had grabbed Debra. Loyalty was a bond of friendship and there was a fellowship between all who had entered the strike together. Wade Rosso was the one who had snatched Debra off the boardwalk, but Wade's name would never be uttered from Richie's lips. "Don't know."

Henry Dodds said, "You stared right at the man, and you don't know? That's fine. I imagine you'll remember quite clearly later. Trust me, we're very good at making tough guys like you tell us whatever we want to know."

"Not me," Richie said through his bloody lips.

The corners of Henry's mouth lifted into a wicked sneer. "Good. The tougher you are, the more I like it."

*⁂*

Matt could see their horses tied to community hitching posts nearest to Richie's cabin and a well-trained mare waiting patiently out front of Richie's with a lead rope tied to another horse. Matt did not want to be on horseback when he confronted Blackburn's men, so he and his deputies tied their horses to the nearest hitching post fifty yards away from Richie's cabin. Matt, Nate and Truet went behind the cottages to remain hidden from view. They reached the back side of Richie's cabin and could hear the men talking through the wall. The cabins did not have back doors or windows to see what was happening inside, but it didn't take much imagination to figure out from what they could hear. Matt sent Truet to the other side of the cabin with his handy Winchester and Nate across the dirt road with a shotgun.

Matt waited until they put Richie in the saddle and tied his wrists so he could charge all the men with attempted kidnapping. With his Colt .45 in hand, Matt swung around the corner of the cottage and set his aim on Wes Wasson while his eyes scanned the others. "Don't move! I won't hesitate to shoot any of you!" Matt's tone was as cold as the ice-stricken Modoc River in the dead of winter.

Truet stepped out from the corner behind the men with his Winchester at eye level while Nate also stepped into the open, aiming the shotgun with both hammers pulled back. The three men had the small group of Blackburn Marshals surrounded.

Wes's chest deflated, knowing he was caught. He had no intention of trying to fight it out against Matt and his deputies. He raised his hands slowly. "Problem, Matt?" he asked.

Henry Dodds snarled. He was protected by the horse from Nate's shotgun but had no chance against Matt in front of him or Truet behind him. Jimmy Abbot and Toby Stearns were in the open mid-stride on the road towards their horses twenty yards away. They were protected by the two horses behind them from Truet but in the open sights of Nate's shotgun and Matt's revolver.

Matt ignored the question. "Drop your gun belts and that rifle," he ordered.

Toby Stearns wasn't in a good or talkative mood. He had gotten far too drunk the night before in the Monarch Lounge to feel his best. "You do know who you're talking to, right? Do you think you'll get away with this, half-breed?"

Henry Dodds spoke with authority, "Toby, just do as he says. Unbuckle that belt and let it fall. You too, Jimmy. He's not our fight." He lowered the rifle in his hands and unbuckled his gun belt to let it fall.

Wes Wasson followed and spoke to his new friends. "Just do it, fellas. Matt's not after you anyway. You came for me, didn't you?"

Jimmy Abbot did as he was told, but Toby resisted with a prideful glare at Matt. "I don't listen to half breeds."

Matt turned his revolver to aim at Toby's chest. "Then draw, dumbass! Let's see if you're faster than my finger. Come on!"

"Toby, unbuckle it now!" Henry yelled, growing irate. Toby was a twenty-seven-year-old man that acted like a sixteen-year-old kid with no common sense, sometimes.

Toby remained staunch in his refusal to remove his weapon like a stubborn child with a pouting glare.

Matt already had the hammer pulled back. "I won't ask again. One...Two..."

"Just do it!" Jimmy Abbot hissed at his friend quickly.

"Fine," Toby agreed and slowly unbuckled his gun belt. It fell to his feet.

Matt held his gun on Toby and told Nate to secure their hands with the two pairs of wrist shackles that he carried. Truet had moved Henry and Wes away from the horses to stand against the cabin, Toby and Jimmy joined them. Nate and Truet went to cut Richie free from his binds.

Matt glared fiercely at Wes Wasson and ripped the badge off Wes's shirt and yelled, "This does not give you the right to kill a man! This," he held his palm open to show the badge, "is garbage!" He threw it over the cabin into the woods. "I want to hurt you! I want to hurt you so bad, but I'm afraid if I started, I'd kill you before I could stop."

Toby spat on Matt. "That badge has more honor

than yours. You half breed…"

Toby's sentence was abruptly ended by a furious right fist to the jaw that dropped Toby like a hundred-pound bag of grain seed to the ground, unconscious.

Matt ordered, "Nate, toss his scrawny ass in the saddle and tie the strings to his shackles."

A crowd of miners came out of their cabins taking notice of Richie and his condition. The few women and children gathered curiously while the men shouted threats and gathered around Richie.

"What's going on?" Joe Thorn asked with concern. A long and thin willow branch used as a fishing pole was in his hand along with his small coffee can of worms and a good-sized trout. "Richie! What's going on?" He demanded as he went to his brother."

Truet collected all the weapons while Nate fetched their horses.

Matt glared into the eyes of Wes Wasson. "You're under arrest for murder. I'll do everything in my power to make sure you hang."

Wes didn't say a word, but the corners of his lips rose into an arrogant smirk.

"You are all under arrest for attempted kidnapping."

Wes snickered. "No one's going to care about a nigger."

Matt shoved his left hand under Wes's chin and rammed his head into the cabin wall to get his attention. "Don't ever say that word around me again! You might get off as your brother-in-law did, but you crossed a line with one of the most dangerous lawmen you'll ever know – me!"

Joe Thorn knelt on the ground where Richie sat, surrounded by their friends. Joe glared at Matt with a burning fierceness in his eyes. "We're not filing charges, Matt. No harm done."

Matt wrinkled his brow. "They were taking your brother and you most likely would never have seen him again."

Joe stood and waved a hand towards Wes. "You're wrong. It was just a friendly jest by our old friend Wes. Isn't that right, Wes?" Joe asked accusingly. There was no friendship between them.

Wes met Joe's eyes just as coldly. "That's right. It was all in fun. These boys don't deserve to be arrested. I'm the only one that shot the nig…"

Matt's elbow struck the side of Wes's cheek bone with a driving force that sent Wes to the ground. Matt quickly dropped a knee onto Wes's back and yanked his arms behind his back. "Shackles!" he demanded as he held a hand out for Truet to hand him a pair. He shackled Wes's wrists as tightly as he could to make the ride into town the most unpleasant.

When he had finished, Truet and Nate placed Wes on his horse to be led into town. Matt spoke, "Richie if you won't testify against these men, it won't do any good to arrest them. If they're not in jail, they could do worse to you or any one of these men next time. Or their families," he added while gazing at a couple of ladies talking with each other across the road.

Richie held a rag over his sliced lip. "There's nothing to say. This is between them and us, Matt. Not you." A general agreement was quickly narrated from the growing group of strikers telling Matt to leave the men there with them.

Matt waved a hand towards the growing crowd. "It's strange to me how none of these men came out to help you, Richie. If we weren't here, you'd be gone. Think about that for a moment. Will they help you next time?"

"You better believe we will!" someone in the crowd answered.

"Absolutely!" said another.

Joe Thorn spoke calmly through a restrained voice, "It was just a bad joke among friends, Matt. You can go now."

"Richie?" Matt asked to verify that was what Richie wanted to do.

Richie answered through his split lip and swollen eyes, "It's all in fun."

Henry Dodds spoke, "Without a crime, you have no reason to arrest us. It was a prank that we took too far."

Matt smiled despite himself. "Joe, you have no idea what you're getting yourself into."

Several strikers quickly backed Joe Thorn. "Matt, we're many and they're few. Maybe they don't know what they're getting into. But either way, the Slaters brought them in to fight and by damn, we'll fight."

Matt shook his head. There was no more he could say. "Truet, Nate, Take that scrawny bean pole off the horse and free him. Free all of them, except Wes." He looked at Henry Dodds. "We'll give your guns back to you fellas in town. I don't care if you leave with us or not, but I doubt you'd get out of here alive if you don't."

# Chapter 21

"Oliver, thank you for coming. Please, come with me and let's discuss our great misunderstanding," William Slater said while shaking Oliver Rohloff's hand and then Oliver's son, Jasper's hand. William had invited them to the W.R. Slater Mining Company office in town. He motioned to the broken windows covered with boards. "As you can see, we have had a very tough few weeks negotiating with our employees, and they decided to strike. It has turned violent, and our office was attacked yesterday, including my daughter, among other employees. I am very grateful for our marshal, or I may never have seen my daughter again. Please follow me." He led the two men upstairs to the conference room where four other men were waiting, including the company lawyer, Delbert Van Arden, Josh Slater, Wally Gettman and Jeff Blackburn.

After introductions, William opened a map and explained how a former employee had changed their map. The result was accidentally, with no deliberate intent, crossing claim borders and the discovery of gold on the Rohloff land.

William sighed. "This is truly a new kind of trouble that we never expected. You'll understand that we are nearly fifteen hundred feet into the bedrock and your small mining venture would not reach it for ten years, if ever, even if you dug a shaft straight down to it," he lied. They were only seven hundred feet underground, but by doubling the distance it would help his cause. "Let me be frank; the gold is beyond your ability as uneducated men to grasp the geological issues at hand, such as the changing structural integrity of the rock. A good geologist and an engineer like Wally are very expensive to hire. The equipment alone for such endeavors are far more expensive than you can afford, and that's just to reach the gold, not including the equipment to extract it and then the expense of processing it. We can agree that Rohloff Mining Works is in no financial position to fund such a monumental task, yes?" he waited for an answer. None came. "We can agree you can't afford a geologist, engineers, the supplies and equipment to go that deep, yes?" he repeated impatiently.

"At the moment, yes," Oliver agreed.

Satisfied, William continued, "Flooding is a whole other issue and it's a constant. I went back through the records of our processing what you have brought out of the ground in the past year, which, again, you have no way of processing any gold or silver you do find, without using our stamp mill. You have low to fair grades of silver ore, but you have only earned a bit more than three thousand dollars in a year of laboring. You could not afford a pump or the hoses necessary to pump out the water to work any deeper than two hundred feet. I imagine that is why your mine is at ground level and working into the mountain and not under it. So here is how I see it: it's your property, but we are the only ones who can access the gold. If I may be direct, I suggest we come to an agreement. Since it is our people, equipment and expense, I believe we are entitled to a larger percentage, so I suggest Rohloff Mining Works receives five percent of the revenue while we do the work. That's five percent for doing nothing. Free money."

Oliver Rohloff narrowed his eyes. "It's my claim, my property. The gold belongs to me. How much have you taken out already? I hear you have a wagon load. That should pay for everything I need to reach the gold on my own. How much gold did you all process from my claim? Silver too? I would like to see your records taken out from that winze."

William almost choked.

Josh Slater spoke clearly, "I wish we could tell you that. As you saw when you came in, our office was attacked, and the strikers opened our files and burned a lot of them in the woodstove. I looked for that information to have it here for you so we could come to an agreement, but that information, along with much more of our financial records were burned. We do not know that answer."

William silently thanked his son for coming

up with a good answer. "Oliver, I wish I could be focused on this, but we are walking on thin ice and wary of our angry strikers. Please understand, we are overwhelmed with all of this at the moment. We are receiving death threats and my daughter was nearly kidnapped the other day. I had to call in special security to keep us safe." He waved at Jeff. "Tell me, what do you want to do? How do you think we should settle this? What do you think is a fair percentage?"

Oliver Rohloff spoke bluntly, "I want my money from the gold you stole. It's mighty convenient they burned those records and not your office down. I'm not going to call you a liar, but I have my reasons not to trust you. Millions of dollars' worth of my gold primarily."

"Oliver, if you think this is a ruse, I assure you it's not. Five percent of the earning will set you up quite well. Young Jasper there will live well for the remainder of his life. But if you want to retire, I'll buy your claim for a substantial amount and still give you five percent of all that's found on that land. I had my lawyer draw an agreement to buy you out. Before you decline the offer, look at the amount I'm offering and estimated future earnings based on our information from the surrounding area. You can retire a very wealthy man and earn hundreds of thousands a year for doing nothing but selling me your claim." William paused to peer at Oliver. "It's more than a fair offer."

Delbert Van Arden slid a series of papers across the table to Oliver. "It is a great offer that will provide you with a very secure future."

Oliver skimmed through the papers. He wasn't a good reader and certainly didn't understand the larger words used in the offer. He knew his son couldn't read well either. He rubbed his eyes and sighed. "I'm not educated enough to understand what I'm looking at here, but I am smart enough not to sign anything until I understand what it means..."

Delbert sputtered, "I'll gladly read the offer to you and explain the ends and outs until you do understand."

Oliver shook his head. "No. I had a friend pen a letter to a lawyer he knows in Portland. When that lawyer comes to town, I will have him read this and see what he says. But you need to understand this, the wagon load of gold you sent off to sell is mine. The lawyer he wrote to will do everything he can to get a piece of it, because I'm offering him a big percentage of it. With the money from that gold shipment, I should be able to hire a geologist and buy all the equipment and men I need to reach what's down there. I didn't come here to hear about your problems or how it happened, I came here to tell you to stop mining on my property, or I'll hire that lawyer to sue you for everything you have. I'll even pay your experienced men more money to work for me. A hundred dollars says I'd treat them a whole lot better than you do and then more of them will want to work for me." He stood up. "I believe that's all I have to say for now. My lawyer will be in touch. I'll keep the offer for the lawyer.

Come along, Jasper."

After they had left the conference room, William put his attention on his company lawyer, Delbert. "Do they have a case?"

"Yes, he does. Accident or not, the gold belongs to him."

William's eyes hardened. "When the money is transferred to my bank, will Oliver be able to find out how much was earned?"

"Mister Rohloff's lawyer can certainly subpoena the bank information. And most likely, you would have to transfer it all to him because the gold is legally his property."

"So, I'm screwed?" William asked, with his sharp eyes peering over his spectacles like a viper about to strike.

"Technically, yes. We could always file a counter claim and take it in front of a jury, but no jury here is going to side with you."

"What about Judge Jacoby? He'll side with me. He always does."

Delbert squeezed his lips and shook his head. "Chances are any Portland lawyer will move to have the case heard in a neutral court where no one can be persuaded by local influences such as bribes or threats. A case this valuable, meaning millions of dollars are at stake, any good lawyer will not take any chances of losing in a local court. Don't be surprised if we fight this in Portland, where your name and reach won't influence anyone's verdict."

William shouted, "Rewrite that offer and offer far less! No! Write a Bill of Sale for twenty thousand dollars and not a penny more for his entire business. No percentage of the future earnings from the property or anything else. Just twenty thousand cash dollars for the whole operation, mineral rights, everything, period! And make sure it has today's date and I want it back by the end of today! Thank you for coming, Delbert. Now, go get that done."

When Delbert left, William stared at Jeff Blackburn thoughtfully. After a moment's silence, he said, "Now you know what Oliver Rohloff looks like, make him sign his company over to me by any means necessary. It must be backdated to today at this time, so we can say he signed it today, the offer accepted, and all is well. We'll write up a receipt for twenty thousand in cash and you stuff a copy in his pocket once he's dead. Beat him up, make it look like he was robbed or whatever you do. Josh will run to the bank and take out twenty thousand in cash from the vault." He spoke to his son, "Make sure the bank has a record of it and mention the sell to everyone in the bank to verify there are witnesses. It needs to be cash so it can disappear in a robber's hands without a trace. Jeff, I need this done as soon as Delbert gets that written up. I can't afford a lawyer to show up and cause me any problems. So, early morning before his employees show up, make sure it's done without a trace back to us."

"What about his son?"

William took a deep breath. "If you didn't notice, Jasper is a little thin on brains. But like his father, they'll only cause us more problems with his lawyer.

Do what you're hired to do, and you can keep the twenty thousand for yourself. Just make it look like an accident. Burn the cabin down or something. I don't care. What's a measly twenty thousand when their mine is worth millions?"

# Chapter 22

Matt stood by the jail cell door holding three pieces of paper in his hand. He spoke to Wes Wasson firmly, "I think you're no better than a cockroach for shooting an injured old man. He didn't do a thing to you or anyone else and you killed him. And then you were coward enough to put his knife in his hand."

"He spoke to a white woman," Wes said. He was reclining on the bottom bunk without a care in the world.

"He spoke to a white woman! You disgust me, Wes."

Wes chuckled. "I suppose I'd be lying dead beside your pal in the mortuary if I had stuck around, right?"

Matt didn't answer.

Wes sat up on the edge of the bed. "I'm not easy to kill, Matt." He stood. "I'm a marshal too, now—a Blackburn Marshal. Don't expect me to be afraid of you, I never was, and I certainly am not now. I'll be out soon. Free of any charges and back to my new career in no time. I'm sorry about your pal. He shouldn't have pulled a knife on me."

"We both know you put the knife there. I won't question why you murdered Jeremiah; because we both know that's who you are. If you knew your friend Jackson Weathers would not indict you, why plant the knife? Was that to impress your new friends?"

Wes grinned but didn't utter a sound.

"Well, justice will be served one way or another. It's just a matter of time."

Wes leaned against the corner post of the bunk-bed with folded arms. "Most folks don't take well to being threatened by a nigger. He had a knife; I had no choice," Wes lied with a nonchalant shrug of his shoulders. "You shouldn't have thrown my badge, though. Jeff, may not have an extra."

"Wes, your badge holds as much authority over anyone as a bottle of piss. But despite that, I do have here an astonishing letter from your dear friend District Attorney Jackson Weathers stating he is dropping all charges against you."

Wes chuckled expectedly.

"I think it's a bunch of crap. Supposedly, according to Sheriff Tim Wright's investigation, it contradicts mine. He has seven unnamed eyewitnesses that state the opposite of what my six witnesses say. I named mine. How odd is that? I feel like I've read something like this before when it comes to your family."

"There's nothing I can do about that. I'm not the district attorney," Wes chuckled.

Matt hesitated to unlock the jail cell. "Listen to me. I don't care if you're afraid of me or not, but those miners are members of my community and that's who I am sworn to protect. I'm warning you, and you can tell your new friends too, I won't let you and your lawless pals terrorize my town."

"There won't be any trouble unless they start it. I don't know what you're warning me about."

"Yeah, you do." Matt unlocked the cell door. "You're free to go."

\*\*\*

Jackson Weathers sat behind his desk, staring at Matt with his mouth open. "Matt, you well know some witnesses don't want to be identified. All seven wish to remain anonymous for now. Rest assured, seven respected members of our community came forward. They all agree Mister Jackson had a knife in his hand and attacked Wes Wasson, forcing him to the ground where Mister Wasson fired a bullet in self-defense at point-blank range into the deceased's chest. I can't argue with seven witnesses, and either can you. The powder burns on Mister Jackson's shirt indicate close contact with the barrel of the gun, which collaborates the story of all seven witnesses. It was self-defense."

"Really?" Matt asked skeptically.

Jackson spread his hands apart innocently. "I cannot control what people say they witnessed."

"That's odd," Matt announced quietly.

"What is odd?"

"Well, you wrote here on this paper that Sheriff Tim Wright interviewed seven witnesses. But Tim told me he never spoke to you or had anyone told him anything different than what I wrote in my report earlier. Why are you lying, Jackson? You did the same thing when Chusi was killed. I have Indian blood running through my veins too. Does that make me less of a man than you?" Matt asked.

"No," Jackson answered, appalled. "The law is the law and there is no crime where no crime is committed. Self-defense is not a crime. It wasn't when Frank Ellison, fearing for his life, killed Chusi Yellowbear, nor is it here. I don't know what Sheriff Wright told you, but he brought to me the sworn testimonies of seven anonymous witnesses who all stated the same thing. Wes had no choice but to protect himself with deadly force. I'm sorry if your information doesn't line up with the facts, but as the District Attorney of Jessup County, I found no evidence that warrants the arrest or detaining of Mister Wasson. I'm sorry. Now, if you'll excuse me, I have work to get done before the day ends."

Matt rubbed his forehead with frustration. "People are going to die, Jackson. Your friend, Mister Wasson, didn't kill anyone in self-defense, nor will he in the future. I don't know what will happen, but I guarantee you this won't be the last time you sell your integrity out for Wes. If one of your family members is killed from a stray bullet from Wes's gun in some shoot-out in town, I'll remind you that your family member died in self-defense. Because Wes should be in jail, tried, convicted and sentenced to be hung in this court of law!" he yelled, angered by the lies and corruption of the Branson court of law.

Jackson stared at him irritably. "I'll remind you that you are a United States Marshal, not a lawyer, district attorney or a judge. You make arrests. We in the court read the evidence and prosecute or not. I chose not to because that's what the evidence says."

Matt stood. "I think you're a liar. A straight-up bought and sold whore of a liar."

Jackson raised his hands innocently without saying a word.

Matt commented, "I hope you can sleep well knowing others are going to die because you decided to cover this up. You don't know the men Wes works for now. You're not doing him any favors, Jackson. You have no idea what they are like, and I won't keep this quiet when the time comes."

"Matt, do you think maybe you shouldn't get in over your head?" Jackson asked quietly.

Matt shook his head. "You don't learn to swim if your feet are always touching the ground."

"Matt, may I give you a suggestion? Flow with the current and enjoy the fruits of your labor. You make the arrests. We in the courts determine the innocence or guilt."

# Chapter 23

Patsy Jane had saved up over two hundred dollars over the years of her career. When she was young and considered pretty, an older prostitute known as Charcoal Sue was being forced out of the brothel for the same reasons Patsy Jane would have been: age, lack of beauty, and less appeal than the younger girls. Sue had no backup plans and no man to marry. Her choices were few and bleak no matter where she looked. Charcoal Sue had taken the only road she felt she could bear – she committed suicide the last night she was allowed to stay in the brothel. Patsy had never forgotten the last words Charcoal Sue had ever spoken to her before going to bed that night. "Save your money, because when whoring is over, you have nothing. Absolutely nothing. Save your money, Patsy Jane, and maybe you'll have something."

At the time, it didn't seem so important, but finding Charcoal Sue's dead body the following day, her words hardened like concrete in the back of Patsy Jane's mind. Patsy Jane decided then to set aside some of her money for the day that every prostitute knew would come for them. The day where she was no longer the young belle of the ball, doll of the evening, lady of the midnight dance or even a woman's soft touch. Instead, she was just a used-up whore.

Grateful to have saved some money over the years, she and John Painter went to see Big John Pederson about renting one of his apartments at the Dogwood Flats. There were no apartments available, nor did he have any other places for rent. They tried talking to Lee Bannister, but he told them to come back the following day because he did have a small two-room cottage available, but he was leaving the office for the day. Filled with excitement about the potential home, Patsy Jane wanted to do something she had never done and that was staying at an upscale hotel. She and John Painter checked into the Monarch Hotel for the night. It was more expensive, but to have some comfort and mingle with a class of people that wasn't at home on Rose Street was an experience she wanted to have. The beautiful room and high-end restaurant might be costly, but it would be worth the occasion to celebrate her life as a whore coming to an end. An evening getting to know John as they lavished in luxury, even for just one night, sounded like a wonderful thing to her.

The evening had started with John anxious to go into the Monarch Lounge and have some drinks. It was a high-class gentlemen's lounge where women were prohibited, and only local members or guests of the hotel could enter. She had given John ten dollars to drink and gamble while Patsy Jane had a relaxing bath with scented soap and shampoo, thick bubbles, and hot water in the finest bathtub she had ever experienced. Leaving the tub, she went to their room and relaxed in the comfort of the thick cotton robe the hotel supplied, chocolate candies and a bottle of champagne. Her moment of basking in luxury ended abruptly as John entered the room wearing his filthy clothing and unbrushed hair, complaining that the ten dollars she had given him had only bought two drinks and played four hands of blackjack. He needed more money. Patsy Jane refused to give him anymore and pointed out they still had a home to pay for along with food, clothing and many other goods to live on until he could find a job. Her refusal to share her money angered him and they had a short and loud argument. Enraged, John left the room, slamming the door behind him.

John went back to the Monarch Lounge and went from table to table and man to man begging for a drink. Begging was not becoming of a gentleman within the lounge's membership and John was asked to leave. John was furious and refused to leave. Typically, such a person would be confronted and taken outside by the hotel's security, William Fasana, but William was taking some time off to escort his uncle Luther and cousin to Portland where William would part ways and visit his lady friend, Maggie Farrell, and his ex-uncle Floyd Bannister. With William absent, John was promptly removed from the lounge by a couple of the visiting Blackburn Marshals playing cards.

Angry at Patsy Jane for her selfishness and being removed from the lounge, John walked purposely over to Rose Street and went from saloon to saloon, begging the men, prostitutes and business owners for any change they could spare. One man bought him a shot of cheap whiskey, but most all labored too hard to give what change they did have to buy a drink for a beggar. With just enough alcohol in him to crave more, he approached two men on the street and asked them for any change. The reception wasn't one of friendly declining or a firm no, but a fist to his jaw and a kick to his gut when he had fallen as a final reminder not to ask the men again. The two men searched John's pockets and took what little change he had collected.

Dejected, angry and desperate for a drink, John left Rose Street and wandered back towards his parents' home. He could have knocked on the door and woken them up, but he already knew they would not give him another dollar no matter what lies he had come up with for needing it. Desperate, his eyes fell on the white church next door to their house. He knew his father passed a collection tray around every Sunday at church for offerings and tithing, but he also did it again at the Wednesday worship meetings. Eli Painter routinely took the week's collection to the bank on Friday morning to give the church board an accurate account at their Sunday meeting before church. Knowing it was Thursday night, John went around to the far side of the church to a window. He used a hardened dirt clod from the street to tap the window just hard enough to crack the glass. John was desperate to get the money, but he also knew he had to keep the noise level down, not to be caught by an alert neighbor. He tapped the glass to create a hole in the center of the window just wide enough to get his hand into comfortably. He pulled a glass section out and set it on the ground beside the building instead of allowing it to fall and break. He ignored the slight cutting of his hands as he skillfully removed one shard of broken glass at a time from the window frame. When he had finished, he climbed inside the church and went to the only door that was kept locked. With a swift kick, he broke through the door and entered the small closet where the wooden box that contained the tithes and offerings was bolted to a tabletop. Years before, the church was stunned to learn someone had broken into the church and stolen the tithing box. To make the tithing box harder to steal, the box was securely bolted to the table and the lid was padlocked. John knew the key was always kept on a nail under the table. He reached down and discovered some things never changed. He used the key on the padlock and opened the box. John counted the coin and paper money in the faint light from the foyer kerosene lamp that was always lit to highlight the now broken stained-glass window covered up with boards. He was thrilled to find over sixty dollars. He unlocked the main door with his pocket full of money and walked out onto the street in the direction of Rose Street.

\*\*\*

Toby Stearns had a bit of trouble brewing in his eyes. He sat in the Green Toad Saloon with his best friends Jimmy Abbot, Henry Dodds and Wes Wasson. Wes's idea was to leave the Monarch Lounge and go to where Richie Thorn and his friends often went to drink. Unfortunately, not one of the strikers had entered the saloon and it was getting late. Any hope of beating up strikers or capturing Richie Thorn was dwindling quickly.

Toby watched the poorly dressed beggar from earlier in the Monarch Lounge enter the saloon and head straight to the bar with a grin and order a gallon jug of wine. Toby watched with interest while the beggar pulled a handful of money out of his pants pocket and paid the two dollars for the jug. The man's hands were partly covered with dried blood trails from minor cuts.

"That stuff will rot your gut," the bartender said, knowing John had bought a gallon of the cheap homemade wine the night before.

"It's my gut. Don't worry about it," John said as he pulled the cork and lifted the jug to his mouth. "Say, give me a shot of whiskey too. I got into a fight with my fiancée. I've been courting her for one day and I'm already tired of her. Give me two shots."

Toby watched him with a curious growing grin. He nudged Jimmy Abbot. "That's the same bum that was in the Monarch Lounge. Wes, you're from around here. Do you know him?"

Wes shook his head. "No. I've never seen him before."

"Look at those hands. Gentlemen, we're marshals. Let's investigate and have some fun." Toby hollered to John with a twisted grin, "Hey, wino, come join us."

John turned towards them with little interest. They were the same men that had thrown him out of the Monarch Lounge. "No thanks. I don't need your money anymore." Having just robbed his father's church, he had no interest in sitting with four men; three of the men wore marshal badges on the lapel of their shirts.

Henry Dodds reached over to another table and pulled an empty chair over to theirs, invitingly. "Come sit down," he said with a forceful tone.

Knowing he could be in trouble, John walked cautiously to the table and sat. He would have to think quickly to answer questions about where he got the money and cut hands.

"I'm Henry. That's Wes, Jimmy and Toby. What's your name?"

"John. John Painter. My pa is Reverend Painter," he offered uneasily.

"Does the good reverend know you're down here drinking wine? And a lot of it by the looks of it."

John lifted his shoulders uncaringly. "He might. We don't see eye to eye on things, you know." He lifted the jug and took a long drink. The reddish liquid dripped onto his beard.

"I see," Henry said.

Toby, with a drink in his hand, motioned toward John. "Those are some interesting cuts. Most folks cut the outside of the knuckles when they hit someone, not their palms."

"Hmm?" John asked, confused. "I never hit anyone."

"Oh. I just thought maybe you beat someone up and took their money. You know you had none earlier, and now it looks like you have quite a bit. Bloody hands, money, it adds up to something suspicious. We'd know; we're marshals. Maybe you better tell us how that came to be. Otherwise, we'll have to throw you in jail, and you might be there for a long time."

John's face went blank as a chill ran up his spine. His voice shook as he answered, "I didn't hurt anyone. I tried to sneak into my parent's house and the window broke. My father loaned me the money to rent a house tomorrow."

Toby laughed with his pals. "Your father must be a forgiving man to loan you so much money after breaking his window."

"I don't believe you," Henry stated.

"I don't either. Wes, what do you think?" Toby asked.

Wes Wasson shook his head slowly. "He's lying."

Toby agreed. "John, here's my deal, you tell us the truth, or we'll go outside and my friends and I will beat some man to death and say we all watched you do it. That's a guaranteed hanging if not an immediate lynching." He paused just long enough for a slight snarl to curl his upper lip. "Convince us not to do that, by telling us the truth."

John grinned, thinking Toby was joking.

Toby peered at him through cold-blooded eyes that made John uneasy. "We're not bluffing."

John's grin faded as his eyes scanned the four men's faces. Not one of them revealed a sense of light-heartedness or a hint of human compassion. John had met wicked men in the past and realized he was in the presence of men that would do just as they threatened to do. His bottom lip began to quiver involuntarily. He was caught in his crime and would be arrested and perhaps facing prison time.

"Start talking!" Henry snapped with a cold scowl.

John stuttered, "I...I stole it."

"From?"

"My pa's church," John told them what he had done and why the cuts were on his palms.

When he had finished, Toby said, "Hand me the money." He counted it, divided it into four portions, and handed his friends their share. "Thank you for being honest, John. Because of your honesty, we'll not arrest you tonight, but as punishment, you have to stay with us, and we will buy you all the drinks you can stomach."

John was relieved but a bit confused. "Thank you."

Toby's lips lifted just a touch. "You bet. Wes, you work at the sawmill, right?"

"I did."

"Right. Hey, do you know Russ over there?" He pointed across the saloon.

"No," Wes replied.

"Come on, you have to meet him," Toby said and grabbed Wes's arm to convince him to leave the table. They walked across the saloon to the corner where a few men sat. Toby smiled at the men and said, "Ignore us. Wes, let's have some fun with this bum. Here's my idea..."

When they came back to the table, Toby sat down and asked Henry Dodds to lend Wes a hand and the two men left the saloon.

"So," Toby asked John to keep him busy, "what room are you and your fiancée staying in at the hotel? We're at the top because we're a bit louder than most folks."

"You're not local marshals?" John asked, assuming they were Matt's deputies.

Toby smiled slowly. "No. We're a different kind of marshal. But let's get drunk. Barkeep," he shouted, "a bottle of whiskey and get it here pronto. John's thirsty."

***

Three hours later, Patsy Jane was woken up by loud knocking on her hotel room door. Angered about being woken from the best sleep she'd had in years on the most comfortable bed she'd ever slept on, she got up and covered her nude body with the soft robe and opened the door with an angry word or two ready to spit out at John. She had time to gasp before four men barged in and one man covered her mouth, while another man with a beard waved a knife in front of her. The blade reflected the faint light in front of her eyes.

The man with the knife spoke, "John said you were pretty. I think he either lied or hasn't been sober yet!" He laughed with his pals. "I guess beggars aren't choosers after all, huh?"

The man that held her from behind spoke in her ear, "Be quiet, and I'll remove my hand." The heavy scent of alcohol was on his breath. Seeing the marshal badges on their lapels in the faint light, she felt a momentary sense of relief to know they were lawmen and not criminals.

"Where's John?" she asked anxiously. She feared something may have happened to him and that was why the marshals were in her room at such a late hour. It was almost three in the morning. She wasn't sure which one of the men was the famous

Matt Bannister, but she was confident they weren't there to hurt her after seeing the badges.

"John's...hanging out at church," Toby answered. The others laughed.

"Huh?" she asked, confused by the answer.

The marshal in front of her put his knife away and reached over to untie her robe. She tried to slap his hand away, but her arms were grabbed from behind and pulled back as her robe opened, exposing her body. The man touched her skin.

She spoke heatedly, "Keep your hands off me. I heard you were a godly man!"

Wes Wasson suddenly understood that she thought Henry Dodds was Matt. He chuckled and pat Henry on the shoulder, "Ma'am, this is Marshal Matt Bannister, I'm Truet Davis, that's Nate, and Phillip is behind you. Matt is a Christian man during daylight hours, but we're the last of your paying customers tonight. I'll leave a dime on the counter. What about you, Matt?" he asked, patting Henry's shoulder.

"Well, John said we could stop by for free," Henry said with a wicked grin as he pushed her slowly back towards the bedroom. "He owes me money for all the whiskey I bought him tonight and he said you'll pay it back. We're here to get our money's worth."

"Please, don't..."

He slapped her face brutally. "Call me, Matt."

# Chapter 24

A loud pounding on his door woke Matt. "Matt, open the door," Nate Robertson shouted urgently.

Truet Davis yanked the door open with a scowl on his face. "What?" he shouted. It was still dark outside, but dawn was breaking over the eastern sky.

Nate didn't wait to be invited inside; he stepped into the house and closed the door behind him with a strange expression on his face. "Sorry. Truet, you and Matt need to follow me to the Branson Baptist Church right now."

Matt came out of his room holding his revolver as Truet asked why.

Nate hesitated as his head moved side to side silently. He was breathing hard from running. "I can't explain, but you need to hurry." The uncommon urgency displayed on Nate's expression didn't need any more of an explanation for both men to know there was something terrible that had happened. It took mere moments for both men to ready themselves and run across town to the church, where they came to a sudden stop. Breathing hard from running, both men's mouths dropped open, horrified by what they saw.

The church had been defaced with red paint in large letters that spelled out the words, 'Thy shall not steal from thy father' followed by a red arrow that pointed towards the church's front door. Two eight-foot boards nailed together in a wide X had been nailed across the doorway and John Painter was stripped naked and tied to the boards at his wrists, ankles and waist with twine. His head leaned against his left arm, held in place by his long hair tied in a knot firmly around his bicep. Whoever had placed him there took a moment to paint a red arrow from his chest down to his belly button, pointing at his exposed crotch.

On the other side of the door on the church exterior wall were the words painted in red, 'John, son of Rev. Thief, drunkard, beggar. Robbed church for wine'. To make the humiliation just a bit worse someone removed the lantern used to light the stained-glass window from inside the church and set it outside on the ground in front of John. It was a quiet street, and it was doubtful anyone had walked by until he was discovered that morning.

"I think he's dead," a neighbor lady said, horrified by what she was seeing. She was with a growing crowd that gawked at the horrific sight. "It's the reverend's son," Matt heard someone in the crowd whisper to another.

Robert Fasana spoke to Matt immediately upon his arrival. "I haven't let anyone go near him until you arrived. I haven't woken the reverend up either." Robert had pounded on Nate's door and sent him for Matt.

Matt approached John and used his knife to cut John's hair to loosen his head from his arm. John was alive but drunk, passed out and cold.

"Robert, get me a blanket for him. Truet, let's cut him down and take him home." Truet and Nate helped hold John as Matt cut the bindings that held him to the makeshift cross. The way John had been tied was reminiscent of being crucified, which was a direct mockery of the church. They wrapped a blanket around him to cover his nakedness, draping his arms around their shoulders. Matt and Truet half dragged, and half carried him to his parents' front door. Matt knocked with his free hand.

Beatrice Painter opened the door part way in her robe to peek out but was suddenly pushed back as Matt and Truet barged in without being asked. "Sorry, Missus Painter, but we have to get your son out of the cold. He's been hanging there all night."

"What? What's wrong with John? Is that blood? Eli!" she shouted in a near panic.

Eli Painter came out of his room in his undergarments. "Matt?" He watched them lay John down on the davenport. "What happened to my son?"

Matt motioned a thumb towards the door behind him. "Your son is drunk and passed out. But someone defaced the church and had him tied up naked across the doorway. Whoever did it had tied his hair around his arm to make him look like a crucifix, I'm guessing. He's cold, but he'll be okay, I'm sure."

Beatrice covered her mouth with a flurry of moisture that filled her eyes. She quickly pulled herself together and went to a closet to get a few blankets. Eli stared at his son and shook his head, trying to grasp what he had heard. "Is that paint?"

"Yes, sir. They painted on the church too. It isn't flattering, Reverend Painter. Do you want to get dressed and come next door with me?" Matt turned to Nate, who lived around the corner. "Will you run home and grab a hammer or a breaker bar to pull those boards away from the church door?"

Outside, sorrow filled Reverend Painter's expression as he stared at the X nailed across the door and the painted words on both sides of the church door. Nate removed the large X and tossed it aside, allowing the reverend to enter the church. His cheeks reddened with humiliation; Reverend Painter refused to look at the crowd of gawkers that gathered at the church to see the vandalism and hear about what they had missed.

"Give me a few minutes. I want to be alone for a while," Eli said to Matt and went to the church door to unlock it but was surprised to find it opened. He entered and closed the door behind him to find some solitude. He covered his face with his hands and began to weep. He slid slowly down the door to the floor and wept into his hands. The humiliation was awful, but his heart broke for his son and what had happened to him. After a few moments, he stood up and it only took a moment to notice a broken-out window and lock on the closet where they kept the tithes and offering box. He was startled to find it empty, except for a few bank notes that would not do anyone any good since they were made out to the church. Anyone could have done the break-in, but seeing the padlock set on the table with the key in it, narrowed it down to his son. His broken heart shattered then and there. His son was a thief, just as the vandalism outside had stated. He stepped into the sanctuary and sat down on the front pew, a defeated man. He cast his eyes on the large cross behind the pulpit. He shook his head, feeling a sudden exhaustion that emptied him of any feelings.

His hands opened towards the heavens, offering a silence that may have spoken louder than any sound could. "Jesus…" he began to weep and could not continue. He had no words to say, just utter silence that cried out deeper and stronger than he could verbalize.

Matt entered the church alone and quietly sat beside his friend.

"It's true," Reverend Painter said with a sniffle. "John robbed the tithes and offering box."

"It may not have been him," Matt offered, having seen many setups within his career.

"It was. John is the only one who knew where the padlock key was. It was hidden. I want him arrested. It's only right."

Matt nodded in agreement. "Truet's going to get some white paint and repaint the church today and board up the broken window. What happened to the stained-glass window?"

Reverend Painter shook his head, overwhelmed. "John thew a jug of wine through it the night before last. I want him arrested, Matt. We may not have a church left if he's free one more night."

"I'll get a hold of Sheriff Wright and have him arrest John. This is the town's jurisdiction, not mine."

Reverend Painter patted Matt's leg appreciatively. "Thank you for your help. I don't know where we went wrong with John. He was such a nice young man when he left here. We had so much hope for him." He shook his head with a father's disappointment which was a depth that kept sinking deeper into a pool of muck and mire that felt bottomless.

Matt offered softly, "He's still breathing, so there's still hope that he can change his life around."

Reverend Painter smiled sadly while his eyes pooled with deep wells of moisture as he stared at the large wooden cross on the wall. "All my life, I felt called to preach the Gospel. I was a poor farm boy from rural Kentucky, and I saved and scraped enough to go to seminary. I worked and lived in a small loft in a livery stable all through school, studying by candlelight and eating scraps for four years to learn the secret of salvation. Our creator gives no more important calling than teaching his sacred word and sharing the secret to the most vital decision that anyone could ever make in their lifetime – the salvation of Jesus.

"For all these years, I have faithfully served this

church family and others as I worked my way west. I've helped families through hard times and introduced many people to Jesus. I've watched those people grow and give their lives to the Lord, and the Lord work amazing blessings in their lives. I've comforted hurting families during grief, sickness and health. Times of celebration, times of sorrow and times of disheartening circumstances." He shook his head discouragingly. "Beatrice and I have labored to raise John to be a Godfearing and believing Christian. In my youth, I may have been harder on him than I should have been to be good representation of our family."

He looked at Matt with a single tear gathered at the corner of his eye. "Your reverend shouldn't have disobedient and disrespectful children. The Bible makes it clear that if a reverend can't control his family, how can he control the church? John is my son. I hate what he has become, but he is still our son, and we love him." His bottom lip quivered as he fought the sobs that waited to erupt. "I failed him. I didn't build a strong enough foundation in him before we sent him off. It didn't stand tall when the world knocked him off his feet. I don't have a choice, Matt. To be scripturally obedient, I must retire from preaching. I can't stand up there behind the pulpit and speak of holiness, obedience, and repenting from sin while my son is a mockery of all I stand for and speak about. The only thing he isn't that I know of is a homosexual, but he did have sexual relations with a woman in our home."

Matt listened as his friend hesitated. He could

see Reverend Painter was struggling to keep his composure.

Reverend Painter continued, "We already have a pigeon coop of gossipers that will have a hay day as it is. John coming home is a novel's worth of gossip that will ruin this church if I stay. This Sunday will be my last day preaching here. I don't know what we're going to do, but the Lord will be faithful, and we'll trust him day by day. It just isn't right for me to be leading this congregation when I can't even lead my own family in living a godly life."

Matt exhaled as he rolled his head with a hint of frustration. "Your son is thirty years old. He isn't a child and you're not responsible for his decisions. He is a man. He decided, for whatever reason, to walk away from the Lord. He chose to become a drunk. Maybe he's hiding from pain, maybe not, I don't know. What I do know is if he murdered someone, he'd pay the penalty, not you. On the other end of the spectrum, if he saved the life of the President of the United States, he'd be rewarded for it, not you. If he worked in a mine and discovered the biggest solid acre of gold, he'd become a millionaire, not you. If he labored at the silver mine and worked his way to the company's president, he'd be the one that earned it, not you. We all get what we earn, and our choices affect our lives too. Not just good and bad choices, but even more importantly, how we respond to our circumstances no matter what they are. You'd be a fool to quit preaching because of your adult son," Matt said firmly.

"You don't understand, Matt. He's my son and

he's... I don't know. I obviously didn't teach him how to handle living life as a man. Life is hard. I don't know if I ever showed him how tough it could be or how to handle life when things get tough."

"Are you kidding?" Matt asked with a scowl. "John grew up in your church week after week, hearing about death, sickness, starvation and every other kind of hardness that hopeless people bring into church to find some hope. If that didn't teach him about the world we live in, then he's just plain stupid! He knew and gave up because it got hard and didn't want to work. There are people like that. Look at my cousin William Fasana. He hates real work, and he grew up working in the granite quarry. He knows how to do it just as well as Robert across the street, but William doesn't want to. He's a gambler, a womanizer and I would say a drunk, but he's not. He is absolutely nothing like my uncle Joel whatsoever at all. Robert, across the street, is like Uncle Joel, but not William. And they're brothers. William is closer to my family than his own because he fits in better with us for whatever reason. John would be the same as he is no matter what you did or didn't do. His life choices are his decision, not yours!"

"John's not stupid, Matt. He...I don't know. I just know he needs help."

"Then help him!" Matt snapped. "But for crying out loud, don't give up what you love to do and were called to do. You help so many people in this community, Reverend Painter, that the devil would like nothing more than to destroy you and your ministry. Don't be shocked, but he'll use your son to do it until your son wakes up and realizes what a fool he is. Last night may just wake him up when he's sitting in jail humiliated. We'll see. I'll talk to him. In the meantime, get the thought of quitting because of him out of your head. He's an adult man and you are not responsible for your adult children or what they choose to do. That is between him and God, not you and God. You lead by example just as you have always done, and let God have the room to intervene. That means, back off! Don't give him any more money, or a place to stay, and allow the Lord to work within John's heart. I believe he will."

Reverend Painter wiped his eyes. "Everyone in our congregation is going to hear about this, Matt. What am I supposed to say?"

Matt hesitated and spoke softly, "You are a father. A human being with a family that has tried to do the best you could. Tell them the truth, you are just a human being and even a reverend's son can get in trouble and make bad choices. But as the Lord does for all of us when we fail, you will accept him back at home when he comes home on the right path. As your congregation and fellow Christians, the people in your congregation should realize their family isn't so perfect either and offer grace to you, your missus and John as well. Maybe they'll be more understanding than you know." Matt smiled empathetically. "As for others in the pigeon coop of gossip, wash your hands and leave that between them and God."

Eli exhaled a heavy sigh. "Thank you, Matt."

"Anytime."

"Will you do me a favor? Catch the men that did this to my son."

A slow smile formed on Matt's lips. "That's what I do best. Let me ask you a question, should I quit my job if my adult son stole an apple?"

The reverend shook his head slowly.

"Then don't you either. You raised a good family. Just walk in your integrity and perhaps that wandering son of yours will see the honor in that and come home to do the same." He patted his friend's leg before standing. "I'll send Nate to get a wagon and we'll haul your boy to the city jail. It's best if he wakes up there."

After Matt left him alone, Eli stared longingly at the large wooden cross. "I have no answers, Lord. All I can do is let my agonizing heart be opened to you and ask, please, bring my son back to you." The single tear slipped down his cheek, followed by another.

# Chapter 25

Owning the Rohloff Mining Works sounded impressive in conversation and perhaps those from out of town were impressed, but the mine itself wasn't too much more than a hole in the mountain dug by hand tools and black powder dynamite. The rock was hauled out by either wheelbarrows or a homemade wooden cart with solid oak wheels with iron bands on the edge that a mule pulled. A wagon outside the portal collected any silver ore they found and took it to the Slater stamp mill to be processed and sold. The digging was slow with only four men working the mine, but the adit reached sixty yards into the mountain at a five-degree incline to allow any ground water to drain out naturally. There were a few short exploratory drifts and a good-sized stope where they had discovered a good quantity of low-grade ore. No shafts or winzes were cut down due to the water level and the lack of finances to invest in a pump, donkey engine, or any other large equipment that helped other mines reach greater depths.

The mining venture started six years before with Oliver and his two sons. Knowing there was plenty of silver ore in the area, Oliver searched along the cliff beside the river and found hints of silver along with a series of veins of white calcite. Oliver filed a claim on the promising spot and staked out his hundred and sixty acres across the river on a gentle hillside where a wide meadow broke up the heavy forest. To make the mine accessible by wagon, he built a log bridge north of the mine's portal over the narrowest section of the Modoc River. The bridge was eight feet above the waterline to keep it accessible when the spring thaw increased the water level. The logs and sawn timber to build the bridge, support beams and other needs inside the mine were cut from the forest rather than the expense of purchasing lumber.

Money was earned, but monthly wages for the employees took a large portion of the mine's earnings after deduction for the processing at the stamp mill. It wasn't a profitable business, but it was Oliver's business. He was saving his money to acquire a small donkey engine and a pump so he could start cutting down to reach the higher-grade ore that he was confident was there.

With the gold the Slaters had discovered on his claim, Oliver could transform his small operation into a massive corporation and expand his mine to the size of Slater's mine. Oliver was content knowing the future lawsuits for the Slater's transgressions would be large enough that he could buy the Slater Silver Mine and possibly even the Slater mansion on the hill. William Slater and his pompous son would be begging him for a loan to start a hog farm by the time his lawyer was finished with them.

Oliver and Jasper lived in a small log cabin in a meadow that rose gently above the Modoc River. The cabin had two separated bedrooms, one had a double bed where Oliver slept, and the other had a bunkbed where his two boys once shared a room. The top bunk remained empty since his youngest son, Monte, was killed when a tree splintered as it fell and kicked back, striking Monte's chest and head. He had lingered for a few days but passed away from his internal injuries two years before. A white cross at the top of the meadow indicated his gravesite. The two boys were as different as salt and vinegar. Jasper was the oldest at twenty-nine, tall, thin, blond hair that fell like glue on his head straight down without a single hint of a wave or curl. His blue eyes were bright and handsome, but the boy never smiled and seldom said anything. What he did say was pointed, sharp and direct.

Monte, on the other hand, was twenty-five when he passed. He was a quick-witted and verbal young man whether you wanted to hear him or not. Unlike Jasper, Monte liked being around people and was engaged to a proper young lady named Nancy Culpepper, whose parents owned the C & A Culpepper Grocery Store on Main Street. It was a tragic loss to lose such a bright and fun-loving young man. It was still a loss deeply felt by both Oliver and Jasper.

Mornings were quiet in the Rohloff home. Oliver wasn't a talkative man and Jasper took after his father in many ways, including the idea that if there was nothing to say, then there was simply nothing to say.

Oliver fried some eggs from the chicken coop and a slab of elk he had canned in a mason jar the summer before. Their survival depended upon their chickens, garden, and wild game, including fish and crawdads from the river. Oliver flipped the meat in a frying pan. His heart was heavy this morning. "Monte would be twenty-seven today," Oliver stated without taking his doleful eyes off the stove top where a smaller cast iron pan fried the eggs.

Jasper didn't look up from his bent-over position, tying his boot laces to begin another day of working the mine. "Yep."

"He would have been married by now. Probably had a kid or two," Oliver reflected. "I suppose those are the only grandkids I'd ever have."

"Yep." Jasper answered in agreement.

"Maybe you should track down Nancy and see if she's still available. She was a nice young lady."

Jasper turned his head to look at his father with a stunned expression. "She couldn't cook. Monte told me she was going to college to learn to cook. I don't know if she ever did learn. You can teach a dog to fetch a dead duck or tree a coon, but you can't teach a woman to cook if she's eighteen and hasn't learned yet. That's what Monte told me anyway. She was going to a special kind of school to learn to cook." He switched legs to tie his other boot. "I don't know what's so hard about throwing food onto a pan."

A slight smile grew on Oliver's lips. He missed the humor and quick wit of his second-born son. "I think Monte was jesting with you. Nancy was a fine cook, from what I understood."

"I don't think so. Besides, she wouldn't have the strength to shovel rock or push a wheelbarrow," Jasper said. He put on his coat and pulled his Henry bolt action rifle from a rack on the wall. "I saw bear tracks on the other side of the knoll last night. I set a trap. I'll be at the mine in an hour or two, depending on if I caught it or not."

Oliver frowned as Jasper walked out into the early morning air. The young man loved to hunt, fish and provide, but Oliver doubted Jasper would ever have a family to provide for. He seemed oblivious of the idea of romance or courting a woman. Oliver wasn't a romantic himself, but he had made the mistake of marrying a woman that he would regret marrying for seventeen years of his life. She hated being poor, she hated being a mother and she hated her husband the most. It was no great loss when his wife wanted a divorce and moved back to her father's ranch. It merely meant a more peaceful home, but they had to cook and wash their own clothes since then. It had been nearly twelve years and Oliver hadn't missed her. It had been that long since he mentioned her name. She wasn't aware of Monte's death, and Oliver wasn't going to spend a penny to notify her. If she cared, she would have tried at least once in twelve years to communicate with her sons. She knew where they were; Oliver had written to her father's ranch to tell her, just in case she ever wanted to write to her boys. She hadn't.

Oliver figured that might have something to do with Jasper's reluctance to court some of the young ladies in the community. It was too bad, but Oliver was pretty sure the Rohloff name would end with Jasper.

Oliver finished cooking his breakfast and furrowed his brow when he heard a chicken squawking on the side of the cabin. It wasn't the usual clucking of the chickens that roamed around the cabin but a painful squawking. Foxes, coyotes, bobcats and other predators were a constant burden that took a while to trap and kill enough of to leave their chickens alone. He left the table and opened the door and was startled to see Jeff Blackburn and his marshals standing at the door, ready to knock with his knuckles raised.

"Can we come in?" Jeff asked. He didn't wait for an answer and entered the cabin, followed by his men. One of whom, a young man with reddened eyes, held a chicken in his arms. He smiled arrogantly and snapped the chicken's neck by grabbing its head and twirling its body in a circle. A few hard rotations and the body flew onto the floor and flopped around headless for a bit. The man chuckled, humored by it.

"What do you want?" Oliver asked uneasily. His

old dog had passed away about a month before, but he wished he had gotten another so he would have known the men were on his property. One of the marshals closed the door after coming inside with a slight grin as he watched the chicken's body flop around.

Jeff put an arm around Oliver's shoulders and escorted him to the table. "Sit down. We haven't been properly introduced. My name is Jeff Blackburn, and these are my marshals. Mister Rohloff, I'm offering you a chance to settle the issue with William Slater." He stayed behind Oliver with his big hands firmly placed on Oliver's shoulders, pressing downward.

"There is nothing to settle," Oliver exclaimed uneasily.

Jeff stepped aside to allow Ed Bostwick to take his place behind Oliver. Jeff moved the other chair closer to Oliver and sat. He removed the breakfast plate from in front of Oliver and slid it down the table. Jimmy Abbot picked it up and started eating.

Jeff pulled a two-paged offer from his inside coat pocket, unfolded it, and laid it on the table in front of Oliver. One of the marshals set a bottle of ink and a quill pen next to the paper. Jeff spoke, "You'll be saving all of us a whole lot of trouble if you just read and sign." It was already predated for the day before.

"I'm not signing anything until my lawyer says to! You can tell William to take this and shove it up..."

Ed Bostwick, standing behind Oliver, grabbed

him by the chin and brought a knife to his throat. "Sign the paper!" he snapped.

"Ed, put the knife away," Jeff said calmly. "Mister Rohloff won't be convinced to sign papers that way. Old men don't value their lives quite like a young man does. Toby, take Wes and Jimmy and follow Mister Rohloff's son that walked up the hill. Take your rifles and put a bullet in his legs so he can't walk. If you hear me fire off one shot, come back. If I shoot twice, kill Mister Rohloff's son and leave him out there for the crows and vultures."

"Okay, boss. Wes, Jimmy, let's go," Toby said obediently.

Oliver sputtered, "Please, don't hurt my son!" he pleaded at Jeff frantically. He knew Jasper had his rifle and was a good shot while killing wild game, but against three experienced gunmen with rifles, he knew Jasper would have no chance against them. "Promise me you won't hurt my son if I sign this. I can't read, so please, just tell me what it says, so I know."

Jeff tapped the paperwork with a heavy finger. "It says sign your name at the two x's and we'll leave."

Henry Dodds pulled his revolver and pointed it at Oliver with a scowl on his face. "Just sign it!" he shouted. He and the others had not gotten any sleep after spending some time with Patsy Jane. Henry was exhausted and in a foul mood. The day was already going to be long, and it irritated him all the more, knowing the day was just beginning.

"Will you read it to me, so I know what I'm signing?" Oliver asked sharply.

"Do you want us to wait or not?" Toby Stearns asked Jeff about following Jasper.

Jeff was already upset with Toby for keeping his men up all night indulging in childish things that were assuredly going to get Matt Bannister's attention. It was the last thing they needed on the day William Slater wanted the Rohloffs dead to stop the threat of future lawsuits. Jeff would not risk his future retirement by giving the twenty thousand dollars in cash money to the old man seated in front of him. "Hold on a minute," he answered Toby. "Mister Rohloff, this is your last chance. Sign the papers, or your son is going to be hurt at the very least."

"Tell me what the papers say!" Oliver shouted. He flipped to the second page and saw the numbers for twenty thousand dollars. "Is this an offer to buy my mine? Tell me that much, at least!"

Ed Bostwick spoke from behind him, "It is, Mister Rohloff. They're offering you twenty thousand in paper money right now to sign that paper, pack up and leave the area. That is what the offer says. Show him the money, boss."

Jeff bit his bottom lip irritably. He had no intention of mentioning the money, let alone showing it to motivate the old man. He would have a private conversation with Ed a bit later. Jeff reached into his coat pocket and pulled out a thick wad of rolled-up money held tight with a pair of rubber bands. "Twenty thousand dollars could be yours. But you better sign your name."

Oliver's bottom lip shook with emotion. Everything he worked for was being taken away from him for pennies on the dollar. "What if I refuse?"

"Just sign the thing!" Henry Dodds shouted. He wanted nothing more than to go back to the hotel and get some sleep.

Jeff answered Oliver's question softly, "You should already know that answer. You don't have a choice."

Oliver closed his eyes and took a deep breath. "Once I sign this, you're going to kill me anyway, aren't you?" He stared into Jeff's eyes and could see the answer for himself.

Ed Bostwick answered before Jeff could speak, "Once you sign that paper, you give up all rights to the mine and there would be no reason to kill you or your son. But I can't promise what these boys will do if you don't."

Oliver's hand shook, but he reached for the quill and dipped it in the ink bottle. He slowly signed his name on both lines marked with an X. He laid the quill down. "It's signed."

Jeff picked up the papers and blew on the ink to dry it. "Thank you. I would appreciate it if you would follow these men down to the mine. I need you to show Henry and the boys around Mister Slater's new claim."

Oliver did not miss Jeff putting the wad of money back in his pocket. The feeling of dread flowed through him, and he knew he would never make the walk back up to his house from the mine. His breathing quickened and his mind flashed through so many memories of his youth, his parents and siblings, and courting his bride-to-be. It had nothing to do with how foolish he was, but purely nostalgic and a longing to do it all again. The birth of his boys and the years of raising them came to mind and brought a mist to his aged blue eyes. His life had been difficult and rare of smiles, but now at the end, he wished he had spent more time enjoying the life he was given. His lifetime of work and the gold discovered in his ground meant nothing now. He was thankful to the Lord for Jasper going to check his bear trap when he did. "Can I ask one thing before I go? Will you let my son live? Please? Keep the money. All I ask is just leave Jasper be."

Ed patted Oliver's shoulder. "No one's going to die. Let's go see that mine."

Jeff glanced at Henry Dodds with a nod of his head. "Make it look like an accident."

"What about my son?" Oliver gasped.

Jeff clasped his fingers together as he rested his hands on his stomach and cast a thoughtful glance at Oliver. "I'm a fair man. We'll leave it up to fate. If your boy doesn't come back while we're here, he'll be fine. But if he returns while we're here, well, there won't be any witnesses. You have my word on that. I hate to mention it, but the longer you sit here, the greater the chances he'll return. Or one of your employees."

Oliver stood on quivering legs. "Let's go."

Ed Bostwick narrowed his brow with a troubled expression. "We were hired to get him to sign that contract, and he did. I read the offer; it protects the Slaters from a lawsuit. There is no reason to kill him." Ed was a former U.S. Deputy Marshal and knew a bit about contracts and the law.

Jeff bit his bottom lip irritably. "Henry, take the boys and escort Mister Rohloff to the river. Ed, you and I need to talk in private. Sit down."

\*\*\*

An hour later, David Ferry and Ben Macken crossed the bridge to begin their day at the mine. With alarm, they discovered the body of Oliver eight feet below the bridge lying face down along the edge of the river on the river rock in three inches of water. Blood from an open head wound faded into the moving water.

"Jasper!" Ben yelled. He had seen Jasper walk down the hill to the house moments before. "Jasper, come quick! Your Pa!"

They pulled Oliver's body to the bank just as Jasper arrived. He knelt beside his father. "What happened?" he asked the two men. He could see the bruising and a gash on Oliver's head.

"He must have fallen off the bridge. He was on the rocks over there. You can still see some blood where his head hit."

"We need to get the marshal," David Ferry offered, not knowing what to do.

Jasper stared at his father as a wave of a rare liquid filled his eyes. "What's the marshal going to do? An accident is an accident." He closed his eyes and took a few deep breaths to control his emotions. "David, go get a wheelbarrow and some shovels.

We'll bury him beside Monte."

"Don't you want to have a funeral or something? I mean, aren't we supposed to tell someone?" David asked with a sense of panic. He could not believe his boss was dead.

"What's to tell?" Jasper asked. "There's nothing anyone can do, except for us, and that's burying him." He stood and removed his hat before turning away to hide his eyes. "If you would take him up to Monte's grave. I'll be there shortly to show you where to start digging." Jasper quickly walked downstream and sat on a large boulder to be alone.

"Aren't we supposed to tell someone?" David asked Ben.

Ben shrugged. "I don't know. Let's just do as Jasper says."

# Chapter 26

Deputy Mark Thiesen was the youngest deputy sheriff at twenty-five years old. He was a handsome young man with a clean-shaven square face and light brown hair cut neatly and combed to the side. His soft blue eyes and youthful looks occasionally invited some teasing about his chosen career path, but when it came to drawing the truth out of people, especially women, no one was more inviting because, beyond his handsome face, he also cared.

Patsy Jane had been beaten up and was afraid of anyone wearing a badge. She had never met Matt Bannister, but she had heard he was a nice man. She had heard wrong. He was an unusually cruel man that took pleasure in hurting her. His deputies were no better. She had been a prostitute for years and was abused, raped and forced to do many things, but she was never treated as brutally. Who could she tell, the young man in front of her? He wore a badge and the sweet face of a young man that was only a cover for a bed of nails. She could trust no one and it was best to recover alone, and hope Matt Bannister and his deputies didn't return. They would if she said a word, they promised her. Patsy Jane sat on a comfortable padded chair with a trembling lip and breathing shallow quick breaths as she held a wet cloth to a cut just below her swollen black and blue eye. The rag went back and forth from the cut below the eye to the swollen and split lip. Other areas hurt worse, but her face was what wasn't concealed below her clothing. She avoided the soft blue eyes of the young man that knelt in front of her.

"Miss, who hurt you?" Mark asked softly. "We can arrest them and make sure nothing happens to you again." She had stated four men had forced their way in and raped her, beat her and left early that morning. She knew who they were, but she was refusing to say.

She shook her head silently while her face scrunched together as she began to cry. "Just go away. There's nothing you can do."

Mark waited patiently. "Maybe I can't do anything, but I'd sure like to help in any way I can. I can talk to the sheriff or Matt..."

Her eyes aligned with his quickly as she reached for his wrist urgently. "No! Don't talk to him! I don't want him coming back. Please, don't tell him. Just go and forget about me!" she pleaded with terror in her eyes. "Please, don't tell him you came here!"

His brow lowered curiously. "Miss, are you saying it was Matt?"

She nodded quickly and covered her sore mouth and split lip with her rag. "Please, just go."

\*\*\*

John Painter had been woken up rudely with a glass of water thrown on him by Matt Bannister. He was in the city jail, but he couldn't remember how he got there or why he was naked, with a red arrow painted on his chest. He figured he passed out from too much whiskey, which his new friends supplied plenty of. He didn't remember a whole lot else after leaving the saloon.

He did remember breaking into his father's church and stealing the money, which he discovered was why he was arrested. What he did not remember too clearly, other than a few blurred memories of being cold and perhaps some laughter from blurred faces in the lantern light, was being tied to a large X in front of the church. His new pals obviously had some fun at his expense after he passed out. It was humiliating, but he found a strange humor in it. John refused to tell Matt who he was with. He didn't know what kind of trouble they could be in if he squealed like a kicked pig, but John had few friends and his new ones had treated him well as far as alcohol and laughter went. He could only imagine how horrified his father and mother must have been to see his hairy nude body spread-eagled in front of the church. John found it relatively humorous. A part of him wished he had the manpower and resources to do something of the kind to his passed-out pals in the past.

John shook his head with a grin. "I'll bet my Pa was not happy about that." He chuckled despite the growing headache.

Matt sat in a wooden chair in front from the bunkbeds of the city jail. "No. He wasn't happy about that. Reverend Painter is an amazing man with a gift for teaching the Bible. He loves doing it and everyone loves him. Because of you, your father wants to quit his God chosen path. I have a father I wasn't proud of for a long time, but I hope I never find myself in a position of being ashamed of my son."

John's eyes transformed from humor to agitation. "What do I care what my father thinks?"

"You don't!" Matt snapped with widened eyes. "So why are you here? Why did you come back?"

"To see my folks."

"Why? You don't care about them, so why would you come back here?"

"What's it matter to you?" John asked sharply.

Matt leaned forward and peered intensely into John's eyes. "Because I care about them! I don't appreciate you coming back here and humiliating them with your stupidity. Do you want to be a bum? Go to Portland and be a bum. I'm sure you'll get more change for a drink there. But don't think you can stay around here and bum off your parents or anyone in the congregation because I promise you, they aren't going to help you. You owe me ten dollars and lucky for you, I know how you can pay it back."

John grinned defiantly. "Oh? How?"

"Hard work. You get a choice, work eight hours a day for ten days at the granite quarry for a dollar a day to pay me back. And then work for another sixty days to pay the church back while you stay in my jail. I'll be honest; this is a luxury hotel compared to my jail. Or you can stay here and go to trial and face three to five years in the state prison. The choice is yours."

"That's seventy days!" John shouted.

"Do you think robbery is a minor thing around here? You didn't steal a muffin from the bakery. You broke into your own father's church and stole the offerings and tithes given by hard-working citizens to the Lord. You're a piece of crap thief that would steal from your family and a church. How much lower can a man go? I have no empathy or mercy for you. You cannot be trusted, period. I heard you left here as a great kid with a world of potential. But now I have to ask, do you ever look in the mirror and question what kind of a man you have become? Honestly, do you ever think you could be a better man? Is this what God had planned for you, John? A beggar?"

John's eyes hardened. He raised his voice, "Who do you think you are to question me about anything? Huh?"

"I'm one of the people whose money you stole.

I'm a lawman and your parents' friend. Does that answer your question?"

"No," he answered with a scowl.

"I didn't think it would. I don't think you can see beyond your reflection and somehow, you think it looks good. I think you're a complete asinine fool. You have parents that love you and a community that would stand behind you if you tried to change your life. But I think even after they gave you their last dollar, you'd piss on all of them. I don't think you'd care if your parents lost their home trying to help you. You'd siphon their last dime away and wouldn't care less. I don't think there is any help for you, so I won't even try. But you will work what you owe the church and me off or enjoy your long stay in the Oregon State Penitentiary. Personally, I don't care which."

"Do you think my father is going to press charges against me?" John asked with a hint of a defiant grin.

"He already has. And yes, I believe he'll see it through. You're not a child or his responsibility. You're a thirty-year-old man with hands and feet of your own. He's tired of holding your hand and so is your mother. They're done, and they're not going to save you. You can thank me for that."

"You're not the judge."

Matt smiled just a touch. "That's true." He stood up to leave. "But Judge Jacoby likes thieves as much as I do. I'd accept the offer if I were you because it's the only one you'll get. You see, this is a pretrial agreement. If you refuse, you go to trial and a jury will convict you. If you accept the offer and try to run, I'll find you and you'll face a longer prison sentence. The choice is yours."

"I'm engaged! How's that for trying to change my life, huh?" John shouted. He turned towards Sheriff Tim Wright. "Did you send anyone to get my fiancée? She doesn't know where I am!"

"Yes, Deputy Thiesen went to notify her. I'd listen to Matt if I were you."

John added hurriedly to Matt, "I'm getting married!"

Matt shrugged uncaringly. "Great. Maybe she'll wait for you to complete your seventy days. Understand it's seventy *workdays*," Matt emphasized.

"Where is your Christian charity, huh? I thought all you Christians were supposed to be forgiving and full of mercy and grace. I should've known you're all a bunch of hypocrites! You know that's why I quit going to church. All of you hypocrites!"

Matt slowly grinned. "So, you quit going to church and gave up on the Lord because of us hypocrites? Is that right?"

"Yeah. You all think you are so high and mighty."

"I have a question for you. What do we hypocrites have to do between you and the Lord?" Matt asked.

"What?"

"You heard me. What do I have to do with your relationship with the Lord? How do I interfere in that relationship you have with God? The whole principle of Christianity is having a personal relationship with Jesus. That means it's a relationship between you and Jesus. How do I, and my relationship with Jesus, interfere with yours? At the judgment seat, are you going to point at me and say, 'Matt was a hypocrite, so I refused to serve you, Jesus'? Is that how it's going to work?" Matt chuckled. "Good luck with that."

"My relationship with the Lord is none of your business!" John snapped.

"That is kind of my point. If your relationship with Jesus is none of my business, then why are you blaming me and others for your not being a Christian? Our lives are none of your business. It's supposed to be a relationship between you and God. A direct line that no one else can interfere with, right? What someone else does or how they are or what you may think is hypocritical is between them and God. You don't know what they may be dealing with or struggling with. You have no idea what their weakness might be or if they're just having a bad day. You ought to know not one person is perfect and we all fail from time to time, and the last time probably won't be the last time, after all. If you're looking for perfection and the perfect church with the perfect congregation, it's in heaven and nowhere else. For now, hurting people, struggling people, and non-perfect people who love the Lord come to church. If you're too good for them and think you're the perfect Christian, then please show us. Undoubtedly someone will think you're a hypocrite and point out your weaknesses or something they disagree with. Personally, I just shrug and say, that's between them and the Lord. Do understand; the Lord works from the inside out, not the outside in. So, what you see isn't always as hypocritical as you may judge it to be."

Matt paused. "But it is very hypocritical to cast judgment on someone else for the same struggles and sins that you do and use that as your excuse for not serving the Lord. Because some day, when you and I stand before the Lord, that excuse isn't going to work. Anyway, you have until the end of today to make a decision. Go to prison or start working on Monday. Just like becoming a Christian, that choice is yours to make." Matt carried the wooden chair out of the jail cell and closed the door before turning the key to lock it.

Mark Theisen entered the office. "Tim, we have a…" he paused when he saw Matt standing near in the jail cells.

"We have a what?" Tim asked. "Did you notify the unlucky fiancée that her husband to be, is in our jail?"

Mark nodded awkwardly. "I did." His eyes glanced nervously at Matt. He spoke slowly, "She was attacked last night in her room and violated. She says it was Matt." He pointed a slight wave to Matt.

"What?" Tim gasped.

"Who?" Matt asked.

Mark continued, "She was beaten up pretty bad.

She was terrified when I mentioned Matt's name. She begged me not to say anything."

Matt was taken off guard. "Who?"

"Who was attacked? Patsy Jane?" John demanded to know.

"Your fiancée," Tim answered. He looked at Matt with a stunned expression, surprised by the accusation. "Why would she say it was you?"

"You touched my wife! I'll kill you!" John shouted and raced to the iron bars of the jail to get a hold of Matt through the bars. He latched onto Matt's shirt and tried to jerk Matt into the bars, but it merely ripped Matt's shirt as Matt turned his body into John's extended arm and stepped forward to pry the extended arm against the iron bar breaking the clutched fist of material and forcing John's shoulder and face into the bars by the pressure.

Matt turned to hold John's arm between his ribs and over hooked his left arm. "John, I don't know who your wife is or what Mark is talking about. I understand you are upset, but it wasn't me." He let John's arm go. "Mark, what are you talking about?"

\*\*\*

Matt went back to the Monarch Hotel with Mark Thiessen, but Patsy Jane refused to answer the door once Mark identified himself. She didn't want to talk to him again. Wanting answers, Matt called upon Pamela Collins to unlock the door without Patsy Jane's permission, and they entered.

Patsy panicked, had backed into a corner and held a small knife in her hands while she shook in terror. "Stay away! You have no right to come in here."

Mark spoke with raised palms to calm her down. "Miss, we're not here to hurt you. We just want to talk and find out who did this to you."

Matt closed the door and asked Pamela to stay in the room with them to comfort Patsy Jane. He spoke gently, "Miss, please, sit down." Matt sat down on the davenport. "Do you know who I am?"

She shook her head frantically, skeptical of Mark and him.

"You don't know who I am?"

She remained in the corner and shook her head again.

"Miss, I am Matt Bannister."

She paused and furrowed her brow as she studied his face. "No, you're not," she answered meekly.

Mark spoke, "Patsy Jane, this is Matt Bannister."

Patsy Jane's frightened and unsure eyes reached out to Pamela questionably.

Pamela reassured her, "Miss Ohlund, I've known Matt for a long time, and this is the real Matt Bannister. You're safe now."

Matt spoke gently, "Please have a seat. Mark nor I are here to hurt you. What I do want is for you to tell me why you said it was me?"

Pamela approached Patsy Jane and gently put her arm around Patsy's shoulders to lead her to the cushioned chair. "It's okay. Matt is here to help. I know him and you are safe. Please, sit and relax. Can I get you anything at all? Some food? Something to drink?"

Patsy looked at her with appreciative eyes. "I haven't left the room and I'm starving. Those men were here, and I don't want to leave."

"I'll be back with some food for you."

Matt asked, "What did those men look like? What did they say?"

A little more relaxed and recognizing that Matt was not one of the men that attacked her, nor were any of the men Matt's deputies, she told him what had happened and what they said. Patsy Jane did her best to describe the men and wept a good portion of the way through what they had done to her.

When Pamela returned with a platter of food, Matt said, "Pamela, we need to change Miss Patsy Jane's room number. Put her in another room and let her stay here for a few days to heal and make other plans. I want her meals brought to her room from now on. No charge." He wasn't the hotel owner nor had any authority over Pamela, who was the hotel's assistant manager. However, he was Lee's brother and a U.S. Marshal, and no one argued with his authority.

"Of course," Pamela agreed. "Right after you finish eating, how about I take you to the bath so you can clean up. We'll move your things to another room while you bathe and then you can get some sleep."

"I'd like that. Matt, what about John?"

What Patsy had told him was disturbing. Matt had not said so, but he knew who the men were. The identifying feature of an ugly scar at the base of one man's hairline who had identified himself as Truet left no doubt that it was Wes Wasson. Despite the sickening feeling in his stomach, a tug of a smile pulled at the corners of his lips. "John's going to either work or prison. It's up to him. I'll know this afternoon when he decides." He paused. "Miss Patsy, I can't arrest those men unless you file charges. But I'll be honest; even if you do, they'd probably be released because the District Attorney wouldn't charge them. The reason why has nothing to do with you, as much as it does with their being friends with our faithful district attorney."

She was troubled. "You know who those men are?"

He nodded slowly. "I do." He paused. "I would love to throw them in jail and see them sent to prison for what they have done to you. But after I arrest them, it's out of my hands and I can tell you right now, they'd be free by closing time."

"Who are they?"

"Four of the Blackburn Marshals. Three are staying here in the hotel and one lives across town."

"Here?" Patsy exclaimed with a panic in her voice.

Matt answered calmly, "That's why we are changing your room and I want your food brought to you. Pamela will be the link between you and me or for anything else you need. If you want to see John, I'll walk you to him or one of my deputies will. For now, you rest." He stood and warned Pamela, "You need to keep a watch on your female employees. If you have any trouble, let me know immediately and I don't care what time it is." He exhaled. "I wish William was here."

Pamela agreed. "It figures he'd take time off when there's actually some work to do."

Matt chuckled. "It sounds like you know him." He listened as a strange sound grew faintly from outside. "What's that?"

# Chapter 27

Joe Thorn led a loud caravan of strikers into town. They carried empty metal buckets of various sizes, steel rock drills of different lengths, two-pound sledgehammers, which they beat on the buckets, pails and steel barrels, creating an annoying racket. Two wagons lumbered behind the crowd with an upright large iron plate supported by a solidly-built wooden frame in the center of the wagon beds. The two iron plates were about a quarter-inch thick and four-square feet with bolt holes along the four sides where they had been stolen from inside the stamp mill. Two men, one on each side of the iron plates, repeatedly slammed their sledgehammers into the plate. Together the four men pounding on the iron plates created a loud clanging of steel that could bring on a migraine headache in a short time with the ringing of the metal. Fifty or sixty others pounded their hammers or rock drills against metal containers to increase the noise level. The noise was a loud, high-pitched clanging, ringing and constant banging with no rhythm or a moment's worth of silence. Shouting and curses were directed at the W.R. Slater Mining Company office building, where they assembled and beat on their iron on iron make-shift drums.

Several wives and children joined them with cotton plugging their ears that carried painted wooden signs stating such words as, *strike*, *don't tread on us*, *rights to the workers*, and *we'll stop when Slater stops*.

Joe Thorn and others were angered by what had happened at Richie Thorn's cabin and wanted to strike back. However, they knew the risk of using violence and guns would lead to another miner's death from the hired gunmen the Slaters hired. Some things are worth dying for, but Henrietta Hendricks, the wife of Walter Hendricks, who had broken his hip in the mine disaster, convinced them that violence would be met with violence. It was best to protest peacefully, non-violently, but hound William Slater with the most annoying noise in the world day and night until he relented and ended the strike.

The idea became a full day's work of planning, making signs, and stealing two panels off a hopper in the stamp mill. The men knew the hired guards were guarding the mine, so they approached Ron Dalton with their idea, and he was happy to help by keeping the guards busy at the other end of the mine property while Joe and others unbolted the two panels and carried them and some heavy lumber to a waiting wagon on the main road. They had spent the day before building the heavy frames to hold the plates upright. The planning and work would be for nothing if a single man carried a weapon or caused a fight. Rules had to be made and agreed upon. Noise and persistence would be their weapon of choice to end the strike. Not one man carried a weapon other than perhaps a small knife.

Every man that worked in the mine as a rock driller took a five-minute turn swinging their eight-pound hammer to hit the iron plates at a constant pace of about twenty hits a minute to keep the continuous ringing of the hammers going. Like in the mine, the men switched places to rest every five minutes. Their ears filled with compressed cotton; the hammers swung just like they would in the mine to drive a drill into the face of the rock. With one man hammering on both sides of the iron plate while standing on makeshift scaffolding to create more room to get a full swing, it was necessary to use heavy beams, iron brackets, wedges and bolts. Carpenters, millwrights, blacksmiths and just anyone with a skill or knowledge jumped in to help design a solid frame and scaffolding to make it work. The men worked together as their livelihood depended on it because it did.

Matt covered ears while his eyes scanned the strikers for weapons or any sign of pending violence. The only thing he could detect was the miners' sense of determination and satisfaction to be as loud and annoying as they possibly could. Matt stood in the middle of the street outside of Slater's office, watching. He was soon joined by the city sheriff, Tim Wright, and his deputies.

"Matt," Tim shouted over the noise, "Can I get your help to shut these people up?"

Matt shook his head. He hollered, "They have the right to protest and that is what they are doing."

"It's disturbing the peace!" Tim yelled with annoyance.

"Let's just be glad it's peaceful so far. They're staying on the public street. There's nothing you can do about it, except maybe cover your ears because they're sure not musicians." Matt grinned.

"William Slater is going to demand we shut them up," Tim stated with a worried expression on his face.

Matt shrugged. "He can end it anytime he wants to. Read the signs."

Tim rolled his eyes. "You don't know William Slater the way I do. He won't put up with this."

"He's going to have to because I'm not going to interfere unless it turns violent. But I am going to watch and see what happens," he hollered.

Deputy Bob Ewing held his index finger in his right ear. "We'll go deaf if they don't stop! That ringing hurts my ear."

"Then go back to your office, Bob," Matt replied.

Suddenly, at the wave of Joe Thorn's hands to get the striker's attention, the pounding came to a stop and silence had never been more noticeable. Joe stood on a wagon's bench seat and shouted to William Slater through cupped hands, "William Slater, we're going to do this day and night until you agree to meet our demands! We'll follow you home and pound that steel all night long. We have three shifts in the mine, and we have three shifts here. If you hope we'll get tired and stop, I'll remind you we do this all day, every day. So, when you're ready to meet our demands, we're ready to go back to work! Until then, just try to work, eat and sleep! Pound those hammers, men!"

\*\*\*

Jasper Rohloff had buried his father and sent his two employees home with instructions to work tomorrow. He couldn't understand how his father had fallen off the bridge. He had walked across it a thousand times and never once came close to the edge. Jasper didn't know what to do now other than keep working the mine. He didn't mind the work, it was hard, but he enjoyed it. He could go home and sit in his house and mourn for his father, but he was still in shock and felt numb. He didn't feel like working or sitting alone. He didn't have any friends to speak of, but the urge to talk to someone nagged at him.

Jasper didn't mind working in the mine, but he didn't want to make the decisions that his father did or worry about numbers or paying this and that. He just liked to do his day's work and go home to fish or hunt, trap or whatever he wanted to do. He didn't want the responsibility of being the owner, which he supposedly now was.

He sat on the ground beside the wooden cross

he had nailed together for a grave marker for his father, just to the left of his brother's grave. He gazed over the river, cliff and mine that his father had built along the river's edge. It was all his now, but it felt empty without his father's presence beside him. He just sat with a numbness that reached deep within him for a few hours. Thinking was a time-consuming occupation when one had nothing else to do. He was alone now with no one else in the world to think about but himself. There was always work to do, a bear to kill, and before long, the salmon would begin to spawn in the river. He hadn't checked his crawdad trap yet today. Usually, he brought it to the house at lunchtime to fry the tail meat in butter for lunch. He'd save the crawdads for dinner that evening.

There was gold on his property, but he did not have the resources to reach it. He had disagreed with his father; it was better to let the Slater's mine it and take a percentage than to hope for riches and labor for it. It was not a tough decision considering that he didn't want the responsibility of owning a mine to see if the Slater's would buy their mine and perhaps hire him and his two employees to keep working it. The only thing Jasper wanted was to own his property still, but not the mine itself.

He patted the fresh dirt of his father's grave. "I never said it, Pa. I don't think once." His eyes clouded with rare tears. He took a deep breath and nodded emotionally with tightened lips. "Love you," he said lightly. He stood and walked past his cabin to the road and walked past the Slater Silver Mine without hearing the steady pounding of the stamp mill. The silence was uncanny, but the closer he got to town, he could hear the noise and then covered his ears with annoyance as he walked to the front door of the W.R. Slater Mining office. He went inside and there was no one behind the counter to greet him.

\*\*\*

William Slater sat behind his desk with a snarl on his thin lips. The strikers had interrupted his afternoon in a way that he never expected. It was too noisy to do any work and all his office employees had moved upstairs to the conference room for their safety just in case the strikers broke into the office. William remained downstairs in his office with his son, Josh, and Jeff Blackburn.

Jeff had given William the signed bill of sale for the mining rights of the Rohloff mine and property. The news that Oliver Rohloff wouldn't be a threat was a significant relief off William's chest. He was afraid of being sued, but that threat had been extinguished like a wasp nest in a carriage door. The news put a bit of warm sunshine on his day and was well worth the money spent. It was an investment that paid a thousand-fold on the dollar. His morning couldn't get any brighter until his employees showed up with a caravan of pots, pans, buckets and pounded on them like a five-year-old child beating on his mother's cooking pot. William peeked outside and questioned where the men had stolen the iron panels. There was no doubt the heavy iron plates came from some piece of equipment that he paid for and most likely would have to replace. It angered him while the ear-piercing pounding was beginning to give William a headache.

"Where is the marshal? Where are Tim and Matt? Why haven't they stopped this?" William shouted. He cast a harsh glance at Jeff. "Go out there and shoot one of them. That'll make them stop!"

The noise suddenly stopped.

William sighed. "Thank goodness."

Jeff Blackburn spoke, "I glanced outside and…"

"Shh!" William hushed him to hear what Joe Thorn was yelling.

Joe's voice was just loud enough to be heard in his back office with the door closed, "William Slater, we're going to do this day and night until you agree to meet our demands! We'll follow you home and beat that steel all night long. We have three shifts in the mine, and we have three shifts here. If you hope we'll get tired and stop, I'll remind you we do this all day, every day. So, when you're ready to meet our demands, we're ready to go back to work! Until then, just try to work, eat and sleep! Pound those hammers, men!"

The annoying pounding began again.

William cursed. "What were you saying?" he asked Jeff bitterly.

"I was saying I looked outside, and the sheriff and Matt are standing on the street watching them. None of my men will do a thing with them there."

William ordered Josh impatiently. "Go fetch Tim

and Matt. Tell them to get in here! Jeff, go with him to keep my son safe."

Tim Wright and Matt followed the two men into William's office minutes later. William was not cordial. "Why haven't you two stopped this? I've heard you both were standing out there gawking at them! You must have heard what they said? Now go out there and tell them to leave town before I have them shot!"

Tim Wright nervously stuttered, "I..."

Matt spoke over Tim, "There's nothing Tim or I can do legally. They are protesting and have that right as long as they remain peaceful. They are not on your property and haven't done anything wrong. I'm afraid you're just going to have to endure them."

"What?" William shouted. "We have noise ordinances. Arrest them for disturbing the peace. Do something! We do have city ordinances."

Matt shrugged helplessly. "And if it was after nine at night, we could make them stop. But there are no city ordinances for being quiet during the daylight hours. And to make matters worse, I studied the city limits carefully to know where my jurisdiction ends and where Tim's begins. The city limits end on Lincoln Street, which means all of you folks that live on King's Point, are not technically within the city limits. Which means your strikers can follow you home and there is nothing Tim or I can do about it, even after nine tonight. Because the county has no noise ordinances."

William cursed. "You've got to be kidding me! How in the hell can this be legal? Look, you two had better do something to stop them or I'll have Jeff have his boys do it! And by George, they will get that racket stopped." He slammed his fist down onto his desk angrily. "What good are you two if you can't do what needs to be done? Did I waste my money and time investing in you two incompetent fools?"

Matt's eyes narrowed. "First of all, Jeff Blackburn has no authority to tell those men out there to do anything. If any of the Blackburn Marshals cause a bit of trouble, they will be arrested. I know you have Jackson Weathers in your pocket and he'll neglect any charges, but I'll be contacting the governor about that. So go ahead and have Jeff and his goons start trouble because they will be squaring off against my deputies and me." He moved his attention to Jeff. "If you want that, we'll be outside."

Jeff shook his head slowly. "I told you, Matt, we didn't come here to cause trouble."

Matt's eyes hardened. "Trouble's already been caused. John Painter was strung up in front of his father's church, naked, I might add. And his fiancée was assaulted in her hotel room by four of your men. Of course, I didn't bother to arrest them because I already know our district attorney wouldn't charge them. But that doesn't mean this is over."

"That sounds like a bit of a threat, Marshal," Jeff said calmly.

"A warning, perhaps. I won't let four jackasses pretend they're my deputies and me while assaulting a woman and get away with it. If the court of law is too afraid to bring some justice, then I will."

He turned to William. "I am petitioning the governor to remove Jackson as the district attorney. And I'm watching Judge Jacoby, just so you know."

"That's a court matter. I have nothing to do with them or the courts. I'm a business owner, not a lawyer. Do what you got to do, but I want those idiots outside stopped," William demanded.

"You can want, but there's nothing we can do until nine tonight. If you want them stopped, negotiate with them and end the strike. But just so you know, and you ought to know, you sure as hell don't own me and you don't own Tim. Don't sit here and pretend that you do."

William shouted, "I can't think with all that racket! My people can't work, and I have a lot to do. Please, go tell them to stop! Tell them they're breaking a sound ordinance or disturbing the peace! Certainly, there is something you can do!"

"Not until nine tonight."

"So what are you going to do? Just let everyone in town suffer?" William asked with a shout.

Matt shrugged helplessly. "That's on you."

There was a loud knock on the door, and it opened.

"Who said you could enter?" William yelled and paused when he saw Jasper Rohloff enter the office. He scowled as he closed the door behind him. He stood by Matt and Tim uneasily.

"Jasper," William said with surprise. "What are you doing here?"

Jeff Blackburn turned his head with interest.

"I came by to tell you my Pa is dead."

There was a short moment of silence except for the loud banging from outside. It was non-relenting and maddening.

"What?" William asked, trying to look shocked. "How?"

"He fell off the bridge and broke his head open on the rocks. I don't know how."

"I'm sorry to hear that. He was a friend of mine, as you know," William spoke softly.

"No, I don't," Jasper answered. "He never considered you a friend. I came to see if you still wanted to buy the mine? I don't want to be an owner. I just want to work."

William frowned and raised his eyebrows, perplexed. He wasn't sure how to tell Jasper that he already owned the Rohloff mine. "I made your pa an offer."

"I know. He rejected it. But I'm not my pa and I suppose the property goes to me now. I'll sign that paper for the money and five percent. I also want to keep my house and property. You can have the mine and gold. Deal?"

William appeared frustrated. He shot a stern glance at Jeff Blackburn.

Matt listened closely and caught the glance from William to Jeff. "Excuse me. I'm Matt Bannister, U.S. Marshal. Who is your father?"

William's nostrils flared. "Matt, perhaps I will speak to those idiots outside. Right now, I have some business to discuss with Jasper. If you wouldn't mind stepping out?"

Matt ignored William. "Who's your father?"

"Oliver Rohloff," Jasper said without much interest.

"He died?"

"Yes," Jasper said impatiently.

"When?"

"This morning."

"Did you see him fall?" Matt asked.

Jasper was in no mood to keep talking about it. "No."

"Did anyone?" Matt asked.

"No." Jasper's irritation over the questions was evident with a quick annoyed glance at Matt.

William rubbed his hands together nervously while Jeff's foot fidgeted crossed over his leg. Both men paid close attention to Matt's questions. "Well, you have my sincere condolences. I recently met your father. He seemed like a good man."

Jasper ignored him making it clear that he had no interest in talking to Matt and wanted to continue with his conversation with William.

"I'll leave you two alone. What's your name again?" Matt asked.

William sputtered, "I should have made introductions. This is Oliver's son, Jasper. Jasper, that's the famous Matt Bannister you're talking to. He's just leaving to shut those idiots up, hopefully!"

Matt snickered under his breath and shook his head. "Good day, gentlemen."

# Chapter 28

Jasper covered his ears as he left the Slater's office and turned south to leave town. He felt good knowing he would not have to worry about his mine anymore or take on any responsibility that he didn't have to. William Slater needed a day or two to write up a new contract for him to sign. The price was fair, it could have been better, but for keeping his house and land and a job in the mine, it wasn't too bad. Ten thousand dollars in his pocket and staying on his mountainside was all he could ask for. He was content.

Jasper walked across the first bridge on Premro Island and neared the second bridge close to the sawmill when he saw Matt Bannister sitting on the other side on a stack of lumber.

"Jasper, can I ask you a question?" Matt asked as he approached.

Jasper shrugged uncaringly.

"How high is your bridge? I've never been to

your mine."

"Eight feet or so."

"He was about five foot eight or so, right? That puts his head up around thirteen and a half feet above the rocks. That's a pretty good distance to fall," Matt stated thoughtfully.

Jasper watched him with annoyance.

"Did you bring his body to the mortuary?"

Jasper's brow lowered. "No. I buried him just as good."

Matt sighed inwardly. He had hoped to get a look at the body. Uncanny accidents were often a suspicious incident that quite frequently was a bit more than an accident, especially when money or jealousy were involved. "You already buried him?"

He nodded.

"No one seen your father fall?" Matt asked to clarify.

He shook his head.

"Were you working at the time? What about any employees?"

Jasper took a deep breath and closed his eyes. "No. I went to check a bear trap and the fellas found him when they came to work, about the same time I came back. Pa fell and he died. There's nothing else to say." He started to walk towards home.

"You didn't see anyone else around? No strangers? Nothing uncommon?"

He shook his head. "He just fell off the bridge."

"How narrow is the bridge?"

He shook his head. "Not very."

"That doesn't seem strange to you?" Matt asked

frankly.

Jasper shrugged. "Accidents happen. He could've tripped and tumbled over; I don't know. I just know he fell and landed on the rocks." He started to walk home.

"Jasper, one last question. Did William buy you out?"

He turned around and nodded without any interest in talking to Matt.

"When did your father refuse William's offer to sell?"

"Yesterday."

"That doesn't seem coincidental?"

He shrugged. "Coincidences happen."

"That they do. I'm just in a career field where sometimes it's not as accidental as it may seem."

"He tripped and fell off the bridge. That's all there is to it," Jasper stated and turned towards home.

\*\*\*

Jasper had never come home to an empty house in his twenty-nine years of life. His mother was always at home when he was growing up, although she was never very welcoming. After she left them, his father and brother were always there, but now both watched over the house from their plots above the cabin. It wasn't often that Jasper ever felt loneliness, but he was never alone until now.

It was strange to see the cabin pipe chimney empty of smoke as he made the hike up the side of the meadow. His father always had the cookstove burning at this time of day to heat some coffee, if not cook a meal. He carried his crawdad trap with sixteen or so good-sized crawdads inside. He had hit a crow with a rock a few days before and let it start decomposing before tossing it in the trap for bait that morning. The crawdad tails and pinchers had a bit of good meat, and the remains would be tossed out for the chickens to consume. Crows also came to get a bite, and a pile of smooth stones was placed beside the house to throw at the birds. They made good crawdad bait once they started to decompose.

He entered the silent cabin and set the wooden cage he had made from thin willow branches on the table. He started a fire in the cookstove and began breaking the claws and tails of the crawdads to pull out the bits of white meat. He tossed the meat into a frying pan with a glob of butter and opened a mason jar of peaches before carrying his meal to the table to eat.

He paused when he noticed his chair had been moved to the side of the table and in an angle facing his father's chair. He furrowed his brow and looked around to see what else might have been moved. A chicken's head was on the floor with a blood trail of droplets that led to the dead chicken's body against the wall. He moved his chair back to the end of the table and sat down to eat. A black drop of ink had stained the table in front of his father's chair. His father wasn't the best house cleaner or all that formal of a man, but the cabin wasn't all too big, and he always pushed his chair under the table when he left the table. His chair was left farther away from the table than where it usually set when he ate.

The buttered crawdads were a meal he could never get sick of, but it wasn't always filling. He forked a side of a peach and put it in his mouth. Someone killed the chicken near the door. It wasn't his father. In their home, no meat was wasted, and eggs as well were too valuable to kill a hen and leave it to waste. The chicken carcass wasn't good for anything except bait now.

He clasped his hands together and rested his chin on his hands. Someone had been there that morning. All the questions Matt Bannister had asked him began to make sense now that it appeared someone had come by the house after he left that morning. Matt had obviously had suspicions and perhaps knew who it may have been. Jasper had already walked four miles into town and four miles back home. He had no desire to walk to town again, but he would in the morning and find out why Matt had suspicions and who he suspected.

To think his father had been pushed off the bridge or murdered angered Jasper. He had never hunted a man, but if he discovered someone had caused his father's death, he would treat the man no different than a doe in the sight of his rifle or a trout at the end of his knife. If his father had breathed his last at the Lord's timing, he could understand that, but if his life was cut short by another for reasons that were not understandable, then it was only fitting that retribution had to be paid.

His jaw clenched and his breathing quickened as he grew angrier at the thought of someone stealing the only person away from him that mattered in his life. There was no reason and nothing to gain from killing his father; nothing at all without killing him too.

# Chapter 29

"Matt, you have company," Nate hollered from the front of the office.

Matt set his pen in its container and stepped out into the main office. His sister Annie Lenning stood on the backside of the three-foot partition wall with an annoyed smile on her face. As soon as he saw her, Matt knew that he had forgotten to wire her not to come to Branson on Friday. His left hand automatically swept over his hair in response, and he began to laugh.

"Hi, jackass," she said with a slight smile that could quickly become a snarl. "I just came from the dance hall where I was supposed to meet Christine and be measured for a dress that I'm apparently not going to wear any time soon! Maybe you'd like to explain something since I came all this way to be here?" Her slight smile faded.

"I'm sorry. I forgot to wire you about that." He laughed uneasily.

"Really?" She paused with a coarse stare. "I might be able to appreciate that if I didn't take time away from the ranch duties to come here to be sized, measured and handled like a calf at branding time for my brother's future wife and she's...where?" Her head tilted to the right while her brows furrowed irritably.

Matt wrinkled his nose. "Indiana."

"Yes...Indiana. I sure am glad I got to hear that from Bella on the dance hall steps and not from my brother." Her eyes hardened. "You have no idea how busy we are at the ranch. I told you and Christine that spring was a busy time long before you decided to marry in May. But, now that I'm here, when are you getting married, Matt?" It sounded more like an exclamation than a question.

He shrugged. "I don't know. We'll decide that when she comes home."

"When is that?"

"I don't know," he answered honestly. The heaviness in his heart was revealed in his voice.

She rolled her eyes. "She probably ran for the hills as soon as she could to get away from you. I know I would."

"You don't have to waste the trip. You can still get measured," Matt offered.

Her eyes narrowed, and she spoke slowly so her bovine brother could understand, "Yeah, why don't I do that? Think about it. Maybe by the time I wore the dress, it wouldn't fit, perhaps?"

"I think you're done growing."

"You're dumb. I can't wait for you to get married

and learn a thing or two about women. Anyway, since I'm here, I guess I might as well make the best of it. We needed to get some supplies anyway. We're heading home tomorrow morning, because like I said, we have a lot of work to get done. But you're buying my dinner tonight at the Monarch Restaurant. I don't care what it is; I will order the most expensive dish. So will Rory."

"Did Rory come with you?" Matt's expression changed.

"Of course. She's looking at material up the street…"

"Who is with her?" Matt asked with concern.

"No one. She's just going to the fabric store, not a saloon. Steven dropped us off and went to get his order of iron bar before we pick up supplies for the ranch. I was going with Rory before the store closes but figured I'd come in here and yell at you first."

"What store did she go to?" Matt's countenance had changed.

"Henson's Mercantile. Why?"

Matt pointed a finger at Nate. "Nate, go find Rory and stay with her while she shops. Bring her back here when she's done. Phillip, go with him."

Phillip shrugged. "I don't know who Rory is."

"She's the only young black lady that will be there," Matt answered.

"I know who she is," Nate said.

"She's fine," Annie said simply.

"Go, gentlemen!" Matt demanded with harshness in his eyes that Annie wasn't accustomed to seeing. He explained once the two deputies left,

"There are some dangerous men in town that will mistreat Rory if they see her. That's a chance I'm not willing to take." He was hesitant to mention Darius's brother being murdered. Matt had his uncle Solomon embalm Jeremiah Jackson and planned to take the body to Willow Falls, where at least Darius could look at his brother's face one last time before Jeremiah was buried.

"Are they ones making all that racket?" Annie asked about the miners banging on the iron plates and buckets. "I'd say they need to spend some time with the Indian side of our family and learn how to drum. If Uncle Luther was in town, he could show them how to work a drum."

"That he could," Matt agreed. "I do apologize, Annie. I had every intention of wiring Willow Falls to tell you to wait. I got busy and neglected to do so."

"No kidding?" Annie sarcastically remarked. "You don't know when Christine's coming back?"

Matt shook his head. "No. Her grandmother lives with her niece, who is apparently wealthy enough to hire a private detective company to track Christine down. Her grandmother is supposedly in her final weeks or months, so Christine went to Indianapolis to spend some time with her while she could. She might come back soon or maybe she'll stay longer. I told her I'd be here waiting."

Annie frowned questionably. "You might be waiting like a sturdy corner post, but you do understand that she's going to a big city and staying with a wealthy family. Christine will probably meet family friends, attend fun parties with a lot of dancing. She's a beautiful woman with an inviting personality and will fit in well with that type of society. So, my question, brother, is, what will you do if she meets some sophisticated wealthy gentleman who sweeps her off her feet with flowers, gifts, quoting poetry and Shakespeare? You know some successful college-educated professional over there is bound to ask Christine what her fiancé is like. Her answer's going to be, he's as faithful as the barn's corner post, right before she sits down to write you a letter apologizing for breaking your heart, but she met the man of her dreams."

Matt chuckled lightly. "Well, she'd have to explain what a corner post is first and foremost. And growing up on a farm herself, she'd realize despite the big eastern city boy's college education, his roots and hers don't come from the same kind of tree," he said with a shrug of his shoulders. "To answer your question, if she were swept off her feet and fell in love with someone over there, I'd be heartbroken. Fortunately, I think Christine's heart is solid and loves me enough to come back. If not, I'd miss her. Thank you for the thought, though. It's not like I don't have enough to worry about."

"You're welcome," Annie said with a pleased smile. She added quickly, "Honestly, I don't think Christine will be gone all that long. I like Christine a lot, but she's not all that tough, if you don't mind me saying so. Emotionally, I don't think she's tough enough to endure missing you for very long. I think she'll cut her trip short and be back within a month."

"I wouldn't mind that. I just hope she stays long enough not to regret anything. And I know she would if she stayed here to marry me. Our wedding can be postponed for a bit. Christine never knew her mother, it was her grandmother that raised her, and I believe Christine needed to go see her grandmother while she could."

The corners of Annie's lips rose a little. "That's nice of you."

"It only seemed right."

Annie asked, "Where is Truet?"

"He is painting the church and repairing a window," Matt said as he watched his two deputies escorting Rory Jackson by the window. She appeared as beautiful as always, with her long curly black hair pulled into a loose braid at the bottom of her neck. Her dark oval face, large brown eyes and timid smile always brought a hint of a smile to Matt's face. He enjoyed her quick wit and plain common sense to see the obvious that may appear complicated to others. "Rory, come on in and you and Annie have a seat back here at the table. I need to talk to you," he said as Rory entered.

Rory stared at the tabletop quietly. She had listened to Matt describe what had happened to her uncle Jeremiah Jackson when he came to Branson and how the killer had escaped justice. It wasn't hard to read Rory's expression. She was as genuine as a person could be and sadness filled her eyes. "Can I ask the man's name? My father will want to know."

"Wes Wasson. He was hired as a Blackburn Marshal the night before."

Annie's brow lowered. "Isn't that one of Billy Jo's love interests?"

"It was. He's one-half of the reason Uncle Luther took her to the coast. The other half is down the street pounding on an iron plate," Matt said with a nod towards the racket being made a few blocks up the street.

Annie chided with raised eyebrows, "I can't wait to see what kind of man she brings home from the coast."

Matt focused on Rory. "I had your uncle embalmed and bought a coffin. I was going to bring him to the ranch today, but I have too much going on and must remain in town. I'm sorry about your uncle. He was very excited to see Darius and you."

"I never met him. I looked forward to meeting him, though. I feel terrible for my father. He is so excited to see him again."

"Rory, with such people around town right now, you're not safe being alone, not even in a fabric store. I know you both planned on staying at the Monarch Hotel, but I insist you stay at Lee's, Albert's or my place."

"Steven is with us," Annie said.

Matt shook his head slowly. "Steven won't be able to stop these men. They know one thing and that is violence, and they respect one thing and that is someone with a history of equal or greater violence." Matt paused. "Me," he added with a sense of shame. "So, if you want to go shopping, you'll have to go with me or one of my deputies. If Truet wants to go shopping with you two, great. Annie, I don't want you walking around by yourself either. Until the Blackburn Marshals leave town, it just isn't safe for any beautiful young lady to be walking around."

"Thank you," Annie said.

"I was talking about Rory," Matt corrected.

"Matt," Nate Robertson interrupted from the front of the office. "Tim's bringing John Painter in."

"Take him straight into the jail. I'll talk with him when I'm done here."

The door opened and Tim Wright led John into the office. "Matt, he agreed to your terms. I don't think he can complete it, but Judge Jacoby sent a conditional letter agreeing to the terms. So, here's your new prisoner."

"Nate will lead you into the jail if you don't mind."

Tim guided John Painter through the partition gate and walked him towards the steel door leading to the jail cells. John lifted his shackled wrists to wave and grinned flirtatiously at the two young ladies at the table with Matt. "Hello," he said as he and Tim waited for Nate to unlock the steel door. "Hey Matt, if you're arresting the whores, can you throw the blackie in with me? I could use a bed warmer. Hell, send them both."

Nate unlocked the door and then intentionally threw it open as hard as possible to slam into John. The door hit John with great force and catapulted him to his back on the floor.

"Geez!" Tim shouted as he jumped out of the

way.

Nate reached down and grabbed John by his beard and pulled him up to his feet. John grimaced in agony as Nate kept a firm grip and pulled him towards the table and then, releasing the beard, Nate grabbed his hair and yanked it back while driving a knee into John's back, taking him to his knees in front the two ladies. "Apologize to the ladies!" Nate shouted. His muscular arm applied more pressure on the hair that began to stretch John's neck.

"I'm sorry!"

Nate turned him to face Matt, who remained seated and glared at John with hardened eyes. Matt reached out, took hold of the beard, and pulled John's mouth open. He spoke callously, "You're off to a bad start. Keep your mouth shut or I'll shove a piece of firewood in there and give it a kick. You're not funny, John." He motioned towards the cell door. "Nate, throw him in the back cell where we don't have to look at him."

"Gladly."

Annie's hardened eyes watched Nate and Phillip lead the man away. "I take it Nate is learning from you?"

Matt smiled slightly. "I've not seen him react like that before. It's about time."

Tim Wright approached the table. "Annie, how are you? It's been a long time." His eyes went to Rory. He hadn't seen the two women since Annie's husband Kyle Lenning's memorial dinner after his funeral back in July.

Annie's expression was cold. She had not forgotten his ploy to frame Christine Knapp with murder charges if she refused to be his private prostitute. At the time, she could not have cared less, but it disgusted her even more since getting to know Christine. "Sheriff Wright, have you framed anyone since I saw you last?"

His cheeks reddened a bit. "No, Ma'am." He turned to Matt. "The Blackburn Marshals are all out front of the Slater's office challenging the strikers to a fight."

"Let's wander down there." He went into the jail and spoke to Nate, "Escort my sister and Rory wherever they want to go. Do not leave them until they are with Truet or in one of my brother's homes. Even if Steven finds you, do not leave them."

"It would be my pleasure."

# Chapter 30

"Pa!" Josh Slater shouted as he opened his father's office door. "When are you going to end this? Everyone has a headache or an earache, and we can't get any work done! We have everything we want, so there is no reason to continue this. Go out there and end this so those idiots will stop pounding on that steel!"

William had sent one of the Blackburn Marshals to the mercantile to buy cotton for his office employees to wad up and shove into their ears. He pulled a wad of cotton out of his ear. He had been looking over the ore yields from the exploratory winze that intruded onto the Rohloff land, which may have been acquired illegally, but now legally belonged to him. "I thought I'd let them follow me home for a while. I want them to feel like they have won, and I don't want to make it too easy. I won't be a pushover," William Slater answered.

Josh was irritated. His head pounded with every

shrill ring of the four hammers pounding the large iron panels. "Pa, my head is killing me. Can you end it please?"

"Josh, go home and get away from here."

"They'll follow me to my house! This whole town is going to hate us if this continues. Besides, it's Friday; Mother has her weekly tea gathering with that women's club on Friday evenings. She'll tear your head off if you bring this noise home."

A slight hint of a smile lifted the edges of his thin lips. "I forgot about that."

"Yeah, Mother would be furious to have her weekly meeting interrupted."

"That she would. But..." he hesitated as his shifty eyes narrowed with thought. "She hasn't had anything exciting happen in her life in a while. It might be good for her to have something new interrupt her daily routine. Besides, I don't like that Delores Fasana woman, the undertaker's wife. She acts like she's too good for me in my own house, which is four times bigger than her own, which I don't understand. I'd like to see her squirm for a bit."

"Pa, just go outside and end this strike! We started it intentionally to delay negotiations with the Rohloffs, but now that we own their claim, there's no reason for it to continue. End the strike right now and let them think they won."

"Go home if the noise is bothering you too much. I'm not stopping them until later tonight. I want to see how long they'll keep this up. They need to know I won't give in easily if they ever do this again. But being the mayor, I will create a daylight noise ordinance to the city council to approve, just to ensure this never happens again."

"Pa, Mother is going to be furious with you. And you're going to scare Debra too."

William chuckled. "Yeah, I know, but it will be kind of fun. Your mother will get over it. Besides, Mister Blackburn and his marshals will be protecting the house until I end the strike. Right?" He asked Jeff, who sat in a chair reading a book.

"For as long as you need us. The boys are outside right now, just watching. Some are a bit crankier than others, but they should have slept last night instead of drinking."

William chuckled. "Josh, did you hear about what those young men did to the reverend's son?" he shook his head with a laugh.

Josh would have found it humorous, but his headache didn't allow laughter. "I'm going home. I think you are foolish for letting this continue. There's no reason. Just end the strike and send the sheep home so we can get some peace!"

"They are not sheep. If they were, I'd never risk encouraging them to strike in the first place. They're dairy cows. Do you know the difference?"

"Apparently not, because I have no idea what you're talking about," Josh answered bitterly.

William took a deep breath. "Sheep are just stupid enough to be unpredictable. You never know which way they're going to scatter, so the problem is trying to keep them together. Those men out there are like dairy cows. They keep together and as long as you keep them fed and housed, they'll keep coming back to get milked. And, son, we're going to milk them for all they're worth. Now that we own the Rohloff mine, we don't have anything to worry about except ending the strike, which I will do later tonight to let them think they won a victory." He smiled his narrow cunning grin that appeared a bit like a snake. "And then they'll go back to work with the same wage and rules they had before, but because they earned it, they'll work harder with increased morale. And you thought I was crazy to instigate a strike." He chuckled.

After Josh left the office, Jeff Blackburn asked, "So our duties will be ending tonight?"

William smiled. "Tomorrow after I have met with Joe Thorn and the others and negotiate their demands, yes. We will not be needing your services anymore. But I told a friend of mine that I was hiring you and he asked me to let him know when our agreement was over because he may want to hire you. I'll have a wire sent to him now and ask him to meet with you tomorrow evening at my place, for secrecy, of course. Would you be willing to meet with him?"

"Who is your friend?"

"I'll introduce him tomorrow or when he can be here. I do not know what he wants to talk to you about, so I am hesitant to say his name. He may not be interested at all. I can only ask him if he's still interested in hiring you and your men."

"What kind of business is he in?" Jeff asked.

William smirked. "He has a few. As I said, I don't know what he wants, but I do know he might pay extremely well for whatever purpose he wants you for. Beyond that, I don't know."

"I'll meet with him. If the price is right, we'll do what we are paid to do."

\*\*\*

Marie Slater was sixty years old and slight in frame, with brown hair turning silver rather than gray. Her facial features were thin and proportionate, revealing that she was once a beautiful woman in her youth. She was the parent that her two children resembled and got their attractive appearance from. Marie had blue eyes that could cut through the thickest rock if a rock drill refused to penetrate it, and those fierce blue eyes cut into her husband with a cold glare that usually was followed by the firing of a maid or gardener.

William raised his hands helplessly. "I didn't invite them here." If Marie knew anything about what was happening at the mine, it would be from Debra or Josh. William did not talk business with his bride and he had not in years. Marie was furious that her Friday night tea meeting with a group of her friends was interrupted by the loud and annoying racket of sixty-some men banging on iron plates, buckets and anything else that created a high-pitched ring. It was constant and there was no escape even within the large mansion.

"Get rid of them! I don't care what you have to do but shoo them away or I will!" Marie shouted. "I have guests, and this is humiliating. Take control of your employees or fire them!"

"I can't fire them, or we won't have any employees. They want a raise and unless you want a lesser allowance, I can't afford to give them a raise," he explained helplessly.

She reached for a shelf, grabbed a beautiful blue vase used as a decoration, and threw it at her husband. He side-stepped and the vase shattered against the wall. She kept her voice low so her guests would not hear, but the venom of her fury was toxic, "Get rid of them before I have your hired men outside start shooting them! I'm not putting up with this, William. I have a social event happening and your filthy employees are ruining it."

"Let me apologize to your friends."

"You can apologize, but you need to give these dogs whatever they want and send them away!"

"I'd love to, but I am sorry. If I can cut your allowance down by, say, five hundred dollars a month, I could probably end this strike."

"Cut your pay down!" Marie shouted with an angry grimace. "I earn my money by taking care of your home and keeping the place perfect. You're not touching my income for your dogs. They'd only spend it on whiskey and lick their puke up anyway. I want them far away from my house or I'll invite the ladies into your private study to wait this out with you no matter how long it takes."

William smiled. "Marie, do you know how attractive you are when you get mad?"

"Is that why I've been mad at you for most of our marriage?"

William chuckled softly. "Oh yeah." He winked at her. "I'll end it in a moment. But first, I want to apologize to your lady friends."

They went into the library where a group of six ladies, ranging from mid-twenties to the late sixties, sat in a circle around a table with a teapot. It never made sense to William how it could be so intriguing to come to their house every Friday night, sit in a circle, and chit-chat about nothing important for a few hours while drinking tea. The same idle chit-chat week after week that only a group of cackling women could find relevant in a world of business and strife.

"Hello, ladies," William greeted the flock of women. "My sincere apologies for the chaos outside. I hope you're not too scared. I assure you, you are quite safe in our home."

"Thank goodness," Virginia Sorenson said with a relieved gasp while clutching her chest. She was the fifty-five-year-old wife of the Branson Gazette owner and editor, Louis Sorenson. "I asked your Mister Blackburn if he would walk me home when we finish for the night. He is such a nice man. I tell you I will not fear with him at my side. Oh! It was such a horrible thing those men outside tried to do to you and Mister Blackburn." She addressed the other ladies. "Those men brought a dead boy to the newspaper's office and wanted a photo taken to publish. They claimed Mister Blackburn shot the boy in cold blood. It was such an awful thing to say. Louis, of course, refused to write such a vulgar story. Those people outside are such animals to lie like that. The boy tried to shoot William! Thank goodness, Mister Blackburn was there. I think the man is a hero."

"Indeed," William agreed. "I seldom get scared, but I may have been at that moment. What about you, Delores? Are you frightened to leave here?"

Delores Fasana snacked on a piece of celery. "No. Your driver picks me up and drives me home." An arrogant smile followed it.

William didn't like her. "Oh yes, that's right. Well, I'll keep you safe."

"That's very nice of you. But I believe it's probably Mister Blackburn and his marshals outside who are the real men keeping us safe. Isn't that right, Mister Blackburn?" Delores asked. Jeff had been in the library talking with the ladies.

"Well, William is our boss. I'd say he's the one keeping you all safe."

A gunshot sounded, followed by the sudden ending of the pounding on iron, but all hell broke loose. Broken glass, bangs, yelling and more shooting. The ladies screamed as Jeff ran out the door. He drew his revolver as he went.

\*\*\*

Toby Stearns had only gotten a few hours of sleep after returning from the Rohloff mine. He was tired, hungry and in a foul mood. Standing all afternoon in front of the Slater mining office, and now on the Slater mansion porch listening to the onslaught of high-pitched clanging of metal on metal was getting to him. His ears ached and a headache was growing. Boredom, the noise and watching the strikers glare at him, spit towards him and make obscene hand gestures while he stood like a pillar alongside his peers was the worst job they had ever been hired to do. Standing guard wasn't such a strange thing, but the noise level was something they had not experienced before.

Wes Wasson had it worse; a group of the miners knew him and hollered out various insults and obscene things at him. Wes had no alternative than to stand like a pillar and take it. They were given an order not to say a word or harm a single man that was striking. They were to stand still and be a wall of protection for the Slater family.

"This is crap!" Toby vocalized with a roll of his head. "Why can't we just run these cowards back to town and get something to eat? You know those women inside are eating, why can't we? A dollar says Jeff is eating."

Ed Bostwick, the former U.S. deputy marshal and highest-ranking marshal on the porch, spoke casually, "Stop whining, Toby. You'll get to eat and sleep again."

"I'm not whining. I'm not a child, and I don't appreciate you treating me like I am." His red eyes glared at Ed.

"Stop acting like one then. We have a job to do. Just shut up and do it."

"Says you. You're getting soft, old man. This boring nonsense is your kind of job; you didn't want to hurt that old man this morning. I swear, you need to remove that badge and pick up a mop and broom," Toby said with disgust. "You should take the office job Matt offered you."

Wes chuckled.

Ed replied with a hardening of his eyes, "And you need to close your mouth before I do it for you."

Henry Dodds walked over between the two. "Both of you need to settle down. We're on the same team here."

"Not hardly," Toby said irritably.

"I swear I feel like I'm babysitting my nephews," Ed said more to himself than anyone else.

Jimmy Abbot was at the far side of the porch and walked to the others. "Can someone just start a gunfight so we can go back to the hotel? I'm too tired to stand here and do nothing except go deaf."

"Get back to your post!" Ed ordered. "You fellas need to toughen up and just do your job. I've never heard so much whining. This is not hard."

"Shut up, Ed!" Toby growled.

"Or what, you scrawny little runt?"

Toby knew he could not beat Ed in a fistfight. He had never won a fistfight, but with a gun, he never had to worry about that again. Unfortunately, he could not shoot Ed, no matter how much he disliked him. Toby squeezed his lips together and shook his head, silently fuming.

Wes waved to Richie Thorn, who came to the front of the striker's line just off the property line. Richie had a severe blackened eye and stitches in his  lip but didn't look much worse than anyone who had gotten in a fistfight. He stared at Toby and mimicked crying with puckered lips and rolling his hands under his eyes. He pointed at Toby and wiped under his eyes and then laughed. "It looks like Richie is having a little fun at your expense."

Toby lifted his eyes and focused on Richie. His lip began to twitch as he watched Richie mock him. He doubted Richie had heard the whole conversation with Ed, but body language spoke louder than words sometimes. His hand slowly moved towards his revolver and his thumb flipped the leather thong off the hammer.

Richie cupped his hands over his mouth and yelled, "Hey, Wes, you turned to petite little men since Billy Jo's not interested in you, huh? Well, he's cute!" Richie laughed.

Toby was humiliated and growing more furious as the laughter spread like a communicable disease. Toby wanted to kill Richie on the spot, but he knew he couldn't shoot Richie, but there was nothing saying he could not scare him. Toby drew his revolver and fired from the hip in an upward angle above Richie's head. The shot rang out and Richie dove like a frightened rabbit. The pounding stopped as a roar of angry yells began to rise. A two-foot-long rock drill twirled through the air towards Toby and hit a window, shattering it upon impact. It was followed by another short two-pound sledgehammer that hit Henry Dodds in the thigh. He fell to the porch floor.

"Damn you, Toby!" Ed yelled and took cover behind the stone porch rail. He pulled his revolver but didn't shoot. Toby, Wes, and Jimmy Abbot fired their weapons into the crowd of fleeing men, women and children.

A Smith and Wesson rifle fired from the back of one of the wagons. The man shooting hid behind the iron plate that stood upright, creating the perfect shield. Mark Sperry aimed his rifle at the scrawny marshal shooting at Richie. The runt of a man ducked behind the stone pony rail before lifting his head to fire his revolver into the crowd of strikers. Mark pulled the trigger; the bullet skimmed the edge of the rail and ricochet into the side of the house. He turned his rifle to shoot at Wes.

Toby crawled to a stone support pillar and stood to get a better shot as he aimed at the back of a fleeing striker and pulled the trigger. The man fell with an arched back to the ground. Toby's attention went to the sound of a bucket hitting the stone rail and bouncing off into the bushes. Someone in a wagon fired another shot that barely missed Wes. Toby squeezed the trigger and feathered the remaining four shots into the crowd before he braced himself against a support pillar and began to reload. The cry of a wounded miner fed his desire to keep shooting.

One side of the Slater's double door opened, and Jeff Blackburn stepped onto the porch to survey what was happening. Mark Sperry aimed and fired, placing a bullet into Jeff's gut before Jeff could say a word.

Jeff bent over and turned towards the door to get to safety, while one hand held the entry wound and the other clenched his revolver. He fell to the floor inside the house and crawled to safety behind a wall. Jeff removed his hand and stared down at the bloody wound in disbelief. He knew immediately that it was a nasty wound as all gut shots were, but not immediately fatal. The women began screaming when they dared to peek out of the library into the long foyer and saw Jeff bleeding on the floor.

William Slater stood near the door, horrified and in shock. He had never expected the strike he planned would become deadly on either side. He had given Jeff and his marshals explicit instructions not to shoot at his employees. It was staged, a planned ruse, by him and to hear the gunshots, men wailing, and the chaos that was erupting before him was a nightmare.

"Slater!" Jeff yelled to get his attention. "Help me up!"

"You're shot?" William asked more than stated.

"I know! Help me up," Jeff demanded.

William pulled Jeff's arm to help him up. Jeff went to the door and peeked out. Most strikers had either scampered away or were hiding behind bushes, the wagons, or a tree or two. The porch had several hammers and rock picks thrown upon it. All his marshals appeared to be in good shape, except for himself. Henry Dodds limped, and Jimmy Abbot had a cut on his head that bled profusely, but none were seriously injured.

Toby, Wes, Henry and Jimmy all fired their revolvers at anything that moved.

Ed Bostwick stood behind a pillar, yelling, "Toby! Stop shooting." He glanced at Jeff and looked again when he noticed the blood staining his shirt. "You're shot?" His loud question caught the attention of the others and drew an end to the shooting.

Jeff, leaning on the door jamb, nodded silently.

Another shot was fired from a wagon and the bullet hit the edge of the door Jeff leaned on, missing him by less than an inch. A man carrying a rifle jumped from the wagon and ran away with the rest of the running miners. It grew quiet.

A voice echoed up the hill from below. "You want a war? You'll get one! We'll kill you all!"

Toby yelled back, "Come try it! We're not ones running away, you cowards!"

Ed Bostwick holstered his revolver, quickly approached Toby, and hit him with a fierce right-handed fist to the jaw. Toby was knocked into the stone pillar and hit his head on a round river rock and fell backwards, cracking the back of his head on the top edge of the stone rail before landing on the porch, bleeding and unconscious.

Furious, Ed, already in motion, kicked Toby in the head. He turned to Jeff and shouted, "It's his fault! He fired for no reason into the crowd. I'm telling you, Jeff, I'm not riding with him again!"

"Not now!" Jeff shouted with a grimace. "Ed, take the men and see if you can find that shooter."

"Are you okay, Boss?" Henry asked.

Jeff grimaced while holding his abdomen. "I hope." He turned back to William Slater. "Can you get your driver to take me to a doctor?"

William was slow to answer. "Yes." He could see

from his doorway two dead bodies and another man trying to crawl away with a bullet in his back where the strikers were. He never intended for any of his employees to get hurt. "Are those men dead?" He pointed at the bodies out in his yard.

"Don't know," Jeff grunted as he moved slowly towards a chair on the porch.

"I hope so," Henry Dodds said plainly. "We never shoot to wound the enemy."

Ed ran a hand through his neck-length hair. "They aren't the enemy. They're just men that got robbed of their lives." He gave William a cold glare. "It wasn't supposed to be like this."

Henry knelt beside Toby and frowned with concern. "Boss, I think Toby's...dead."

"What?" Ed questioned and knelt beside Toby and felt for a pulse in his neck. Unable to feel one, he checked the wrist for one. He sat against the stone rail in disbelief.

"Well?" Jeff asked from his chair.

Henry held Toby's wrist. "He's dead."

"Was he shot?" Jimmy Abbot asked. He was stunned to hear his friend was dead.

"How did he die?"

"Ed hit him," Wes said. "Toby hit his head when he fell."

Ed stood. "I didn't mean to kill him."

Jeff exhaled heavily. "I need to get to a doctor. Wes, you know this town. Go warn the doc I'm coming."

# Chapter 31

Regina Bannister came downstairs from tucking her two daughters into bed for the night. The two girls wanted to stay up later to visit their Aunt Annie and Rory, but Regina insisted they go to bed. She doubted they would fall asleep with the mine employees striking and pounding on the iron plates and everything else they could find to make a horrible amount of noise. It was frustrating, but Matt made it known there was nothing he could do legally to end it and figured William would soon enough. No man could withstand the noise for very long, especially while at home with his wife and daughter. The miners had followed William Slater home just up the hill from Lee's house.

Regina could hear Lee laughing before she stepped into the family room where Steven Bannister had just told a story. She could always tell when Steven told a story by his animated motions and a big grin. No one told stories quite as well as

Steven could.

"The man walked really weird, like this." Steven stepped forward with his right leg, slightly hunched over while swinging his right arm forward in line with his leg and then stepped with his left leg while swinging his left arm. "I can't do it as well as he could, but you get the idea."

Lee had laughed so hard his eyes watered. He held out an arm invitingly for Regina to join him on a red velvet-covered love seat. Lee wiped his eyes. "Oh my...Steven, I swear, you have the most interesting people come to Willow Falls."

Steven held up his hands. "Oh, you haven't heard the best part yet. The man said his name was Napoleon the Great and he was the king of Ziarra, which is in the middle earth, underground somewhere."

"What?" Matt asked with a perplexed expression.

"Hold on. Napoleon wore nothing except patched together patches of leather. Not buckskin, mind you, but rawhide leather knee-high boots with wooden soles, leather pants tucked inside his boots. A leather shirt, again, not buckskin, but rawhide leather and a long leather coat made from pieces of rawhide stitched together with rawhide string. All of it was thrown together and sewn by him. His hat was about six inches tall, again, rawhide, with a short rawhide bill on the front that was sewn on there. Crazy! I've never seen anything like it. It was all patched together. Honestly, his clothes creaked when he moved. They were so stiff and sweat-stained. He carried a good-sized leather bag with a leather shoulder strap. I don't know what was inside of it, probably leather scraps. That's how I met him. He came into my shop and asked if I had any leather he could have."

Lee, listening with interest, asked, "You didn't say it looked like he had enough?"

"No. He was staring at my blacksmithing apron and gloves like a fourteen-year-old boy stares at his pretty teacher. It was weird. I told him no. But that was just the beginning because then he proceeded to tell me his name and that he was king of Ziarra which is underground. He said dirt fell from the sky and a hole opened and a rope came down and two miners slid down the rope and kidnapped his wife. They just shimmied right back up the rope with her and left a rope dangling from the middle earth sky. He climbed up to our world and he is now searching for the miners that snatched his wife. I had to ask what she looked like in case I saw her…"

"You're making this up," Matt accused.

Lee and Annie both laughed.

"No! I'm not. I swear it true." Steven continued, "Napoleon said his wife shouldn't be too hard to find because she was as beautiful as a middle earth sunset and wears leather like him too. That's all they wear down there." Steven paused and apologized to Matt, "Sorry, brother, but I told him to come to see you. I told him you know a lot of miners and could probably find her because you're a good tracker."

Matt asked without any humor in his voice. "Are you serious?"

"Yeah, I'm serious. What else was I going to tell

him?"

Lee chuckled despite the sad circumstances of the man's delusion. "Well, if I see him, I'll tell him I saw a woman as beautiful as the sunset dressed in rawhide walking out towards the mine, kissing on a couple of miners carrying a rope."

"They left the rope dangling from the sky," Annie quipped. "Remember, that's how he escaped the middle earth?"

"Good point. So, they don't have a rope," Lee said, to get his facts right.

Annie added, "Maybe you could tell him you saw two miners searching heaven and earth for a wife, but now they had a long rope. It looked like they might try grabbing one from the middle earth," she said with a shrug.

Matt shook his head. "Don't do that. He could turn violent, especially if he finds a couple of miners with or without a rope. It would probably be more dangerous for him if he confronted a miner. You're serious?" he asked Steven.

"I'm dead serious. We didn't see him on the road here today, but he might show up at some point. I'm warning you now; he's a character. He didn't seem dangerous, though."

"I'll keep my eyes out for him."

Annie offered, "Maybe he went to Natoma and found the tannery. That would keep him busy for a while," she chuckled.

Steven sat down from telling his story and added, "My wife, the good-hearted soul that she is, offered him some food and clothes. He took the food but didn't want the clothes."

Lee spoke to Steven, "It's nice to hear you say something nice about Nora when she's not here."

Steven scowled. "Yeah. I don't know what's wrong with me. Don't tell her I said that, though. She might start to think I like her or something." He took a drink of his glass of lemonade.

Annie shook her head exaggeratedly. "No, we won't do that." She was sitting on the red velvet davenport between Truet Davis and Rory Jackson.

Matt sat in a red velvet padded chair not far from Steven's matching chair. He missed Christine and it showed in his lack of joy. Matt was fairly certain the word "Misery" was invented by a man like him that missed his own beloved lady. Dolefully, his eyes lowered with a heavy heart as he wished she was there with him to enjoy an evening with his siblings. There was a time when Regina wanted nothing to do with Christine, but since Thanksgiving and getting to know her, the two of them had become good friends. Christine would have enjoyed being with the family and visiting with the three ladies. The sinking sensation in his chest that defined the misery of missing Christine dimmed the light that usually brightened his eyes. Sadness and longing for her presence overshadowed his cheerful countenance. He took a deep breath and yawned.

"Tired, Matt?" Annie asked. She held a glass of wine, along with Regina, Lee, and Rory.

"A little bit."

"You don't even know what tired is. Come work

on the ranch for a day and then you'll know what tired means. So you got up a little early, who cares? Toughen up or get to bed like a little old lady," Annie chastised with a furrowed brow. "It's not even late, you yellow-spined gecko."

Matt was about to respond when the sound of a gunshot eased his smile to a concerned frown as the miners' pounding stopped and a roar of yelling and gunshots filled the noticeable silence. He stood quickly. "Truet, let's go!"

"Oh, my goodness, is that shooting?" Regina asked with great concern. They were only a few hundred yards from the Slater mansion.

"It is. I'll grab my gun," Lee said, standing.

"No! Stay here. The girls might need you," Matt said. "Tru?"

Truet kissed Annie hurriedly and followed Matt quickly outside.

They moved uphill while many miners and their families ran down the hill in terror. By the time they reached the Slater mansion, the shooting had ended, and a few injured miners were lying on the ground with non-fatal wounds, but four dead bodies lay on the ground in front of the Slater home. Matt had not personally known any of them. He approached the porch with his revolver in his hand.

"Matt," Ed Bostwick said, noticing him and Truet. He recognized the expression on Matt's face and knew all too well Matt was deadly serious.

"I was told on my way up here that you all started shooting into the crowd."

Ed shook his head. "No. The dumbass Toby fired

a shot above them, and all hell broke loose. They may have thought he shot into the crowd, but no. They started throwing all this crap." He motioned towards the multiple rock picks, candle picks and hammers that lay on the porch. "They shot at us too. Jeff is gut shot, and you can see the bullet holes on the wall. They should be bringing the carriage around to get Jeff to the doctor. Wes went ahead to let the doctor know."

"And him?" Matt motioned to Toby, who was lying on the porch.

Ed took a deep breath and tilted his head with a shrug. "Dead. I hit him for shooting first and he fell and cracked his head against the stone pillar. It killed him." He was still stunned.

Matt looked across the porch where Henry Dodds and Jimmy Abbot congregated together, solemn for their friend's accidental death. "And Jeff?"

"He's inside. His time may be done too. You can see the bullet holes where they fired at us. That's when we shot back—some more than others. I didn't fire a shot except at the person shooting at me. Jeff gave us strict orders not to engage with these people. Toby did and is probably responsible for most of the deaths and injuries because he was fanning into the crowd."

The carriage was brought around to the driveway. Henry, and Jimmy Abbot went inside to help Jeff into the carriage. Matt went onto the porch, where William Slater stood in horror as he gazed remorsefully upon the two abandoned wagons and bodies lying on the ground. Matt spoke frankly,

"Truet and I are going to take the injured miners to the doctor's office. I suggest you find a way to end this strike before this happens again. The battleground is already at your house. The next one might be inside."

William looked away from the bodies to him with regret showing in his eyes. He nodded heavy hearted. "Can you let Joe Thorn know to meet me at my office tomorrow at noon to put this behind us? I'll meet their demands."

"Is your family okay?"

William nodded. "Yes. Your aunt is inside. Do you want to take her home?"

"What, aunt?"

"Delores."

Delores was his Uncle Solomon's wife and she wanted nothing to do with their family whatsoever. "I have injured men to take care of. When I come back for the dead, I can, if she's still here. Goodnight, William."

"Matt," William said with a troubled voice, "it wasn't supposed to happen like this. These men were not supposed to harm my employees."

Matt could not help but scoff. "I told you a long time ago not to bring the Blackburn Marshals to town when you first spoke of them. I told you they'd only bring trouble. A woman was raped by four of them in the Monarch Hotel last night. I didn't bother to arrest them because I already know you and Jackson Weathers would refuse to file charges. They'll walk away. And nothing disgusts me more than that! Your world up here on this hill is no more important than that woman's world down there in that hotel. And those maggots right over there," he pointed at Henry Dodds and Jimmy Abbot, "are getting away with it! But not by my choice. It's yours! Do not ask me to protect your family if you'll go out of your way to protect the criminals after hurting other families. And right over there are four more lives destroyed." Matt shook his head in disgust. "End the strike and get rid of these animals or more innocent people are going to be raped and killed." He descended the porch steps and said to Truet, "Let's gather the wounded into a wagon. It's going to be a long night."

# Chapter 32

Saturday morning, Matt went to his office and noticed a mule with a pack on its back with a shotgun in a scabbard tied to the hitching post outside his office. The door was unlocked as Phillip was already inside to take care of their prisoner. Matt expected to see Patsy Jane waiting for him as they had an appointment at nine to discuss John Painter's agreement. Matt doubted his mind would change, but she was adamant about discussing it with him. However, it wasn't Patsy Jane waiting for him, but Jasper Rohloff.

"Matt, this gentleman would like to speak with you," Phillip said of Jasper.

Jasper stood up from a chair. "Jasper Rohloff. We met yesterday." His hand was stuck out to shake.

"I remember. What can I do for you?" Matt asked while shaking his hand.

"Why did you ask me so many questions? Do you think someone killed my father?"

"I don't know. I didn't see where your father fell or his body."

"No. But you were asking like you were suspicious. Who were you suspicious of?"

"I can't be suspicious of anyone without some evidence of any kind to point me in that direction. You said he fell. I have no choice but to go with that unless there's something you didn't tell me."

"I hadn't gone in the house yet," Jasper said thoughtfully. "I left when my pa was making his breakfast. I went to check my bear trap and came back and our employees had found Pa in the riverbank beneath the bridge." He paused as Patsy Jane entered. He glanced at her and continued, "So our employees and I buried him by my brother. I sent the men home, and I came to town to tell Mister Slater that I'd accept the offer my father rejected the day before. The only thing I asked was to keep my property and house and have a job at the mine. I don't care about being rich so much. I just want to be left alone and live off the land as I do. It's just me now."

"What kind of offer did Slater make your father?"

"A fair one. It's true. We are too small and poor ever to reach the gold. My father wanted it all and threatened to sue. He was hiring a Portland attorney to sue the Slaters for pirating our claim. They offered him twenty thousand in paper money and five percent of the gold. I settled for ten thousand and one percent of the gold as long as I keep the land we live on. I'm meeting him today at one to sign the deal and get the money. I brought the mule to buy some supplies. But I need to know what made you think my father was killed?"

"You mentioned you had not gone into the house. What difference would that make?" Matt asked.

"That's what made me curious. I left town and went home. Sitting there alone, I noticed my supper chair was moved next to my father's chair. His chair was not pushed under the table like it usually is. Our cabin is small, and he always pushed his chair under the table. Also, there was a dead chicken on the floor; its head had been twisted off by the door. We don't waste meat, especially not egg-producing meat. It was very odd. And there is an ink spot on the table that wasn't there before. It got me thinking and I remembered all your questions. I went to the riverbank and there was a pointed boot print in the soft mud. We don't wear pointed boots, either do our two employees. So now I'm curious, why were you so suspicious?"

Matt frowned. "The men Slater hired to escort the gold are bad men. They are called the Blackburn Marshals and wear generic marshal badges." Matt's eyes went to Patsy Jane as she listened intently. Normally he would speak to someone in the privacy of his office, but since Patsy Jane had first-hand knowledge of how bad they were, she could hear as well.

"You think they killed my father? I saw one of them in Slater's office when my father rejected their offer."

"That would be Jeff Blackburn. He is paid to do whatever William Slater tells him to do. Jeff has four or five marshals here in town with him. Let me do some investigating and I will get back to you later today. Now that I have some evidence of a crime and not an accident, I can check into it. But..." he hesitated and looked at Patsy Jane empathetically. "I can't promise anything. I'll do my best."

Patsy Jane spoke to Jasper, "What he means is don't count on any justice coming. Our district attorney favors them. I know because they hurt me too and told me they were Matt and his deputies. It wasn't Matt." Tears filled her eyes. Her black eye, split lip and bruised cheek were still visible.

Jasper's brow narrowed. "Did they do that to you?" He pointed at her face.

She nodded quietly.

Jasper turned to Matt. "You can't arrest them for hurting her like that?"

"I could arrest them, but the district attorney will let them go. I already tried it."

Jasper reached his hand out to Patsy Jane. "I'm Jasper Rohloff. I think they killed my father."

She shook his hand. "I'm Patsy Jane. I am sorry to hear that; you have my condolences. Don't be mad at Matt. He's taken good care of me since the attack."

Matt spoke, "Patsy Jane, one of the men that attacked you was killed last night. I thought you might like to know that."

"Good. You have three more to go," she said with a twitch of her bottom lip. She took a deep breath before asking, "Matt, don't you think seventy days too long for John to stay here? Thanks to you, I have two more nights in the Monarch Hotel, and then I'm homeless. I don't have anywhere to go. I can't rent a house without John saying he will find work. But he can't work for a dollar a day to pay you and the church back. Can't I pay what he owes? I don't have a lot, but I could do that, and we could start over."

Matt shook his head. "No. And it's seventy workdays, so it's more like a hundred days or so in total. I'm not willing to negotiate on it at all. John's a drunk and he needs to be sober for a while and physically work to pay what he stole back. I believe staying in jail and hard work will have a way of sobering him up and working out his demons so he will be a functioning adult when he is released and have a job already. It's worked for others, and I believe it will work for him. I'm not letting him out until he completes seventy workdays starting Monday. He'll be a better man for it."

Her breathing escalated. "What am I going to do?"

"Patsy Jane, John's parents are dear friends of mine and I'm doing this for them. It's one last chance for their son. And I pray that it works to change his life. I understand you just met him and need a place to live. I don't want to make any awkward suggestions, but why don't you and Jasper go have breakfast or lunch and talk for a while? He might want someone to help around the house and you need a place to live. Maybe you'll get along or maybe not. Maybe you'll hate each other by the end of your lunch, but why not take a chance and go talk for a while? I'll even pay for your meal."

"What about John?" Patsy Jane asked.

"What about him? He's not in love, Patsy Jane. He can't even love himself. Just have lunch or something and talk for an hour or two. If you don't like Jasper or he doesn't like you, I'll help you figure something else out." Matt asked Jasper, "Does that sound okay to you?"

Jasper's face reddened. "I'm not much good at talking to women."

Matt yawned tiredly. It had been a long night. "You don't have to make a decision today, Jasper. I arranged for two more nights at the Monarch Hotel for her. You don't owe her a dang thing and there's no pressure because I'll find her a place and a job if you're not interested in sharing your home. I'm not suggesting you get married, it's just based off needs. You might like someone to cook, clean, and to talk to, and she needs a place to call home for now. I'll make you a deal, I'll pay for your meal at the Monarch Restaurant if you two will go talk for an hour or two. Who knows, maybe each of you will make a new friend. What do you two say?"

Patsy casually shrugged her shoulders. She spoke to Jasper, , "I'm okay with that if you are. The restaurant has really good food."

"I suppose. I have a meeting at one, though," Jasper clarified.

Matt reassured him, "It's not even ten in the morning. You have plenty of time. Let me know how it goes." Matt waited until they left the office and then turned to Phillip. "I'll bet my paycheck that the Blackburn Marshals killed Oliver Rohloff. Write a note for Ed Bostwick to come to see me and take it to the hotel."

"Okay. That's some slick love matching you did there," Phillip chuckled with appreciation.

"When you have cold hands and a pair of warm gloves, they might just match up together. Besides, I didn't want to listen to her cry and beg for the next hour to let John out. How is our new guest this morning?"

"Cranky and unappreciative."

"Good. I wouldn't expect anything different."

# Chapter 33

"Good morning, John. How was your first night in our jail?" Matt asked as he pulled a wooden bench down the granite block wall to sit in front of John's cell.

John was pacing back and forth in his cell. He was aggravated. "Too quiet! It's too silent in here. I want to go back to the other jail. Take me back!"

"Hmm. If I do, you will face a trial jury and most folks around here have no patience for a thief. Especially a thief that steals from a church, let alone their father's church. That just tells everyone that you'd steal from anyone. There are no bounds to your thieving. You'd be sent to prison, John. Do you want to go to the Oregon State Penitentiary? It won't be quiet there at night, I bet."

"I don't care! I want to go back to the other jail!"

"I'm trying to help you, John, believe it or not. I suppose a glass of wine would settle your nerves, yeah?"

"Do you have one? I could use a drink. I won't lie about that."

"I bet not. Sit down and let's talk for a minute. You went to the Andover Theological Seminary in Andover, Massachusetts, which is a prestigious school for a Branson, Oregon, boy. What happened?"

"Nothing happened," John responded irritably. He sat on the edge of the bottom bunk. His hands fidgeted and his knee bounced continuously.

"How do you go from striving to be a theologian, which is a pretty high goal, to a thief, wino and beggar? Something happened, John. Was it too hard?"

"Is that all I am to you? A thief, wino and beggar?"

"No. You're a man that could have a future ahead of him, but that's up to you. How can a striving theological student give up on life and, worse, give up on God? You were raised in a Christian home with a gifted reverend as your father. You certainly overheard men and women talking with your parents about their hurts and life. How did it happen, John? Why did you abandon the Lord when you know so much about the Bible?"

"Have you ever lived in solitary confinement?" John asked.

"Just by my own will when I was running from my own hurt. I once had my gun pointed at my head and would have pulled the trigger if it wasn't for a reverend like your father. Coming back to my family and this community has changed my life from black to white. It could for you too. But we have to figure some things out first."

"Oh yeah, like what?" John asked bitterly.

"Like why you would rather beg for money than work. Why do you want to hide your pain in wine and why do you hate your own Lord and Savior? You don't have to talk to me. You can just labor your seventy workdays, pay your debt and go right back to drinking and begging if you want to, but there won't be another chance. I'll do everything I can to help you get back on your feet and the path the Lord has for you, but you have to have enough care about life and yourself to want to change. You're thirty years old and life is passing you by. Time doesn't stop and before you know it, you'll be fifty years old and either prospering with a family surrounding you or sitting on a city street begging for change to waste it on cheap wine. The Lord has a greater plan for your life than that."

"How do you know? Maybe *this* is God's plan for me. The road God put me on has led me here. God plans all things, right? He controls everything, doesn't he? We don't have choices; we are predestined to prosper or suffer. God condemned me a long time ago and now I'm just trying to enjoy what I can while I can. All those praise songs about how good God is, people like you and my parents sing, can be sung by you. You're chosen. I'm not. I was kicked out of seminary, okay? One of the professors told me that I would never become a theologian because I wasn't smart enough. I was told I would make a terrible reverend, so I would never be like my father. Yeah, he sets a standard I cannot touch!"

John shouted. His eyes filled with tears. "I was ran out of there by my professor, a theologian himself. He told me it was not God's will for me to be there because I wasn't cut out for it. I don't fit the mold." He hesitated. "So, I left. But I couldn't come home."

"What did you do then?"

"I traveled around working from place to place, experienced this and experienced that, but never settled down until I met Sue."

"Sue?"

"My wife."

"Did you love her?" Matt asked.

John's lips tightened. "With all my heart."

"Where did you meet her?" Matt asked.

"Louisiana."

"You loved her and got married. Did you two have any children?" Matt already knew he had two children.

"Two. I have a son and daughter. Eli Junior and Rachel." He covered his face with his hands and sniffled emotionally.

"So you were a family man. Where did you work?"

"I worked as a card dealer on a sternwheeler on the Mississippi River."

"What happened?" Matt asked softly.

"I started drinking, gambling and womanizing. The sternwheeler I worked on was named The Lesser Morality and it really was."

"Was Sue a Christian?"

He nodded. "When I met her, yes. But I had already walked away and pretended to be until we were married. She quit going to church when I did. Her parents weren't too happy with me, but I didn't care. I was working and making good money on the Lesser Morality. Life was good."

Matt set his elbows on his knees and interlocked his fingers to rest his chin. "Then what happened? How come you're not there with them now?"

John chuckled sadly. "Lesser morality. Drink, gambling and women. I gambled my pay away, drank the rest or spent it on the women. There was a brothel on board. I was fired for stealing money from the gambling tables I worked at to take home a paycheck after losing mine. I spent six months in jail for it. Sue had enough, I guess, and took my children and left me while I was there. She sent me a note in jail saying she never wanted to see me again, and I have no idea where they are now. I searched for them for a while, but her family hid her well."

"How long ago was that?"

"Six years."

"John, how does God have anything to do with what you chose to do? The drinking, gambling and all that? How can you put the blame on the Lord when it was your choice?"

"He plans everything, right? We don't do anything without the Lord's knowledge or permission, do we? Even the day we die is written by God." He shrugged.

"I think you forget such words as *repent* from sin, which is a choice, right? It was pretty consistent in the Bible. I'm sure you read that word before. We have free will, we can do anything we choose to do, but that does not make it God's will. How many times does the Bible say flee from sexual immorality? That is a choice and God's will never involves sin. Drunkenness, sexual immorality and gambling are choices you choose to do against the Lord's will. And by doing so, you lost what really mattered in your life – your family. It happens a lot. We often bring hard times upon ourselves, and it might be easy to blame it on God, but that doesn't mean he is to blame. Often, we are. Sometimes there is no one to blame because life just happens and there's no rhyme or reason for it. Accidents happen, criminals commit crimes, being at the wrong place at the wrong time, people get sick, life is wonderful but fragile and painful. But you can't blame God for your own choices when the consequences hurt."

"I'm not!" John exclaimed bitterly.

"No?" Matt questioned. "What I hear from you is you hit hard times and gave up and now, in hindsight, you blame God for not helping you keep your family, which you lost by your choices. And that whole lifestyle is out of God's will. The name of your boat stated it all; it was and is a proud proclamation of sin. God does not tempt his people with sin. But he does say repent from sin. And life is giving you a chance to do that and get right with the Lord."

"It's too late for me. I already told you that."

"By the sound of it, the original crack in your faith was your professors. Let me tell you a little secret. We don't need to fit in someone else's mold of what we should be as Christians. The only mold you need to fit in is knowing Jesus and what the Bible says. What an east coast theologian considers a proper Christian may not be what a west coast small town country boy is. God doesn't care about a person's exterior, as so many Christians judge them by. God looks in the heart and sees the truth of what that person can be, not is. And an east coast reverend may not connect with a small town as a small-town reverend would. That professor had no right to tell you to quit because you wouldn't be a good theologian or reverend. All he did was discourage you and there's nothing more devastating than discouragement. I'm beginning to understand, John."

"I don't," John admitted. "I don't ever fit in. God must not have chosen me because I don't fit in anywhere." He shrugged sadly.

The steel door opened, and Phillip stuck his head in and said, "Ed Bostwick is here to see you."

Matt looked at John empathetically. "The best analogy I have ever heard is a toolbox. A hammer works great to drive in a nail, but it can't drive in a screw. A screwdriver can drive in a screw perfectly, but it cannot drive in a nail. A hammer and screwdriver together can't drill a simple dowel hole, but a hand drill can. The point is it takes the right tool to do the right job. And we are God's tools, John. You are not your father or that professor or the little old lady down the street. You are who God made you to be, whether a hammer, screwdriver, nail, screw, drill or dowel; we all have a purpose and will fit in like a puzzle piece where we are meant to be. Do not cut yourself short. You have the knowledge of eternal life within you, and the world needs to hear it. Don't waste your life begging for scraps when the world is dying and desperate to know what you already know. No, you're not on the path God has chosen for you, but you can be. Stay here with me and work for it. I promise you will walk out of here, standing taller and a very changed man with a purpose. It won't be easy, but it's an investment that will change your life for good. The Lord's waiting to hear from you."

# Chapter 34

"How is Jeff? Come into my office and let's talk a bit," Matt said, leading Ed Bostwick into his private office. Matt waved to a chair in front of his desk and sat down behind it.

"Jeff is going to make it. You have an amazing doctor here. He operated on him all night to repair the damage. Jeff's not out of the woods yet, but hopefully, he'll recover okay. They needed the bed, so we moved Jeff to the Monarch Hotel. I guess he's in your cousin's room by the stairs. It's the only bed on the first floor and we couldn't risk carrying his cot up the stairs. The manager said it would be fine."

"Jeff Blackburn is sleeping in William's bed. William will be back next week, and I'd like to be there to see his expression when he hears that. As you know, I am not a fan of Jeff or his men. I have to admit, I was surprised to see you riding with him. Why are you?"

Ed Bostwick grinned. "Money. You made as much as I did as a U.S. deputy marshal and it was pitiful pay for the dangers we faced and the men we killed. The wounds we carry," he added softly. He took a deep breath. "I make far more now than I ever did without half the worry or danger. Now I have men watching my back."

"Men or friends?" Matt asked.

"Both, I guess. We ride together."

"I notice you don't drink and gamble with them."

"No. I'll have a drink here and there, but I'm not a kid and it seems like the last few men Jeff hired were. One I accidentally killed last night. Just as well, you would have killed him before we left anyway. He was hankering to fight you."

"I know. Anyone else I have to worry about?"

Ed shook his head. "No. Toby was the only hasty and stupid one."

"Good. Ed, I know someone killed Oliver Rohloff. He didn't fall off the bridge. I'm asking you who did it and if William Slater hired you to do it? Which is a given, but I need evidence."

Ed chuckled. "Matt, I wish I could give you an answer, but I don't know anything."

"I was expecting more from you, Ed. You were a stand-up lawman with a solid reputation. I didn't expect you to sell out to Jeff Blackburn."

"I didn't sell out. I looked around and realized I was risking my life for pennies and not making a bit of a difference. I wanted to make a difference and bring justice to the west, but the outlaws keep coming and expanding, grouping together and taking

300

over. Kill one, and five more take their place. All that traveling around and sleeping on the ground no matter the weather in the same clothes for weeks on end, just to take a bullet or end a life. Hell, Matt, you know what it was like. Jeff made me an offer and I almost turned it down, but then I asked myself, for what? Why would I turn it down? The money's much better, I hardly ever have to sleep in the rain, and I can afford a better meal than beans day in and day out. Killing is the same whether you wear your badge or mine."

"No, it's not. One is justice and the other is murder. Oliver was murdered, plain and simple. I'm asking, was it you?"

Ed stared at the desktop. "It wasn't me I can tell you that much."

"But it was your friends or the men you ride with?"

Ed shook his head. "What's the difference, Matt? No matter what I tell you, your court system won't prosecute us. We are above your law for all practical purposes, and we know it. And that's part of the reason I chose to join Jeff and his marshals. We protect each other. It's the marshal code. You won't get any answers from me or any of the others because if we talk, it becomes the duty of the rest to kill the codebreaker. Old friend, you're wasting your time."

"So, it was you fellas. I figured as much." It irritated him that once again, the law was bought and dismissed when needed to bring justice to a family. "I'm getting tired of you and other marshals. The

Blackburn Marshals bring nothing except trouble and since justice is missing, that only leaves one other option and you know what that is. This is my community, Ed. I won't allow you and your pals to terrorize it. I won't sit here with my hands tied because our court system is cowardly. I'll bring it myself." Matt's hardened eyes stared coldly into Ed's.

"Matt..." Ed answered hesitantly. "We didn't want any trouble here. Toby instigated everything that has happened so far. He's gone. We should not have any more problems. I'm in charge while Jeff is down until Ira Kelly comes back. I'll make sure all is sweet, my old friend."

"Ed, why don't you join us here? My budget is thin, but I can request more from the county commissioners to hire another man. My brother is on the board, and he'll make it happen."

Ed chuckled. "I must be a man of great reputation to have so many offers."

"I offered a position to a young city deputy I met in Arizona, but he rejected it. I also have a standing invitation for TJ Tolbert to join us, but so far, no. You see, he is a man that honors his U.S. deputy marshal badge because little by little he is making a difference over in Oklahoma."

"TJ is a good man."

"So were you. The question is, are you still?"

Ed tilted his head in thought. "You can't pay what Jeff pays."

"I'm not paying for a gunman. I'm paying for the character of a lawman who wants to keep his community safe and serve the people. I'm paying for a good man with honor and integrity. That's the only kind of man I will hire. You had it; I'm just questioning if you still do."

"Of course, I do," Ed said plainly.

Matt reached over to the corner of his desk and picked up a wooden frame that Truet had made him that contained a silver dollar. He showed it to Ed. "This simple silver dollar doesn't look like much. You probably have three or four in your pocket yourself. But this is a symbol of why I do what I do. I gave this coin to a five-year-old little girl named Eva Crawford for her birthday a couple of months ago. Her mother's name is Kellie. They're a wonderful little family over in Natoma. One day, an outlaw named Jude Maddox invaded their home, tied up Eva and her siblings, and kidnapped Kellie. I tracked them to Willow Falls and killed Jude and saved Kellie. Little Eva gave me back this silver dollar for saving her mother. Ed, this silver dollar is why I love my job and why I do it. I'm not talking about the value the government puts on it, but the value of saving a little girl's mother and keeping a great family together. Old friend, you will never get that sense of satisfaction working with Jeff Blackburn, but you would here." He set the coin frame back on his desk. "Now you know what I'm offering, family, friends, loyalty, love and appreciation along with a decent salary and a place to call home. Think it over."

Ed smiled sadly. "I like kids."

"Do you? Because what you and your pals do

is kill the fathers of little girls like Eva for coins like that one. How many children's hearts and lives have you fellas broken since joining Jeff? Think it over, Ed."

They stepped outside of the private office and Jasper Rohloff and Patsy Jane were waiting for Matt at the table by the woodstove. Matt said good-bye to Ed and approached the table. "How was your lunch?" he asked.

"Good. Thank you," Jasper said awkwardly.

Patsy Jane grinned. "We are going to try it out for a bit in separate rooms, and if we get along okay and he likes my cooking, we'll get married. And if we do, I'm going to invite you, okay?"

"Of course."

"But I'm staying in the hotel for the next two nights if you don't mind? I feel spoiled there. Okay?"

Matt chuckled. "I don't mind."

"Can I speak with John and let him know our engagement is off? I think it's only right."

Jasper said, "I have to go to the Slater's office anyway. I'll meet you at the hotel in an hour and you can help me shop for food stuff. Okay?" he asked Patsy Jane.

"Yes."

Jasper left the office and she looked at Matt with a grin. "I really like him. He's shy and needs to learn how to do a lot of things, I think. But his heart is a good one. Thank you for buying us lunch."

# Chapter 35

William Slater shook Joe Thorn's hand. "Again, those men were instructed not to harm a hair on any of your heads. I don't want my employees hurt. I'm thankful we could come to an agreement and end this strike. You won't hear me say this too often, Joe, but I am heartbroken for the families of the men that were killed last night. It was needless and the man who started it is dead. As I said, I'll make restitution for what happened, and it will be fair. Thank you, Joe."

"I'll let the families know. We'll replace those panels and get back to work Monday. Sorry, I'm not jumping for joy, but we lost some friends and we tried to keep it peaceful."

William frowned. "I understand that. The noise was breaking me anyway. I was just about to call you inside my house to make this appointment for today. I waited five minutes too long and the cost was lives. Please, let their families know I am truly sorry."

"Will do." Joe Thorn carried a signed and dated agreement of changes to rules and regulations that he and William had agreed upon. The strike was over, and they even got a small pay raise and Christmas day off to spend it with their families. He walked out of the mining office, raised the paper into the air, and yelled a victorious yell. Thirty other men waiting with sidearms and rifles cheered.

Jasper Rohloff ignored them and entered the office. He walked down the hall where he had found William the day before. He knocked on the door and entered.

"Right on time," William said with a grin. He had set a prepared agreement several pages long on his desk. "That is one thing about your father that always impressed me. He was always punctual. My sincere condolences to you and your..." he paused. It occurred to him that Jasper had no more family. "Well, my condolences to you. Let's get this signed, shall we?"

Jasper sat down with William. "Is it what we agreed?"

"Of course. We are buying your mining rights for ten thousand in cash, which I have right here. You will no longer have ownership of the mine, but as to our agreement, you receive one percent of the total value of minerals processed from the Rohloff mine. The name Rohloff Mine will remain intact as you asked. And your two employees will retain their jobs, as requested. You will retain all property west of the river as the owner but agree to allow us access to and from the mine on the road. And that pretty much sums up the contract in short."

"What about me working in our mine?"

William frowned. "I didn't think you were serious about that. You do realize that one percent revenue will be more than you've ever made. The gold alone will undoubtedly put you at five figures, if not six figures almost immediately, depending of course, on the total value. Jasper, I am not shorting you or intend to do you wrong. You can check the numbers when they come in, but you'll never have to work again. This is a lifetime or life of the Rohloff Mine, agreement."

Jasper shifted in his chair. "If I don't work, I don't know what I'd do."

"Well, if you want to work, then you're hired. But you don't have to. You won't need to."

"I'd like to."

"That's fine. Shall we both sign it? I have a copy for you and me both. You can double-check, but they are identical. Do you want someone else to read it before we sign?"

"No. I'll take you at your word. But your word better be good."

They both signed and dated the contract and William handed Jasper the money owed. Jasper put the agreement in his shirt pocket and then asked, "Did you have my father killed?"

"What?" William was shocked by the question.

Jasper pulled a small caliber .32 caliber pocket pistol out of his pocket and pointed it at William. "Did you have my father killed?" he asked louder with a menacing appearance in his eyes.

"No! What are you doing? We're partners in a business, Jasper," William stated urgently. He was seated in his chair but leaning back with his hands held out in front of his face.

"My father didn't fall off the bridge. Someone was there. Who was it?"

"How would I know?" he shouted.

"Last chance! Who was it?" Jasper pulled the hammer back until it clicked.

"Jeff Blackburn and his men! Jasper, listen, I didn't want anything to happen to your father. He was my friend! I just wanted Oliver to sign the sales agreement and they went there to ask him again! It was not my idea to kill him. I had nothing to do with that. That was Jeff Blackburn's idea!"

Jasper held the gun on William a second longer. He lowered the gun and took a deep breath. "Thank you for telling me. If this agreement is different than you said or if you break your word, I'll come back and pull the trigger. I'll ask now, is it different than you said?"

William shook his head. "I told you the truth. I'm not shorting you or lying in any way. I have been straight with you."

"Better be. My men and I will keep pounding rock until you all show up. Good day."

## Chapter 36

Matt rested his chin on his hands as he sat on his front steps watching the last rays of orange light disappear over the roof tops of his neighbors' homes. He could have ridden up to the top of the hill to watch the setting sun, but it wouldn't be the same without Christine beside him. There was a time when he did not mind being alone, but it wasn't being alone that brought the loneliness that plagued him; it was not having Christine near him. He had lain on his bed when he came home from the office and stared at the side of the bed that Christine had slept on when she escaped from Pick Lawson back in October. He remembered waking up and seeing her sleeping peacefully on his arm. How he longed for that moment to never end. He had been looking forward to their wedding day so that every morning he could wake up beside her. If there was such a thing as heaven on earth it had to be living with the one person that you loved enough to want to spend the rest your life with them. Matt could not think of a greater display of love than committing the rest of his life to being with Christine.

It hadn't even been one week since she left, but it felt like several weeks. Annie had commented that she didn't think Christine was emotionally strong enough to withstand being away from Matt for too long. However, Matt was the one sitting alone melancholy and heavily burdened with the weight of the sadness of not being near her. Even in the presence of his siblings the night before with all the laughter and good conversation, he could not shake the hollowness in his chest where her presence had earned his love and affection. Love is the most unique thing; it stirs in the heart like a whirlpool in the river bringing new life and excitement into a man's life with colorful dreams of a bright future together. Love is nurtured, watered and blooms over time like a flower garden with the sweetest aroma and beauty. Love is truly like a diamond in a coal mine and a magnificent gift to find, but love sure longs for the other half when she's three thousand miles away without a date of return. It's said distance makes the heart grow fonder, but there was no room in Matt's heart to love Christine more, it was already full to capacity and overflowing to the point that it hurt when she was away from him.

Matt stepped out into the yard and looked for the moon as darkness settled over town. There was a small star near the moon that Christine had once referred to as *her* star. It was a constant that she could locate as a child and believe her mother was watching over her. He stared at the little star and perhaps, just maybe, on a train somewhere she might be peering out a window at it too. Perhaps she was even missing him as much he missed her.

Matt took a deep breath and prayed, quietly, "Lord, I pray that you will keep Christine safe. I miss her, Jesus. I miss her a lot. This might be harder than I thought it would be. I hope and pray she has a blessed time with her grandmother though. I hope it is something she will always be grateful for. It is such a wonderful blessing for her."

\*\*\*

It was too beautiful of a night to sit at home alone dwelling on his loneliness for Christine. Truet had driven a wagon to Willow Falls to escort Annie and the others while taking Jeremiah Jackson's casket to Darius. Matt went for a walk around town and found himself on Rose Street. He walked on the street, avoiding the boardwalks filled with men of all ages enjoying themselves from a week of hard work. Laughter, loud teasing and occasional arguments and fighting were nothing new. It was always about the same.

Matt stepped into the Green Toad Saloon and scanned the saloon from one corner to the other with a sweeping of his eyes. He recognized Wes Wasson, Jimmy Abbot and Henry Dodds sitting around two tables pulled together with Vince and Jack Sperry in a back corner. Two other men joined them that Matt did not know. At the bar holding a glass of whiskey was the rough exterior of Morton Sperry. He was staring at Matt in a mirror behind the bar. He nodded with a faint hint of a smile.

Matt stepped forward and casually swept his thumb over the thong that held his revolver securely in the holster. He approached Morton's right side to keep his gun hand at a distance and to put Morton between his brothers, the marshals, and himself. Matt knew he wasn't liked by either group and alcohol could quickly spark a fight.

"Morton," Matt said.

"Matt. Do you want a drink? I'll buy."

He shook his head. "No, thanks. Are you all making friends with the marshals over there?" Matt asked, watching the men converse and laugh.

Morton shook his head. "No. Wes wired us to work as Blackburn Marshals against the silver miners. We came to hire on, but we're just a little late. I hear the strike ended and the boss got shot."

"You sound disappointed."

"I am. I wanted to join up against the miners."

Matt shook his head.

"It's not what you think," Morton said. "Our older brother works at the silver mine. He was striking. We were joining up to be spies and let the strikers know what the Blackburn boys were planning. In truth, my brothers, Cass, Elliot and I would have killed every one of the Blackburn Marshals if they raised a gun towards a single miner or one of your boys," Morton said, looking at Matt. "I told you I consider you a friend."

"Do you?" Matt asked. His eyes studied Morton

carefully.

"I do."

"Then I'm going to ask you to watch my back. I have some personal justice to dish out."

Morton's brow rose. "Really? Well, lead the way. I'll watch your back."

"Matt!" Wes Wasson said with a grin as Matt approached their table. "Hey, when I see your hair, I just want to..." He used his flat hand as a knife blade and sliced through the air with a whistle.

Vince Sperry laughed, as did a few others.

"Anytime you're ready to try." There was no humor on Matt's face.

Morton Sperry watched from a distance.

"Later, sometime," Wes chuckled. "I don't want to ruin my love interest with your cousin, you know. Someday we're going to be related, you and I."

"Doubtful. Wes, I want you and your two friends, Henry and Jimmy, to come outside with me. We need to talk."

"What about?" Henry asked and swallowed a shot of whiskey.

"A lot of things. Come on out."

"Are we under arrest?" Henry asked, and then slapped Jimmy Abbott in the chest with a laugh.

Wes stuck his wrists out to be arrested. "Please do. I love that expression on your face when Jackson frees me."

Matt raised his eyebrows and smiled slowly. "I bet. You're not under arrest. I just want to talk."

"Oh, hell, why not?" Henry stood. "It's getting too hot in here anyway. Come on, Jimmy."

"We're playing cards," one of the men Matt didn't know said callously to Matt. He must have been holding a good hand as he was irritated the card game was being interrupted.

"Keep playing. I wasn't talking to you," Matt answered, sharply.

Morton Sperry spoke, "Cass, this doesn't involve you."

Matt remembered Pick Larson had warned him to watch out for Cass Travers before Pick was hung over the granite pit. Now he could put a face to the name. It made him uneasy to know cutthroat men and outlaws surrounded him. It wasn't wise to trust a murdering outlaw to watch his back, but Matt trusted him despite Morton's reputation and past.

"Matt, that is Cass Travers and that's Elliot Zook. They just got back from wintering in Texas. Gentlemen, this is Matt Bannister," Morton made introductions.

Cass watched Matt like a wolf, searching for a weakness. Elliot Zook's eyes scanned Matt up and down to size him up as well. "Marshal," Elliot said with a casual nod. Both men were hardened and experienced killers, no doubt.

"Gentlemen," Matt replied to the two gunmen. He put his attention on the three Blackburn Marshals. "Wes, Henry and Jimmy, let's go outside."

"Fine, but if this is about who killed the miners last night, I don't know," Henry said.

"It's all a haze, now. Isn't it?" Jimmy stated.

Matt walked out into the street and stood in

front of the three men that stood side by side. He could see Morton talking to his brothers and two friends on the boardwalk quietly. "Which one of you said they were me the other night?" His eyes scanned their smug faces as they either grinned widely or tried to hide their humor.

"What are you talking about?" Henry asked, trying to play dumb.

Wes chuckled. "If you're talking about the drunk's whore, it was just a freebie."

Matt stepped casually with his left foot and then brought a swift kick using his shin bone just above the ankle to connect with Wes's groin as hard as he could. Wes collapsed to his knees, unable to breathe. Matt drew his revolver and swung it backward, slamming the barrel into the side of Henry's head. Henry fell to the ground with a deep gash just above his ear nearer to the back of his head. Matt's revolver froze on Jimmy Abbot. "Don't move!" Matt warned fiercely.

Matt stepped in front of Jimmy. "I talked with her. She told me what you did. Close your eyes. Isn't that what you told her? Close your eyes!" he ordered.

Jimmy began to shake under the barrel of Matt's gun. He tightened his eyes. His hands moved towards his crotch, indicating he expected to get kicked. Matt swung the revolver and bashed it against Jimmy's skull. Jimmy went down and landed hard. He laid there unconscious.

"Drop it!" Matt heard Morton Sperry shout. He glanced over and saw Morton holding his gun on

Henry Dodds, who had grasped his revolver. "I'll blow your damn head off if you don't let it go!"

Matt didn't wait for Henry to decide; he kicked Henry's face with brutal force that knocked Henry back, bouncing his head off the hard ground. Not finished, Matt stomped on Henry's head and then kicked him in the ribs. He took a few steps away and then came quickly back with a hard kick with the point of his boot into Henry's groin. Henry turned to his side and curled into a fetal position. Matt pulled Henry's revolver out of his holster and did the same with Jimmy's and carried the two guns over to Wes.

Wes was starting to stand, and Matt swung Jimmy's revolver and cracked it against Wes's head. Wes fell with a new cut on his scalp. Matt unholstered Wes's revolver and carried the three guns to a water trough and threw them into the water.

He grabbed Wes by his hair and yanked him to his feet. "Just because your bleeding doesn't mean I'm done, Wes. I'm just beginning. This is for Chusi!" He pulled Wes by the hair across the street quickly and slammed his head into a support post of an overhead awning of the boardwalk. Wes fell like a falling tree to his back. Dazed, but still conscience, Matt yanked him up by his hair again and pulled him to the water trough and shoved Wes's head underwater at the opposite end of where the guns were. Matt held him there long enough for Wes to begin to panic. Matt yanked his head up to let Wes cough and try to catch his breath.

Matt leaned down next to Wes's ear. "I'm having

a great time, Wes. What about you?" Matt asked with a sneer. He shoved Wes's head underwater and held him there. He pulled Wes out of the water, lifted him to his feet, and hit Wes with a right cross to the jaw that sent him back to the ground. Matt lifted him back to his feet. "Come on, Wes put your hands up. Let's see how tough you are."

Wes wavered on his feet with his jaw opened to catch his breath. He opened his palms in a surrendering fashion to wave Matt off. "No more," he said. He lowered himself to one knee to rest his weary body—blood mixed with the water and seeped down his face from a fresh cut on his head. A knot formed on his forehead from his collision with the post.

Matt shouted, "Stand up and fight!"

Wes stood with a painful grimace. "Matt…"

Matt drove another solid and brutal kick into Wes's groin. Wes dropped to his knees and fell over face first while convulsing to get his breath. He began to vomit.

Matt knelt and put his face next to Wes's ear. "Get your ass out of my town! Jackson Weathers might keep you out of jail, but I promise you every time he does, it's going to get worse for you. He can protect you from jail, but he can't protect you from me. And I will hurt you! Try me one more time and see. This is child's play!" He pushed Wes to his back and ripped the new generic marshal badge off Wes's shirt and tossed it into the water trough.

He approached Jimmy Abbot, who was just becoming alert enough to realize Matt had grabbed both of his ankles and lifted his legs straight up and spread his legs. "Wh...what..." Jimmy stuttered as he stared in horror at the hardened and merciless eyes of Matt.

Matt dropped his hundred and ninety pounds straight down with a bent knee onto Jimmy's groin. The young man grunted and rolled to his side when Matt stood. Not finished, Matt kicked the tip of his boot into Jimmy's crotch. Matt stepped around and kicked Jimmy's face with a powerful kick.

A few feet away, Henry was starting to stand. Matt ran forward and drove his knee into the side of Henry's head. Henry was driven into the ground again and laid there trying to get his bearing. Matt pulled Henry by the shirt collar to his feet. "So you are the one that pretended to me? Say yes."

"You're going to..."

Matt brought his right palm upwards in a fierce uppercut and hit Henry's chin with the edge of his palm and continued the strike upwards through where Henry's head was. Henry's head snapped back as his teeth slammed together and he fell to his back unconscious. Two teeth fell from his profusely bleeding mouth, onto the hardened ground.

Matt stood between the three men laying on the ground in pain. He shouted to a large crowd watching him, "These three men raped a woman, and our district attorney won't prosecute them. As you can see, I still did. There's three free guns in the water trough, take them. These rapists don't need them anymore."

Six men raced to the first to save the weapons

from the water.

Matt ripped the marshal badge off Jimmy's shirt and Henry's before throwing them into the water trough with Wes's.

"Nothing like a fair fight, huh?" Morton asked with a grin. "Three against one and somehow, it seemed fair enough to me."

Matt took a deep breath to slow his breathing. "Thanks for having my back."

Morton patted Matt's shoulder. "Anytime. If I had known about the woman, I would've liked to have helped you."

Matt waved a hand at the three men. "Have at it. Just don't kill them."

Morton's lips curled upwards. "Cass, Elliot, let's help my friend teach these men how to treat a lady."

# Chapter 37

Ed Bostwick shared a room at the Monarch Hotel with Henry Dodds, but like usual, Henry was out drinking with his two pals and the newly hired man Wes Wasson. Ed had done his time drinking and things of such rowdy nature. Now he preferred to spend his evenings reading and getting some sleep early. Ed was thirty-eight years old, never married and had no children. He had brothers and sisters spread out around the prairie states mostly, but he hadn't seen any of them in years. There were times he could grow lonely for home and the big thanksgiving dinners and Christmas mornings with his family, but those days were long past now.

The idea behind the word *home* was a life he had not known in about twenty years. He joined the military and while serving, his parents were killed in a house fire. Being the youngest in his family, his older siblings were starting families and staking their homesteads in various places. Life had already changed, and the distance only grew the longer he remained in the military. He no longer had a home to go back to and when he was discharged, becoming a Deputy U.S. Marshal seemed like a logical decision. He joined up and met the bitter young deputy marshal with a growing reputation for brutality and a bloodhound-like tenacity that never quit tracking a man down or quit fighting. The name Matt Bannister meant one thing and it was death. For an outlaw to hear Matt Bannister was trailing him meant death was coming if they didn't surrender immediately.

Matt was cold, unfriendly and never smiled. He never laughed and his brown eyes were sharp, penetrating and angry. He wanted to be alone, worked alone and lived alone. For many, including Ed, Matt Bannister was untouchable, unfeeling and a solid rock of incorruptibility. It took a long time to get to know Matt, but he was a man with a burden and trusted no one. Ed would talk about his home as a child, but Matt was always hesitant to talk about his home or childhood. He'd rather not talk at all. Ed had worked with him a few times and Matt's reputation was well earned. Little by little, they became distant friends, but Matt kept everyone he met at a distance. No one was allowed to get close to the man. Ed did know that Matt stayed on the trail constantly to avoid being home alone.

Ed could not believe the changes he saw in Matt now. He had expected Matt to be the same cold and dangerous man he was before, but he was different.

He smiled. He cared. He had a home and spoke of family and friends. His eyes shined with joy and the purpose of wearing his badge wasn't about seeking justice with his gun like it used to be but protecting his community.

It was hard to believe that Matt Bannister had been promoted from the ranks of a deputy marshal to a U.S. marshal. Such promotions didn't happen too often, and a good portion of federal marshals were mere politicians that had some help along the way to get appointed. Many of them never left their office or did much at all as a lawman goes. The further west a man went, it seemed the more hands-on and experienced they were. Matt's experience surpassed Ed's own, and a more dangerous man Ed had never known. The changes in the man were stunning, like the difference between night and day. Matt appeared alive, happy and excited about life. Maybe it had to do with being in love, but the fact was, Matt was a changed man.

The invitation to work with Matt as a deputy marshal again was tempting. Ed swore he would never wear a deputy marshal badge again, but it wasn't the same here as it was in Cheyenne. He wouldn't be on the trail as often, have a livable pay, and a place to finally call home with friends and a sense of family. The town was beautiful, and the people seemed pleasant enough. It was a good town, and it placed a longing in Ed's heart to have what Matt had, a sense of community and being the protector of it. All that Matt said was appealing and it was a decision that weighed heavily on his mind. The only appeal of the Blackburn Marshals was the money.

Ed found the life of a deputy marshal lonely, exhausting, frightening, bloody and paid little to nothing for the dangers one encountered. Jeff Blackburn was a way out of the life he had been accustomed to and now he stayed in fancy hotels, dressed better, had paper money in his wallet and a bank account where a good portion of his pay was sent after every job. Three years as a Blackburn Marshal had given him a life with a group of brothers, more or less, a family to belong to. They celebrated holidays together, birthdays together and tragedies, like the unexpected death of Toby Stearns.

Ed did not intend nor imagined hitting Toby could kill him. It was a freak accident that was still hard to believe. He didn't like Toby too much, but whether he liked him or not had no bearing on what happened or how bad he felt that it was his fault regardless. Toby was a fragile young man, though. He was skinny as a green bean and had not an ounce of muscle on his bones. The kid had a fiery temper from years of abuse and being picked on, but he did have a fast hand and a decent aim. He was still learning how to be accurate instead of just fast. A fast man had an advantage if he was accurate. If not, he would be dead sooner or later. Ed expected Toby would meet his match sooner than later. A troublemaker always does. But to die from a right cross by a friend, no one expected that. If Toby had ever carried grain bags or labored on a farm, maybe he'd have the strength in his legs to take a punch instead of flying like a snowball into a stone wall.

Now that Jeff had been wounded and in bed for a few weeks to recover, Ed was the boss until Ira Kelly returned from California. He was responsible for controlling his men, which would be easier now that Toby was gone. It was just too bad that he had been the cause of it.

Ed rubbed his goatee thoughtfully. If he were to list all the pros and cons of deciding between staying with the Blackburn Marshals or joining Matt's office, it would become overwhelmingly clear his wisest choice was to join with Matt and learn to enjoy life again.

There was a knock on his hotel room door. He rose from the comfortable chair and opened the door. A prestigious-looking man in his late fifties, dressed in a black suit and silver-rimmed spectacles was at the door. "Can I help you?" Ed asked. He figured the man was knocking on the wrong room.

"Yes." He tilted his head down to the right inquisitively. "Are you Ed?"

"I am."

"Good. Then I have the right room. May I have a word with you?"

"About?"

"Business. I understand Mister Blackburn will be out of circulation for a while. William suggested

I speak with you."

"William Slater?"

"The one and only."

"Come in. So, who are you?" Ed asked as the well-dressed man stepped into the room.

"My name is Robert Fairchild."

Ed shook his hand. "Have a seat. What kind of business are you in, Robert?"

"Oh, many things. I relocated from back east. I am originally from Philadelphia but started a newspaper in New York City. That's the spine of my good fortune, but I also invested in other businesses and fiddled with a bit of everything. In short, I made a fortune and thought I'd retire. However, I'm too young to retire and do nothing. William Slater and I got acquainted through my friend Louis Sorenson who owns the Branson Gazette. Louis and I were friends in our youth and have remained so. He is a partner of mine in some of my corporate endeavors. Let me just say that marshal's office downtown wouldn't be there if it were not for my casual acquaintances in Washington DC. So, *that's* who I am."

Ed remained silent for a moment. "Do you want a drink?" he asked to be polite. He was still waiting for the reason the gentleman came by.

"I never touch the stuff. I bet you're wondering why I came to see you?"

Ed nodded curiously.

"I decided to retire from the busyness of my life in the east. I don't want to sit on the porch and grow old, I like to be active, and business is my first love. Money, Ed, can be consuming and I am not consumed enough. I want to build a woolen mill and produce wool for the market. I believe there is a large market worldwide and this area is perfect for it. I bought a large sum of acreage, about twenty thousand acres north of here, and had my home built before I came here. Cattle ranchers have used my land, a lot of it as free-range land. I brought in my five thousand sheep and there seems to be an issue with the cattlemen. Another five thousand are scheduled to arrive in mid-June."

Ed began to chuckle. "You brought sheep into cattle territory?"

"Yes. I have every legal right to do so. I have shepherds to protect the flock, but one of my shepherds and two hundred of my sheep were killed. Our local sheriff in Hollister shrugged his shoulders and didn't seem to care. One of the federal marshal's deputies came to investigate, but two hundred dead sheep and a dead man without any witnesses didn't leave much for him to do. Cattlemen did it, but who among so many?" He shrugged.

"Mister Fairchild, are you wanting to hire us to protect your sheep?" Ed asked.

"My sheep and my shepherds. My shepherds are from Peru and don't speak a lot of English. I speak their language. I spent several months vacationing in Peru, among other places. I am a bit of a world traveler and collector," he added. "Anyway. I need men with enough, how do you say, grit and firepower to let me raise my sheep in peace. And I am willing to pay top price for the right group of men. The job could take time, months, maybe? Or maybe just the title Blackburn Marshals will be enough to back the cattlemen off."

"How much?" Ed asked. He never discussed contracts, Jeff Blackburn always did, often assisted by Ira Kelly.

"You're a man of few words and direct. I have written a proposition down with full details of what I expect for the money. How you men deal with the cowboys is up to you and you alone will be responsible for any legalities that come from whatever procedures you follow." He pulled a sealed envelope from his jacket pocket. "This is only the proposition. I do understand Jeff is recovering, but do you suppose we could go see if he is awake?"

"We can check." Ed descended the three flights of stairs to the courtesy desk, which was attended by a young man of a stocky build. Ed grabbed the door handle of Jeff's room when the young man said, "Excuse me, that's a private room. The Monarch Lounge door is over there,"

"I'm Ed Bostwick, and I'm checking on my friend. Thanks for watching his door, though."

Jeff was sleeping soundly. His pillow had fallen off the bed. "Jeff, are you awake?" Ed asked quietly as Jeff continued to sleep peacefully. Ed picked up the pillow and gently lifted Jeff's head just enough to set the pillow under his head.

"Let's let him sleep. I was hoping he was awake,

but we can talk to him tomorrow," Robert Fairchild stated. "Do you have plans for the rest of the evening? If not, I invite you to join my precious wife and I in our room for some tea? I'll drink tea, but you can drink whatever you wish. My wife enjoys wine. We can discuss in more detail what I want. And maybe I can help you turn the Blackburn Marshals into something much bigger. What do you say?"

"Sure. I have nothing else to do." They closed the door behind them as they left.

The closet door opened a crack, and Jasper Rohloff peeked at the entry door to make sure the two had left. He had almost been caught red-handed and would have if the young man had not questioned the two men at the courtesy desk. It gave Jasper the moment he needed to duck into the small closet and close the door.

He heard the older man say to the desk clerk, "Young man, can I trouble you to make me a pot of hot tea and bring it to room nine. And maybe a bottle of your best wine. Ed, what would you like to drink?"

"I don't drink much myself. Wine is fine."

"Then two bottles of your finest wine, young man. What is your name?"

"Joshua Bannister, sir."

"Bannister?" Robert Fairchild grinned. "The son of the owner?"

"Nephew."

"You're not the marshal's son?"

328

"No. He's my uncle too."

"Very good. Joshua Bannister, if you can get the tea and wine upstairs within, let's say twenty minutes, I'll tip you very well. After twenty minutes, I'll start reducing the tip every minute. Sound fair enough?"

Joshua grinned. "I'll hurry."

"Good boy. Well, come with me, Ed. I'll introduce you to my missus."

***

Jasper Rohloff had dinner with Patsy Jane at the Monarch Restaurant that evening. They were seated near the door close to the reception desk and watched the doctor and other members of the Blackburn Marshals walk in and out of a room and overheard it was where Jeff Blackburn was recovering from being shot. The doctor had stated Mister Blackburn was on a heavy dose of morphine to keep him sleeping throughout the night. It was an uncomfortable dinner for Patsy Jane to recognize the men that had abused her, but her back was turned to them and they did not enter the restaurant or notice her. Jasper quietly watched and ate his dinner.

After dinner, Patsy Jane invited Jasper to her room to talk. In truth she was afraid of being alone after seeing the men that attacked her. They talked for a few hours, and then Jasper descended the stairs and found the front foyer empty and the clerk with his back turned to him. He quietly stepped into Mister Blackburn's room unnoticed and closed the door silently. Jasper watched the old man sleeping for a bit.

"You shouldn't have killed my father." Jasper pulled the pillow out from under Jeff's head and covered his face with it. It was only a moment later that he heard two men talking and approach the door before they were stopped by the front desk clerk.

Panicked, Jasper let the pillow fall to the floor and quickly ducked into a small closet and closed the door as the entry door opened. His heartbeat quickly as the two men talked momentarily and left the room. He could hear them talking to the front desk clerk about making some tea and getting some wine.

Jasper stepped out of the crowded closet and waited until the two men could no longer be heard. He locked the door and went back to the bed. He pulled the pillow from under Jeff's head carelessly and held it in his hands and placed the pillow over Jeff's face and pushed down with all his weight. Jeff did not put up a fight. Five minutes later, Jasper removed the pillow and made sure Jeff wasn't breathing. . Satisfied that Jeff Blackburn was dead, Jasper returned the pillow under his head.

Cautiously, he opened the door just enough to peek out to see an empty foyer and left the hotel as casually as he had walked in.

# Chapter 38

Beatrice Painter sat in her rocking chair humming a praise tune while she crocheted a blanket for a young couple in the church who were expecting a baby. There was much to pray about and one of the most urgent prayer needs was encouragement for her husband, Eli.

John's coming home was like a hammer to the chin that busted out a few teeth too. It happened in a flash and the damage was too severe to repair in a day. The hurt he caused them was deep, real and perhaps permanent. If it had been contained within the four walls of their home, maybe they would heal from John's indiscretions and foolish choices, but like a blazing fire that sweeps through a forest, the gossip of the reverend's son had overwhelmed the town and certainly the church. The humiliation did not define the shame that shadowed the hearts of Beatrice and Eli. To make matters worse, someone in their congregation had written them a note demanding Eli to retire from the pulpit and get control of his family. The note had hurt, but not as bad as the looks and knowledge of the gossip in town.

Their future was suddenly unknown, all because of their wayward son. They had done all they could, but it didn't matter. The ministry was the only profession in the world where the father and mother were responsible for the choices of their son or daughter in the eyes of others. There was a reason to worry because Eli and Beatrice didn't have an income or a home to live in without the church. Eli had been the reverend for years, and just days before, there was no discussion of his retiring or leaving the church. Now it was, for some people, non-negotiable.

Beatrice could fear, she certainly had a reason to, but instead remained calm and praised the Lord while she crocheted. If she knew any one thing, it was the Lord was with her and Eli. They had lived long enough and rested upon the Lord more than enough times to know for a fact that they could trust Jesus and he would somehow take care of them.

A knock on the door brought her out of her thoughts. She laid the blanket down and went to the door. No one was there, but a sealed envelope wedged into the exterior door jamb fell to her feet. She picked it up and looked around the dark street but didn't see anyone. She closed the door and returned to her rocking chair. Sitting, she opened the envelope and pulled out a letter inscribed to

Reverend Painter.

She gasped and covered her mouth with her hand as the tears filled her eyes. She stood and stepped towards the small den filled with books and a desk where Reverend Eli Painter studied and wrote his sermons. She knocked on the door and entered.

Reverend Painter narrowed his brow with concern when he saw her emotional expression. "What is it, my love?" he asked.

She handed him the letter with her lips closed tight. She would start to sob if she spoke a single word. She turned and walked out of the office quickly.

Concerned, Reverend Painter opened the folded letter and began to read. He set the letter on his desk and the room became blurry as the moisture filled his eyes. He took a deep breath and wiped his eyes. He approached Beatrice in the family room, where she was standing in front of a wooden cross on the wall crying. Eli wrapped his arms around her and smiled sadly.

"Why are people so mean?" she asked emotionally. "They're supposed to be Christians."

"Oh, sweetheart, that's between them and the Lord."

"What are we going to do?" she asked with a broken heart. A tear slipped down her cheek.

"I'm not giving the sermon I have been working on. It would be pointless at this point."

"Are you going tomorrow?"

"We're going, sweetheart. And we're going to hold our heads up. We did our job and sent a Godly young man to seminary. The Lord knows our hearts and we are going to stand on our integrity. We can do no more than that. Let's pray and try to get some sleep. Either way, the Lord will take care of us. He always has."

# Chapter 39

The news came early. Jeff Blackburn was dead. Matt stood in his cousin William's room with Doctor Ambrose and Ed Bostwick, along with Tim Wright and a few other men. Doctor Ambrose had verified that he died during the night. Nothing looked unordinary to him.

"His body just…didn't survive the surgery. It was an invasive surgery and high risk. My condolences, gentlemen." He closed his doctor bag and left the hotel.

Ed pulled the sheet and blanket over Jeff's head. "Rest in peace, my friend."

"Do you know who shot him?" Tim asked Matt.

Matt shook his head. "No."

"Are you going to investigate who?"

Matt took a deep breath. "I already did. They're not saying anything. No one knows."

Ed clicked his tongue. "They're not going to talk. We killed four of theirs and injured five more that we know of. They'll only celebrate. I know you didn't like him either, Matt."

"No. But I don't celebrate anyone's death whether I liked them or not. So now what, Ed? Did you consider my offer?"

Ed slowly nodded. "I have another opportunity that I am going to take. I appreciate the offer, though."

"May I ask what?"

"I can't tell you yet, Matt. It's not around here, so I'll be leaving town sooner than I expected. The boys and I will be heading out today."

"Have you talked to any of your marshals this morning?"

"No. They're still sleeping. I guess I'll go wake them up and let them know about Jeff."

Matt grinned. "Well, do me a favor; tell them thanks for the good time last night for me."

"I will," Ed said with a curious look at Matt. "What's the grin for?"

"You'll see. Remind them, if the law doesn't seek justice, I still do." He winked at his old friend. "I hope your new opportunity works out for you. I suppose this is the end of the Blackburn Marshals?"

"It might be. I don't know what Ira Kelly and those fellas will do. Maybe they'll join me, maybe not. But I'm not taking orders from anyone again. I better go see what you did to my men." He paused. "They'll be able to travel, won't they?"

"Oh yeah. Just get them out of my town."

Tim Wright asked, "What did you do?"

"I just showed them a little hospitality. I didn't

hurt them too badly myself," He paused. He declined to add that Morton Sperry and his friends worked the three men over a bit more. "I need to go. Church is almost starting. You should come along, Tim."

Tim declined. "It's not for me. You go ahead."

# Chapter 40

Reverend Painter sat his bride on the front pew and took his position behind the pulpit. For a moment, he stood still and stared at the notes to a sermon that he spent all week writing. He looked up at the many faces of his congregation staring at him. Some, no doubt, waited to hear him apologize and resign.

The silence was deafening as he could not quite find the emotional strength and courage to speak. He pulled the letter out of his suit jacket pocket and unfolded it.

"I got this letter last night. I think I'll read it to you.

> "Dear Reverend Painter,
> "With a saddened heart and a sorrowful soul, I sit at my table to pen this letter consisting of a message God has placed on my heart.

*"The city of Branson has greatly bene-fitted from your ministry service for many years. However, when I heard that your son John came home a begging vagabond, drunkard, sexually immoral man, and a godless thief, I am astounded that you have not shuffled away from the pulpit with your tail of shame tucked between your legs. Your son, John's nakedness, has tarnished the church's very doorstep. The community will not soon forget that, and our church is now a mockery around Branson. Your son also broke into the church and stole the offerings and tithes from the hard-working folks in our church to feed his constant drunkenness and whoring. I imagine you did not give your son money from the church to feed that fire, which I can appreciate. But there is no more straw to burn; the last straw was you not volunteering to quit the pulpit already.*

*I will remind you since you seem to be forgetting. Apostle Paul wrote in 1 Timothy 3:5:*

*'If an elder cannot rule his own house-hold, how can he rule God's church?'*

*"Tell me, Reverend Painter, is it right for you to remain a reverend when you cannot control your own son? Surely, you, of all people, should know that answer. Are you going to argue with God?*

*"Your situation reminds me of Eli and his two sons in the Old Testament. Ironi-*

*cally, your name is Eli too. Let me ask, being trained in Biblical accuracy, do you feel the same kind of shame that Eli felt because of his sons? I doubt you do or you would have quit by now!*

"*Reverend Painter, you and Beatrice have failed to raise a Godly son and manage your household. Therefore, I must demand that you resign from the pulpit of the Branson Christian Church and move out of the church home so a new reverend with Godly parenting skills may take over.*

"*A false teacher can spread misleading lies like yeast through dough. Likewise, it can be said the same way about a reverend whose life is a false teaching. You and your wife, Reverend Painter, are the yeast that is going to destroy God's church. Our church!*

"*I expected the pulpit to be empty on Sunday, but I understand you will be there. I will too, and I expect to hear an apology, the money returned from your pay, and a prompt and immediate resignation.*

*Sincerely.*
*the congregation.*"

Reverend Painter glanced at his wife, who was sobbing quietly but seemed loud in the silence that followed the letter. He tightened his lips and took a deep breath. He tried to speak, but nothing came out.

He cleared his throat. "It's signed 'the congregation.' That means all of you. My sermon today is pointless." He raised his notes and set them down. "Let me say a few words and then my bride and I will leave and let you, the congregation, decide if I should go or not.

"You all know what this letter is about, right? Gossip gets around faster than the black plague did through Europe, which is just evidence of how bad it is, even though I preached about it so many times. So, what's the deal? The deal is our son came home. We haven't seen him in twelve years and the gossip is true. John broke into our church and stole the offerings and tithes. The letter's true; he used the money on alcohol. Our son is not a Christian anymore. He is a beggar, a drunk, a womanizer and a thief. He didn't learn this from his mother nor I!" he exclaimed loudly.

He continued, "We raised John in our home. It is and has always been a Godly home. We sent John to seminary in Massachusetts, and we didn't see him after that. He came home this week, and we were as shocked as anyone to discover how corrupted and…" He paused before adding softly, "ungodly he is. I won't lie to you. He is troubled, lost and broken. But he is still our son. We love him and want to help him. We pray he'll see the light and come back to Jesus. Pick up his mat and walk again because he once was a wonderful person and I think deep down he still is. He just needs to find that light." He wiped his eyes.

"I love my family. I love this church building and I love all of you. But this letter is right. A false teacher ruins churches and lives. I have spent my career being very careful not to teach anything wrong or different than it is translated in the Bible to the best of my ability. Beatrice and I raised John in a Godly home and he  left our home with the Lord in his heart. I will not beg you to let us stay here. This letter and another like it have cut me deep and broke my and Beatrice's hearts. She asked how people can be so hateful. It's a good question, I think. You see, we did kick John out of our house because of the life he was living. We don't agree with it, nor are we the ones living it. But you know, I would hope the congregation, our friends, would be more willing to pray for our son and hope with us that Jesus would touch his heart and resurrect that fire in his heart, rather than condemning us. But we didn't get any letters offering prayers or encouragement. We got two letters demanding I resign.

"Well, I'm here. And I'm putting it in your hands. I ask you to vote and Jim O'Neil will come to the house and give us the verdict. My resignation will be handed in today if you want me to leave. But if you want us to stay, then I only ask that instead of hateful, angry and bitter letters to me or anyone else in this congregation for something you think is so horrible, before you write it, look in the mirror. Could someone write to you about your faults? Your struggles? Your sin? Your family? I'm the reverend; I'm an easy target. You expect Beatrice and I to be perfect, our children too. I got news for you. We're just as human as you are and have the same problems, pressures and faults. But unlike you, we are greatly concerned about our son. And I think that's the right way to be. Not critical, hateful or mean-spirited. We're supposed to love each other, not tear each other down. Whoever wrote this letter, thank you. Because you just showed me where my sermons are failing." He left the pulpit and held his hand out for Beatrice. "My lady, let's go home. Jim, it's your show."

Jim O'Neil was an elder and walked to the pulpit as the reverend and his wife left the church. The sadness on Jim's expression showed his uneasiness to be the man chosen to relay the news of the vote no matter the verdict was to his best friend. "Any words? Does anyone have anything to say? Someone wrote that note. Does that person speak for all of us?"

Matt Bannister had listened to his friend read the letter and glanced around as he was accustomed to doing to find the guilty party. His eyes had landed on a woman in her fifties named Gail Lamb. Gail's cheeks had reddened, and her lips puckered just slightly as she stared straight ahead, trying not to be noticed. Gail shuffled uncomfortably in her seat while blinking a few times. Her eyes picked up on Matt staring at her and she looked away immediately. Gail and her husband, Israel, owned a barber and beauty shop where she shampooed, cut and styled the women's hair on one side, along with selling ladies' products of various kinds while Israel shaved and cut the men's hair on the other side of a wall. It was a thriving little business that brought in a wide variety of clientele and undoubtedly a cesspool of gossip. Matt watched her and did not doubt that she had written the note that the reverend read. As for the other one that the reverend mentioned, sixty-year-old Horace Green appeared quite uneasy himself.

"Well, the letter was right. The reverend's son is a reflection on him. What's that say around town?" A younger man in his thirties named David Flinn asked with a shrug.

"He was naked at the front door of our church. That should tell us what he thinks of the church and us."

"It should tell you what he thinks of his father."

"Is Reverend Painter a false teacher?"

"No."

"I think it's rude for someone to write that note."

"I'm glad that note was written. It's obvious the Painters can't control their family. I'm not saying reverend anymore. He doesn't deserve it."

Matt listened to the casual talking as the congregation spoke out. He stood and walked to the pulpit. He waited for the chit-chat to come to an end and all eyes were on him.

Matt picked up the reverend's sermon notes and glanced through them quickly. He spoke loudly, "I listen to all of you talking and I have to ask, how many of you have seen the reverend's son, John, around town in the last few days?"

About a quarter of the congregation raised their hands and offered their uninvited thoughts. Gail Lamb did not raise her hand.

"How many of you talked to John?" Matt asked.

Not one person raised their hand.

"Listen, folks, there's a lot of really good people here and we help each other when we can, which is a great thing. That sense of community and friendship is an attribute that comes directly from Eli and Beatrice Painter. They've been here a long time and I'm stunned to hear so many people question the man's integrity. Is he a false teacher? No. Is his life a false testimony? No. He is exactly what you see, a man who loves his wife and son dearly and has sacrificed and given his life to serve Jesus and teach the Lord's word. Did he make mistakes raising his son? Of course, he did! He will tell you that himself. But if you think he had to be a perfect parent because he's a reverend, then I suggest you take him off the pedestal you made for him.

"There is a difference between raising your children until they are grown and what they do with their independence. While you raise your children in your home, they should respect you first and others as well; they should behave. That is a parents' responsibility. Reverend Painter and Beatrice raised John in the church, and he knew the Lord. John is an adult. He is thirty years old and what he is, is by his own making. It was his choices and his actions that led him to where he is. He came home and refused to obey the reverends' rules, so they asked him to leave. Did you all know that? I doubt it. You see, here's the thing about gossip, it seldom tells the whole story and then some jackass, yeah, I said it, and you know who you are, has the gall to write such crap.

"Reverend Painter is not hiding his son's actions from you. Reverend Painter pressed charges against John for breaking in here. John is right now in my jail. Reverend Painter is doing everything right. He is not feeding his son's bad habits or cuddling him. He wants to help his son, but he won't tolerate the sinfulness. Reverend Painter and Beatrice don't need some hen in the gossip coop clucking away and demanding he quits because his adult son is not living a Christian life. John is not a child living in the Reverend Painter's home, he is a grown man who makes his own choices, and our reverend has no authority over him any more than you have authority over your adult children! Yes, the Apostle Paul did write that no elder or, in our terms, a reverend, should be the head of the church if he can't control his family. That's a reasonable truth. But he's not talking about adult children that don't live at home. He's talking about his wife and children. Back then, maybe older kids did live at home, which would apply, but John doesn't live at home and hasn't in over twelve years. He's been home for three or four days and is asked to leave his parents' home because of his sinful choices, and two of our fellow hens or roosters clucked away with their pen to condemn our friend and demand he resigns. Do know, people like you two hurt more people in the church and run them out, and they never want to come back because of crap like this! That's exactly what happened to John."

Matt lifted the reverend's sermon in his hand. "Here's the difference between a Godly heart and not. Someone would have our Reverend quit because his son is struggling and hurt by Christians. John's downfall began with a professor's criticism. Discouraged, broken and giving up, he quit and was too ashamed to come home. One thing led to another, and he lost his way and got caught up in the snares of life. Our reverend sees that and has hope that the Lord will open his son's eyes and bring him back into the flock like a lost sheep. That's what Jesus says he does and that's what Eli and Beatrice Painter are praying and hoping for. It looks to me like Reverend Painter has been working on a sermon about the prodigal son. What a glorious thing it would be if John rededicated his life to Jesus, cleaned up and eventually went back to seminary to be a theologian. That's the hope of the Lord in the life of a Godly man. It's never too late to serve Jesus. As Christians, shouldn't that be your hope as well? Or is it just easier and more satisfying to criticize, find faults and demand someone else resign for something he has no control over? Get it through your heads, folks. Reverend Painter and Beatrice are not responsible for their adult son's choices. Those are on him alone. And the fact that anyone wrote a letter like what was written without knowing the facts makes me sick!

"In fact, I know of a young lady who got pregnant a few years back. She was unmarried and went to church here with her family, and someone in this congregation wrote a nasty letter to her and a letter to her parents as well. The young lady's letter called her some nasty things and almost drove her to suicide. Worse than that, her parents' letter gave an ultimatum, disown their daughter or be removed from the church. It was signed, coincidently, *the congregation.*" He paused to glare out over the congregation.

"I asked Reverend Painter about that recently. He knew nothing of it! If the person who wrote those letters is here. That young Christian lady was raped! Her pregnancy was not from, in your words, whoring around. You destroyed her faith. If you are her parents sitting in here today, don't be a fool! Go find that girl of yours and love her and your grandchild. She could use your love and your help. Don't worry about what some nosy hen in the gossip coop thinks. Your life is between you and God. Your daughter needs you. And Reverend Painter wasn't the one that condemned her. It was one of you! You have a gold mine with Reverend Painter and Beatrice, folks, don't let them go." He took his seat with a scowl on his face.

\*\*\*

After church, Matt stood in the churchyard alone, watching with a sense of satisfaction as Gail Lamb walked away from church with her husband, red-cheeked and furious over the unanimous vote to keep Reverend Painter.

"Mister Bannister," a soft voice said as a finger tapped on his shoulder to get his attention. He turned around and saw the weepy and pain-filled eyes of Ellie Goddard standing there with her Bible in her hand. "Were you talking about our daughter, Viola?" Her voice was soft yet emotional as she spoke.

Matt spoke softly, "I was."

"It's true? She was raped?" Ellie's lips quivered with emotion.

"Yes. Viola said you didn't believe her. But it is true."

"How do you know?" Bart Goddard asked with a hint of hostile doubt.

"Because Joe Thorn admitted to it when confronted by Billy Jo. Wes Wasson courted Viola for a short time and told Billy Jo. Billy Jo is my cousin, and we went to talk to Viola not long after. Viola told me the story herself. Billy Jo wasn't there when Joe forced himself upon Viola. It wasn't Viola's choice and she tried to fight him. Her life just got worse from there."

"Oh, Lord, what have I done?" Ellie began to cry. "My baby girl needed me and I…" she began to sob. "I was so blind…"

Bart put his arms around her. "It's my fault. God forgive me."

Matt said plainly, "You'll find her and your granddaughter, Bonnie, in the Dogwood Flats. Apartment number two. If you don't mind me saying, Bonnie looks a bit like her grandmother," Matt said with a wink. He smiled. "Go see your daughter."

# Chapter 41

John Painter laid on the bottom bunk of his cell in the silence of the jail. The urge for a drink was strong, but it was impossible to get one. The jail was impenetrable with solid granite block walls, no windows, only a steel barred door, and two feet of bars spaced four inches apart on either side of the door that revealed only an empty bench and another granite wall. There was a bucket to relieve himself and vomit in, which he had been doing. There was very little else except the bunk bed, blankets, and pillows. There was absolutely nothing to do and the only reading material if one chose to read it was the Bible.

Boredom could be a form of torture all its own when a man was left with nothing except his thoughts. He hadn't had a drink of alcohol since the night before his arrest and his body was screaming through the sweat that drenched his body, cold chills and upset stomach that cried out for a drink of wine, whiskey or something stronger than water and coffee with his meals. His hands shook and he was miserable. He had overcome a migraine headache, but his head still ached.

Angry, he did his share of loud cursing, screaming and even tried to grab Phillip that morning when he brought breakfast, demanding to be released. The breakfast tray fell to the floor and Phillip refused to get more food until another deputy was there to keep John at bay. Hungry, thirsty and angry, John ripped the top mattress off the bunk bed and irately crumbled the blankets and sheet and tore the pillow open in his rage.

After expending a few moments of energy throwing the mattress, blankets and pillow feathers around the cell, John picked up the Bible to rip it to pieces as well. He ripped out the first ten pages or so and then opened it to the middle and grabbed the corner of the pages to tear them out, but he froze. His eyes fell on the written word and like in a trance, he sat on the edge of his bunk and read from the 23rd chapter of the book of Proverbs.

*'My son, if your heart is wise, then my heart will be glad; my innermost being will rejoice when your lips speak what is right.*
*Do not let your heart envy sinners, but always be zealous for the fear of the Lord.*
*There is surely a future hope for you, and your hope will not be cut off.*
*Listen, my son, and be wise, and keep your heart on the right path.*

*Do not join with those who drink too much wine or gorge themselves on meat, for drunkards and gluttons become poor, and drowsiness clothes them in rags.*
*Listen to your father, who gave you life, and do not despise your mother when she is old.*
*Buy the truth and do not sell it: get wisdom, discipline and understanding.*
*The father of a righteous man has great joy: he who has a wise son delights in him.*
*May your father and mother be glad: may she who gave you birth rejoice!*
*My son, give me your heart and let your eyes keep to my ways.'*

John's wrath faded like a pond disappearing down a sinkhole. Water filled his eyes as a sudden pain ached from his stomach up to his throat. The words spoke to him as if the Lord himself stood in the cell and spoke them. His chest tightened and his breathing quickened. He did not think about it; he immediately went to his knees and bowed his head on the mattress. There were no words in the English language that could describe the flood of emotion that poured out of his soul like vomit without a word being spoken. A life of abandonment, sin and pain stored up in a warehouse of dust-covered years of mire so deep it was hard to breathe. He wept and began to sob as the shame and years of heartache burst to the surface like an underwater volcano erupting and spouting the steam, heat and pressure out of its depths.

"Jesus, forgive me!" he sobbed. "I have betrayed you. I have no words, except if you will forgive me, I will repent from my sins. I only ask for your forgiveness. Jesus, this lamb is stupid and lost. Oh, Lord, come find me because I'm so far from you. Be my shepherd and my Lord. Help me, Lord, to get it right. Help me to repent and quit drinking, quit it all. Remind me what it is like to be near you. Help me to get back to where I was when it was just me and you." He sobbed.

Matt had come into the jail with Phillip with John's dinner but paused at the door as they heard John praying. Matt waited and put his finger to his mouth to not interrupt by making any noise. They remained at the door.

John began to sing the hymn, Alas! And Did My Savior Bleed in a pleasant voice:

> "Alas! And did my Savior bleed? And did my sovereign die? Would he devote that sacred head for such a worm as I?
>
> "Was it for crimes that I have done He groaned upon the tree? Amazing pity! Grace unknown! And love beyond degree!
>
> "Well might the sun in darkness hide, and shut his glories in, when Christ, the mighty maker, died for man, the creatures' sin.
>
> "But drops of grief can never repay the debt of love I owe; here Lord, right here, Lord,

*I give myself to thee, 'tis all that I can do."*

He sniffled and wiped his eyes. He said, "Yes, Lord, right now, I give myself to thee, for that is all I can do."

Matt walked in front of the cell door and ignored the disarrayed cell covered in feathers. "I don't want to interrupt, John, but praise God. You're on the right path now."

John smiled weakly as he wiped his eyes. He stood. "I'm okay."

"Yes, you are. And you will be."

"We brought you your dinner," Phillip said, and slipped the tray of food in the slot in the door.

"Thank you. Phillip, I apologize about earlier. I'm also sorry about the mess in here."

"You can clean it up after you eat," Matt responded. "You're not the first man to do that."

"Matt, is it possible you could ask my parents to come to see me? I want to tell them that I surrendered to the Lord."

Matt pointed at the tray John held. "Eat your dinner and then I'll take you to them. It'll be a nice surprise for them."

\*\*\*

Beatrice Painter washed the dishes after sharing dinner with Jim and Edna O'Neil. It was good to share a meal with good friends and put the issue of John behind them, within the church at least. It had been a heart-wrenching week for Eli to see his son come home in the shape he was in and make the choices he did. Eli had a gentle heart that always hoped for the best outcome, but Beatrice was a bit more practical and saw things for what they were. She had hope too, but the reality was John wasn't going to change if they supported him and turned a blind eye to his sin. There were rules in their home, just as there were rules in serving Jesus. Just as a child doesn't make the house rules, so mere human beings don't make the rules that God sets over the people that serve him. Kids don't have to like the house rules, and people didn't have to like the laws God established in the Bible, but that didn't change what sin is and what is not.

John's life of sinful choices was not acceptable in their home and if he chose to ignore the rules, he could not stay there. He wasn't a child, and Beatrice wasn't going to treat him like one. He had his life to live, and she would let him live it his way, but pray the Lord intervened and brought him back to Jesus and a life of righteousness.

"Oh, sweetheart, if I had known you were doing the dishes, I would've come in and helped you," Eli said with a cunning smile.

She chuckled. "Well, you always arrive offering to help just when I'm finishing. Perhaps you should go rest your tired feet in your chair and when I finish, I'll come to rub your sore and oh-so tired feet."

"I think I will. Perhaps you could bring a clean bowl of warm water and wash my feet too?"

Beatrice splashed him from the washbowl and grinned. "Get out of here. You should be washing my feet."

He sat down in a dining chair to watch her. "Who do you think wrote that letter?"

She hesitated to answer for a moment. "I'd say someone who may change churches after hearing what Matt said to the congregation."

Eli grinned. "Yeah. That young man deserves a pound cake for what he did for us today."

Beatrice looked at Eli softly. "We need to have him over for dinner this week. With Christine gone, he's probably going to be lonely. We'll invite him over on Wednesday."

Eli frowned thoughtfully. "Do you want to go see John tomorrow sometime?"

Beatrice peered out the back window as she dried a bowl. "No. I don't want to see him in jail at all. But on his last day there, maybe we could arrange it to meet him for lunch and let him know we love him and offer him a place at home if he can abide by the rules and come to church."

"I suppose. I think I will go see him, though. I just want to ask him how he can find any fulfillment in life after leaving the Lord? And remind him that Jesus is still waiting for him to come back and that invitation will always be open arms just waiting for him to say the word."

"You should."

There was a knock on the door.

Beatrice turned her head towards Eli. "If it's another note, just toss it in the fire. We don't need any more discouragement today."

"Oh, Beatrice, if someone took the time to tear

me down, I should at least read what they have to say."

She chuckled.

"John?" she heard Eli say.

"Pa..."

Beatrice set a plate down and grabbed a towel to dry her hands as she walked into the family room. Her fury was building as she wondered if he was stupid enough to escape from jail. She stopped five feet from John when he looked at her. Her mouth opened. She could not help but stare.

"Hello, Mother," John said with a soft smile on his lips. It was a shameful smile with a touch of sadness like he used to have as a child when he disappointed his parents. It was an expression she had not seen since he left Branson over twelve years before.

"Your eyes," she said. "What did you do? They're different."

His lips tightened as a wave of tears filled his eyes. "I prayed," he squeaked.

Beatrice's face contorted into a scrunched, misshaped expression of emotion and she stepped towards him with her arms spread out wide. She wrapped her arms around him and began weeping.

"I love you, Mama," John wept as he hugged her. "I'm sorry. I'm so sorry."

"My baby's back," Beatrice whimpered. "Eli, our baby is back."

Eli's bottom lip quivered, and a tear slowly crept out of his eye.

Matt opened the door and peeked his head inside before entering with a pleased smile. He loved to see a homecoming the way it should have been from the beginning. Reverend Painter quickly hugged him.

"Thank you! Thank you so much." The reverend broke the hug and wiped his eyes.

"Ah!" Beatrice said, breaking away from her son wiping her tears away. "You still smell awful." She laughed through her emotions. "You need a bath and some new clothes. I'll get the tub ready. Are you home to stay?" she asked.

John laughed as he hugged his father. "No. I have to go back with Matt."

Eli asked, "John, did you truly repent and come back to Jesus?"

"Yes, Father, I did. I am putting the drinking and everything behind me and as you always told others, I'm picking up my mat and walking."

"Praise the Lord! John, you could not ever give us a greater gift. Thank you, Jesus."

"Well, Ma and Pa, I just wanted to let you know that and Matt was good enough to escort me over here. But I know Matt has dinner plans of his own, so I need to get back. I'll see you two in about seventy-some days."

Eli frowned. "Matt, now that he's on the right track, can I drop the charges?"

John shook his head. "No, Pa. I need to stay in jail. Matt has a job lined up for me and although it will be hard, I need that time to work and read the Bible. I want to have a solid foundation when I am released. Otherwise, I might give in to temptation and I don't want to do that. So honestly, despite it all, this is a blessing and I know it. I am thankful for it. I'm excited about life again, Ma and Pa. I really am."

Eli smiled slowly while a proud smile formed on his lips. "I'm proud of you, son."

When Matt and John left, Eli held his bride in his arms and quietly wept tears of great joy. Their baby boy was home. The prodigal son had returned. The Shepherd had found the lost lamb and returned him to the flock. Their prayers were answered.

# Chapter 42

Christine Knapp couldn't pull a lot of joy out of her soul as she sat beside her grandmother's bed. It was a blessing to see her again, but Christine was not prepared to find her so weak, frail and appearing so much older than she ever had before. She was never a large lady, but now Christine's grandmother had no weight on her at all and light enough that Christine could pick her up and help her to the chamber pot which was under a chair to make it easier for her to use. Evelyn Harper's body may have been weak, but her spirit was just as stubborn and yet, loving as it had always been. Her grandmother made her smile, but it is difficult and heartbreaking to love someone so much and yet have to watch them fade away day by day.

For two weeks Christine has sat beside her grandmother holding her hand, reading the Bible, playing the piano, singing hymns and talking about her journey west, the loss of her beloved daughter,

Carmen, and then soon after her husband, Richard. Being stranded in Denver and the Lord's blessing of moving Bella's heart to take Christine in and give her a home and a career as a dancer while she mourned the loss of her family. She told her grandmother about moving to Branson and meeting Matt. There had been so much to talk about and the opportunity to do so was a blessing that Christine would never forget.

However, her grandmother was more tired than usual today and slept soundly giving Christine time to sit in the quiet room with only her thoughts to keep her occupied. It was very sad day to be left alone with her thoughts, it was May 31st. It was supposed to be Matt and her wedding day. If she was still in Branson, she would be standing in front of the church holding Matt's hands and saying her vows to always love the man and commit the remainder of her life to him while he made the same vows and commitment to her. It would have been a beautiful wedding and will be when she went back home. She missed being home in the dance hall and the annoying and petty little arguments with the other girls. She missed Matt most of all. His hugs, kisses, and his caring eyes when he listened. She missed the comfort of his presence and security he brought her. He made her feel complete and without him, being so far from him, it just didn't feel right. A part of her was anxious to go back home to be with him, but she committed to staying with her grandmother to the end. It could be days, weeks or perhaps a month or more. Her prayer was that Matt would be patient and faithful. She didn't doubt that he would, but she knew there were some attractive ladies in Branson that might try to steal him away from her. In the quiet of a room three-thousand miles away thoughts begin to form and once considered, can become a repetitive whispering of thoughts.

Evelyn Harper coughed and began to gag in her sleep.

"Grandma, are you okay?" Christine asked with concern.

Evelyn's eyes opened and blinked a few times. She looked at her granddaughter and smiled slightly before closing her eyes to rest. Her breathing was deep but congested.

Christine heard someone walking in the hallway towards the room. For a second the boot heels sounded like Matt's, but she knew the doctor was coming to the house at this time. The doctor was worried that the congestion might turn to pneumonia and the chances were Evelyn would not survive it. But for a second her heart leaped at the sound, but it was most unreasonable to think Matt would travel three thousand miles to see her.

A knock on the door and the door opened slowly. Doctor Pritchard stepped into the room, to Christine's faltering spirit. For just a second, she could have sworn she knew that walk. "How is my patient today?" The doctor asked. His beady eyes smiled at Christine.

"She is tired. She's been sleeping all day. Coughing and gagging over it, but she seems to be breathing well."

"I will look her over. In the meantime, why don't you get out into the fresh air yourself. I know, why don't you go spend some time with this vagabond I found wandering around the halls." He stepped forward and turned to point at the door.

Matt stepped into the room. Christine rocked forward in the rocking chair and dropped her head into her hands and burst into sobs before launching herself into his arms.

He chuckled. "I didn't want to miss the chance to meet your grandmother," he said into her ear.

"I missed you," she sobbed. "I missed you so much." She looked at him and kissed him. "I must look horrible." Her cheeks were wet with smeared tears.

"No, you're the most beautiful sight I've seen in weeks."

"Who is that?" Evelyn asked in a hoarse voice as she stared awkwardly at them.

"Grandma, this is Matt, my fiancé. He's here! He came here to meet you and see me," she said with a renewed passion in her voice. "We were supposed to be married today, but he came to see me instead!"

"Get my glasses. Help me sit up."

"Hello, Missus Harper," Matt said. "My name is Matt Bannister, and it is a pleasure to meet you. I have heard so much about you."

Evelyn put on her spectacles and looked at Matt critically. "You have long hair."

He grinned. "I do, yes."

"A respectful man should have short hair. My

363

husband never let his hair get longer than his ears. Of course, I'd cut it for him."

"I'm sure he appreciated that. I've never been married so my hair just grew."

Evelyn appreciated the wit. "If my granddaughter marries you," she coughed. "I'm giving her my scissors."

Matt knelt beside the bed. "Well, I'll be honest with you. I love your granddaughter very much. When Christine found out you were here, I knew then that I could not marry her without coming here myself and asking you for your permission to take your granddaughter as my bride. Now, if it takes cutting my hair to get your blessing, I'll do it." He added skeptically, "But I'd rather not cut my hair, just so you know."

Evelyn's lips squeezed together emotionally as a cloud of moisture filled her eyes. She patted his arm and took his hand in hers. "You postponed your wedding to let her come see me?"

"Yes, Ma'am."

"Are you taking her back with you? Did you come to get her?"

He shook his head. "No. I came to see her for a few days, but I wanted to meet you and ask for your blessing to marry her."

"You're not making her leave here?"

"No."

"How long can she stay?"

"As long as she wants to."

"So, you're not making her go home with you?"

Matt chuckled. "No. I'm not even here to ask

her to come home with me. I just wanted to see her on what was supposed to be our wedding day and I wanted to meet you. That's the only reason I'm here."

"You won't hurt her?"

Matt's brow narrowed. "No. I love her, Missus Harper. Hurting someone is not love."

"You will take care of her?"

"The very best I can."

"That's not good enough. I am going to heaven soon, and I need to know my granddaughter will be taken care of for the rest of her life. Can you do that? Can you love her until she is as old as I am? When her youthful beauty turns wrinkled and gray, will she still be the only woman that you love?"

Matt smiled slightly. "Yes. I will take care of Christine. I will love and honor Christine until my dying day. If, you give you me your blessing."

She snorted with a quick laugh before coughing a few times. "I think you two will get married with or without my blessing. I don't think it really matters."

"It matters to me."

She looked into Matt's eyes for a moment and seen his sincerity. "You had my blessing when you postponed your wedding to let her come here and you showed up today. I want you to take her home with you."

"Grandma, I'm staying with you," Christine said.

Evelyn shook her head and reached for Christine's hand and placed it in Matt's. "My sweet,

sweet, Christine, I don't want you sitting in here waiting for me to ascend to heaven. I wanted to see you and make sure you were all right. You are. Matt is your family now, sweetheart. Go home with him and start a family. Just cut your children's hair." Her tight smile covered for the tear that slipped down her cheek. "Your grandfather, mother and I will be waiting in heaven for you. We'll have a reunion then."

"But I told you I would stay," Christine stated.

"For what? We've had two very wonderful weeks together and a few more days. I love you and you know I do. What more can we say? I am proud of who have become and I am excited for you to marry Matt. He is a good man, bad hair, but a good man. You need to go home and get married. And may the Lord bless you both abundantly."

"Grandma, I don't want you to die alone," Christine said bluntly.

"I won't because Jesus is always right here with me. Now go, you two go visit. Enjoy the sunshine. I'll see you both…soon."

\*\*\*

Matt and Christine went to a restaurant to eat supper and then walked around the city content in each other's arms. When they returned to the house her second-cousin Miriam informed them that Evelyn had gone back to sleep after the doctor left and had passed away in her sleep. Shocked by the news, Christine went to her grandmother's room and mourned over the lifeless body.

Christine wrapped her arms around Matt. "I'm so thankful you are here,"

"Me too."

"She gave you her blessing," Christine said while holding him tightly.

"She did."

Christine sniffled and spoke through a quivering voice, "When the funeral is over, can we go home and get married?"

Matt closed his eyes as he held her close. "Absolutely."

She pulled her face back and looked into his eyes. "I love you. You have no idea how much you being here means to me. I'm so thankful you got to meet her. I'm so thankful she got to meet you.

Miriam stood in the doorway, and said, "Christine, I think you need to know that your grandmother always said she wanted to make sure you were going to be all right before she left this world. That is why we hired the detective company to find you." She nodded and wiped her tears away. "I believe she knew you are going to be fine." She offered a comforting smile. "So she went home."

Christine closed her eyes as another tear fell. She rested her head against Matt's chest and held him while his powerful arms gently embraced her. Protecting her. Loving her. Comforting her. Evelyn Harper knew her beloved granddaughter would be just fine.

# Acknowlededements

For my family.

This story and the others I've written never would have been without your support, interest and encouragement. To my wife, Cathy, thank you for your constant patience and understanding because being married to a writer isn't the easiest role to be in. To my son, Keith, your devoted interest, care and feedback are absolutely invaluable. I want to thank you for that! I want to thank my daughters and son-in-law's as well for always being supportive and believing in me.

I love you all.

I want to thank Mike Bray, Jennifer Hendricks and the rest of the staff at CKN Christian Publishing for their hard work to make this book possible. You're the best at what you do, and I have so much respect and appreciation for all of you. Thank you.

# A Look At: When the Wolf Comes Knocking

**Some wolves attack when their prey is at its weakest. Some charge fiercely. Others...knock softly.**

When Greg Slater returned home from college for winter break, his whole world changed. After rescuing his high-school sweetheart, Tina Dibari, and helping sentence his best friend, Rene Dibari, to life in prison, Greg fell in love for the first time.

Fifteen years later, life isn't easy, but Greg and Tina are working on their marriage. But an old fear has come back to haunt them...

***Rene has escaped prison, and he's thirsty for revenge.***

As shocking truths unfold, Greg and Tina face a ripple in their faith and in their home. Tina starts doubting her faith and seeks comfort in a friend with lustful intentions. Meanwhile, Greg struggles to navigate this new unrest in their relationship.

*Unfortunately, evil stops for no one, and three very different wolves are after the Slater family.*

**Will Greg and Tina's love be enough to keep them together, and—more importantly—will their faith hold true when the wolves come knocking?**

***AVAILABLE ON AMAZON***

# About the Author

**Ken Pratt** and his wife, Cathy, have been married for 22 years and are blessed with five children and six grandchildren. They live on the Oregon Coast where they are raising the youngest of their children. Ken Pratt grew up in the small farming community of Dayton, Oregon. Ken worked to make a living, but his passion has always been writing. Having a busy family, the only "free" time he had to write was late at night getting no more than five hours of sleep a night. He has penned several novels that are being published along with several children's stories as well.

Made in the USA
Columbia, SC
04 April 2022

58510526R00228